Disney's

TREASURY OF

CHILDREN'S
CLASSICS

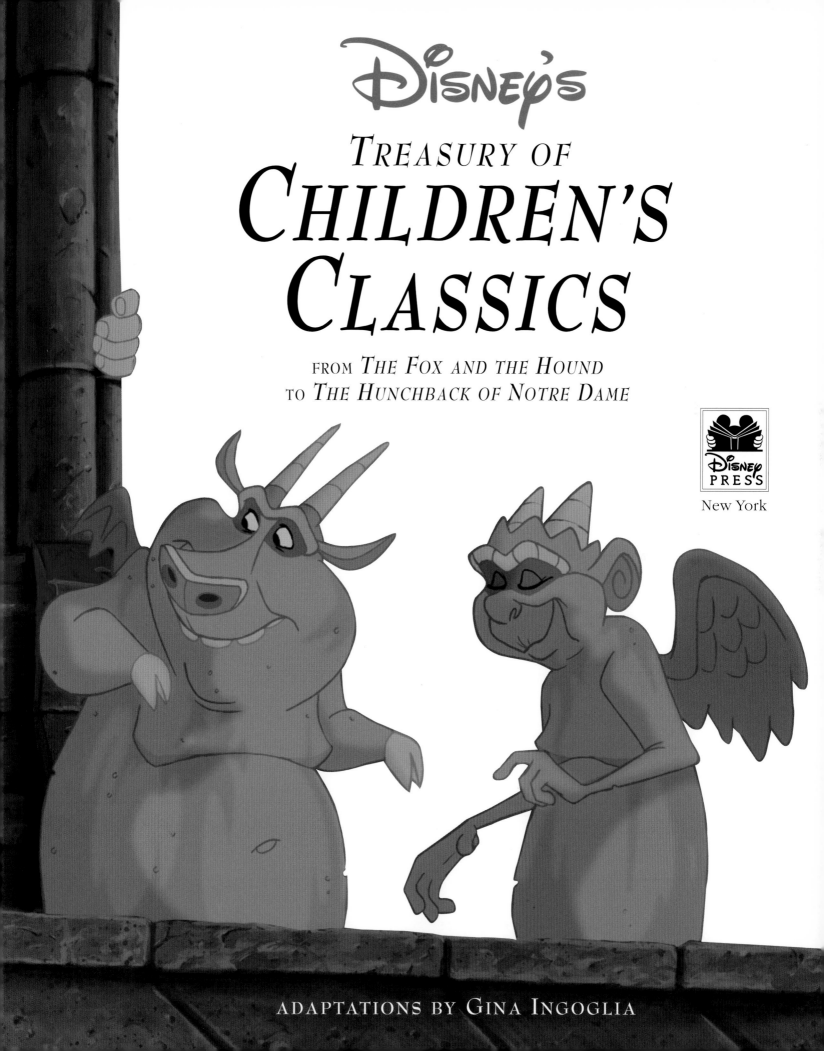

DISNEY'S
TREASURY OF
CHILDREN'S
CLASSICS

FROM *THE FOX AND THE HOUND*
TO *THE HUNCHBACK OF NOTRE DAME*

DISNEY
PRESS

New York

ADAPTATIONS BY GINA INGOGLIA

CONTENTS

PREFACE

The thirteen stories gathered together in this book are at the heart of the remarkable art form called animation. They are the work of hundreds of imaginations and thousands of different hands. They are tales of courage and of hope, of triumph over adversity, of coming-of-age, and of learning to do what's right. They are adventure stories and love stories, and they take us on journeys of discovery, full of laughter and drama, sadness and joy.

The tales come from many sources: storybooks and fairy tales, history and literature, and the pure imagination of the storytellers. From the wide-open savannahs of Africa to the cramped stalls and crowded marketplaces of ancient Arabia, from the streets of the Old World to the forests of the New, from the untamed outback of modern-day Australia to the close, grimy streets of fifteenth-century Paris, the stories carry us places we've never been before. They take us on magic carpet rides and on visits to enchanted castles, to places where animals talk and toys come to life.

Over the last eleven years (most of the period covered in this book) I've had the privilege of watching a collection of earnest young professionals develop into a group of the best storytellers in the world. At first these people were untested artists who had hardly worked together before. Yet over time they have grown and learned from one another and developed, not just as individual artists, but as an ensemble. I've seen the Disney animated feature revive, blossom, and flourish in their hands.

When I walk through the halls of the Feature Animation building, I can see the passion of these artists translated into a wealth of artwork and ideas. An animator labors for hours over a stack of drawings, intent on getting a character's expression perfect. Two directors act out a scene for each other, discussing their roles spiritedly, perhaps even contentiously, until just the right emotional level is reached. A background artist sits in a solitary corner, crafting small paintings that, in a stroke or two of the brush, define the mood of a scene. In one room a group of people watch an artist point to drawings painstakingly sketched onto a dozen or so slips of paper and pinned to a corkboard, as she recites the lines of dialogue from a bit of story she's trying to tell. In another, young artists sit in a circle, their attention focused on capturing at their drawing boards the sinuous contours of a sleeping lion. Or, in a darkened theater, an audience of peers eagerly watches as a finished sequence of animation flashes across the screen. Each of these people shares one simple wish: to tell a great story.

This medium has truly been reborn in the hands of these remarkable artists, who learned their craft after most of the original masters of animation had already left the Studio. They not only rediscovered and revived the knowledge of those great early talents but went on to build on that base using their own extraordinary ideas, skills, and understanding. Fired by their love for this art form, they have pushed the boundaries of animation both creatively and technologically, in ways that we could not, at the start of this journey, have imagined.

The new technologies available to this generation of artists—computer-generated imagery and sophisticated postproduction systems that permit moving cameras, sophisticated effects, and countless variations in color—all serve to create a broader canvas than their predecessors had access to. In the future, technological advances will expand animation's horizon even further. Yet for all those advances and refinements in style, it is the *stories* that stay with us long after the lights come up in the movie theater and the film is over. This book is a collection of fifteen magical years of ideas, visions, dreams, and, most of all, stories. Read on to your heart's content. We look forward to sharing with you many new ideas, new visions, and new dreams in the years to come.

Peter Schneider
President of Walt Disney Feature Animation

THE FOX AND THE

H OUND

From her nest in the oak tree, a plump old owl called Big Mama saw the whole sad affair take place. She was just settling down to a good morning's sleep when a panicky fox, carrying a newborn kit in her mouth, burst out of the woods. She was fleeing from a pack of baying hound dogs. Sensing she might not escape, the fox hid her baby in the grass next to a fence post and then tore across the meadow. Moments later, Big Mama heard rifle shots. She knew that the baby fox was now all alone.

Big Mama flew down to him. "You poor little fella," she said, stroking the shivering kit. "You're gonna need some carin' for." The baby fox snuggled up against Big Mama's soft feathers. "Oh, no, not me, darlin'," Big Mama said, laughing. "But don't you move. Big Mama's gonna be right back."

The owl flew off in search of her two friends, Boomer and Dinky. She found them perched on the branch of an elm tree, trying to prod a caterpillar from its hiding place. Boomer, a woodpecker, was widening a hole in the trunk, while Dinky, a little sparrow, cheered him on.

"Boomer," Big Mama said, "stop that peckin' and listen. I need you and Dinky to help me." She told them about the motherless fox.

"Gosh," said Boomer. "Who'll take care of him?"

Dinky ruffled his feathers and thought. "Hey, I got an idea," he exclaimed. "Widow Tweed's all alone. She'd probably be happy to take care of him. And I'll tell ya how we'll arrange it. . . ."

A few minutes later, Boomer tapped on the door to Widow Tweed's farmhouse.

"Yes?" Widow Tweed answered, looking around bewildered. Just as she was about to close the door, Big Mama and Dinky flew down and yanked her pink bloomers from the clothesline. "My word!" she cried. "You come back with those!"

The birds flew to the edge of the garden and dropped the bloomers near the fence post. Widow Tweed hurried out of her house to retrieve them. When she picked them up, she was surprised to find a little furry ball huddled on the ground.

"Why, it's a baby fox," she said. As she bent down low, the tiny creature tottered over to her. "You're such a little toddler," she said, laughing. "I think I'll call you Tod." She wrapped him in her apron and brought him inside.

That afternoon, Widow Tweed's neighbor, Amos Slade, drove his rattletrap truck past her farm and pulled up to his shabby house down the road. His old gray hunting dog yawned and ambled over to greet him.

"Looky here, Chief," Amos said to the dog, who was busy scratching himself. He grabbed a small sack from the truck. "I've got a surprise—someone for you to look after." Chief sniffed the bag and a brown spotted puppy poked out his head.

"Whaddya think of our new huntin' dog?" asked Amos. "His name's Copper. Just a little runt now, but he'll grow." Chief raised one eye and grumbled. But when Copper licked him on the nose, he decided the little hound might not be so bad after all.

Early in the morning, Widow Tweed put on her rubber boots and trudged out to the barn. Tod followed along curiously. As Widow Tweed milked the cow, Tod wandered in and out of the cow's legs and batted at her switching tail with his paw.

"You're going to have to be patient with Tod," Widow Tweed told the cow. "He's one of the family now." But after Tod chased the pigs through the mud, upset the hens, and knocked over the milk bucket, even Widow Tweed became flustered. "I'll never get my chores done. Run along, dear, and play somewhere else. And try to stay out of mischief."

As Tod trotted past the elm tree, he saw Boomer and Dinky, still trying to catch the same caterpillar. He wandered across the meadow toward Amos Slade's house, where Copper and Chief lay stretched out in the yard.

Copper raised his head and sniffed the air. "I smell somethin' funny," he said to Chief. "I'd better go check it out." Sniffing his way across the meadow, he bumped straight into Tod.

"What are you smelling?" Tod asked.

"Don't know yet," answered Copper. He took another sniff. "Why, it's . . . you!" He raised his head and let out a hoarse little howl.

"Why're you doing that?" asked Tod.

"Us hound dogs are supposed to do that when we find what we've been trackin'," explained Copper.

"I see," said Tod, not exactly sure what tracking was. "I'm a fox, and my name is Tod. What's yours?"

"Mine's Copper."

Tod smiled. "I bet you'd be great at hide-and-seek. Wanna play?"

"Can I use my nose?" asked Copper.

"Sure," said Tod. And from that moment on, they became the best of friends.

Copper and Tod spent the summer playing together all day long. They splashed around in the swimming hole, chased butterflies through the meadow, and played endless games of hide-and-seek. By dinnertime they were always exhausted, but every night they'd drift off to sleep dreaming of the next day's fun.

Big Mama often watched the two of them from her oak tree. "Imagine that! A fox and a hound playin' together! Those little darlin's think life's just one big happy game." She shook her head and sighed. "Too bad nothin' lasts forever."

One fall day, Tod and Copper were playing tag near the swimming hole when they heard a loud whistle.

"Dagnabit, Copper!" Amos shouted from the house. "Get over here!"

"He sounds mad," Copper said. "I gotta go home."

"Do you have to?" asked Tod.

"Sure do," said Copper. "See ya here tomorrow."

But the next morning, Copper didn't show up. So Tod wandered over to Amos Slade's yard, where he found Copper tied to a barrel.

"My master says I gotta stay home from now on," explained Copper.

"Well, we can play around here then," suggested Tod.

"No, we can't," said Copper. "Not with Chief around." He pointed his nose behind the barrel, where Chief lay fast asleep. "Chief's supposed to keep his eye on me."

Tod inched closer and took a good close look at the snoozing dog. Carefully, he peeled down Chief's lower lip. "Look at those teeth!" he exclaimed with wide eyes.

Copper gulped. "You'd better go!" he warned. "Chief's a great guy, but he can get pretty cranky."

Dreaming he was chasing rabbits, Chief took a big sniff. One of his eyes popped open, then the other. "It's . . . it's a fox!" he yowled, and charged after Tod.

"Run, Tod! Run!" shouted Copper. Tod scooted across the yard, squeezed under the chicken coop fence and, with Chief nipping at his heels, raced into the coop. The chickens squawked, and feathers flew everywhere.

Hearing the commotion, Amos grabbed his shotgun and burst out of his shack. "Goldang it!" he cried, firing a shot into the air. "It sounds like a fox is after my chickens!"

Tod squeezed out the back of the coop and started down the road. At that moment, Widow Tweed just happened to drive by with a truckload of milk cans. As she slammed on her brakes and jumped out, Tod leaped inside the truck. "Gimme that, you trigger-happy lunatic!" she scolded, grabbing the gun away from Amos.

"Dagnabit, woman," Amos cried. "Your thievin' fox was after my chickens. If I ever catch him on my property again, I'll blast him. And next time there'll be no warning shot."

Widow Tweed decided it was best to keep Tod inside. "It's getting cold anyway," she told him. "I know you weren't out to harm those chickens. But you caused a lot of trouble and Amos is really upset."

In the morning the smell of the approaching winter filled the air. Boomer and Dinky had already flown south, and the caterpillar they had been stalking all summer was settling down to winter in one of the widow's flowerpots. Widow Tweed watched Amos load his truck with hunting gear, lock up the house, and whistle for his dogs.

"He's going on his winter hunting trip," she explained to Tod. "And good riddance!" Before she could stop him, Tod dashed through the open door to go and say good-bye to Copper.

Big Mama flew down from her nest. "He's gone, Tod, honey. But what are you doin' over here? And what did you expect to do if you ran into Chief?"

"I can outfox that old dog," Tod boasted, sticking out his chest.

"Now hold on one minute," Big Mama said. "Didn't you learn anythin' yesterday?" She flew toward a small shed. "Come here, I want to show you somethin'."

Tod nudged open the creaky door and peered inside. The floor was covered with rusty traps, and rows of animal skins hung tacked to the walls.

"That's awful!" gasped Tod. "Those poor things!" He looked up at Big Mama, who sat perched on top of the door.

"You're gonna be one of 'em, darlin'," she warned, "if you don't keep away from Copper when he gets back!"

Tod's mouth dropped open. "You mean he's gonna become a huntin' dog? He's gonna be my enemy?" Big Mama nodded. "But he's my friend," insisted Tod. "We'll keep on being friends forever."

"Darlin'," said Big Mama, "forever is a long, long time, and time has a way of changin' things."

The winter months passed very slowly. Every morning, Tod looked down the icy road, hoping to see Amos Slade's truck bouncing along and bringing Copper home. It seemed forever, but little by little, the days grew warmer.

Big Mama was cleaning out her nest one fine morning when she spotted Boomer and Dinky flying back from down south.

"Welcome home, boys," she said. "It's been kind of lonesome around here without you rascals."

Tod trotted up to greet them. "Hi, fellas." Boomer blinked hard and stared.

"Say, this can't be the scrawny little squirt we found by the fence post, can it?" asked Dinky.

"He's gotten so big," said Boomer. "Look at that bushy tail!"

A butterfly fluttered past, brushing Boomer's nose.

Big Mama chuckled to herself. "I wonder if they know that was the caterpillar they were after."

"Someone's comin'," Boomer said, cocking his head. They all turned and saw a truck jounce around the bend in the muddy road.

"Big Mama," cried Tod. "Copper's back!"

As Amos drove past, they saw Copper sitting in the front seat.

"He's gotten *real* big," said Tod.

"Uh-huh," agreed Big Mama, catching a glimpse of the backseat. "And look at that pile of skins he helped track down. Your friend Copper's an honest-to-goodness huntin' dog now. Just remember that you're a fox."

"Aw, that won't make any difference," said Tod. "Copper's gonna be glad to see me. I'll go over tonight when Chief and Amos are sound asleep."

As soon as it grew dark, Tod went to look for Copper. He spotted him lying next to the doghouse, with Chief by his side.

"Hey, Copper," Tod whispered, "Over here. It's me, Tod."

"I thought so," Copper said, trotting up to greet him. "It's good to see you, Tod, but you shouldn't be here. You're gonna get us both into a lot of trouble."

Tod's heart sank. Maybe Big Mama was right after all. "We're . . . we're still friends, aren't we?" he asked.

Copper sadly shook his head. "Those days are over. This winter Chief taught me how to track rabbit and other stuff. I was kinda clumsy at first, but I got good at it—real good. I've become a huntin' dog, Tod. In fact, my master says he's got the two best dogs there are!"

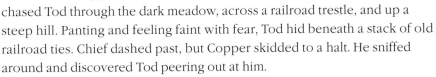

A sudden yowl startled them both. Turning around, Tod saw Chief charging straight at him. Right behind was Amos toting his gun. "It's that durn fox again!" he cried. "Well, now I've gotcha!" He fired at Tod. Tod streaked out of the yard and disappeared under the fence.

"Track 'im down, boys!" Amos shouted to Chief and Copper. The two dogs chased Tod through the dark meadow, across a railroad trestle, and up a steep hill. Panting and feeling faint with fear, Tod hid beneath a stack of old railroad ties. Chief dashed past, but Copper skidded to a halt. He sniffed around and discovered Tod peering out at him.

"Tod," Copper whispered, "I don't want to see you get killed." He could hear his master lumbering up the hill. "I'll let you go this one time." He ran off after Chief.

Tod held his breath until Amos wheezed by. Scrambling from his hiding place, he raced back down the hill and headed for the moonlit trestle. Just as he began to feel safe, Chief sprang out from the shadows.

Tod ran for his life. Halfway across the trestle, he heard a shrill whistle. As a train thundered onto the trestle, Tod squeezed himself flat. But Chief stood frozen in the engine's blinding headlight.

"Jump, Chief!" yelled Amos, running down the hill. At the last second, the old hound dog jumped out of the way. He fell from the trestle, tumbled down some rocks, and landed in the water below. Copper raced down to help but saw that Chief's leg was broken. Looking up, he glared at Tod. "If it's the last thing I do," he growled, "I'll get you for this!"

Amos lugged his injured dog back home and immediately stormed over to Widow Tweed's house. "I know he's in there!" he roared, banging on the door. "That fox of yours almost killed Chief. And I'm gonna get 'im!"

"Amos Slade, you're an old friend," Widow Tweed hollered through the window, "but you can't come barging onto my property!" Still she knew the time had come. She'd have to do something to save Tod.

As soon as the sun came up, Widow Tweed got dressed, put on her coat and flowered hat, and carried Tod to her truck. She drove past Amos Slade's house, past Big Mama's oak tree, and past Dinky and Boomer's favorite elm tree. Tod gazed silently out the back window, watching it all slowly disappear. After driving several miles, Widow Tweed pulled onto a road that led to the local game preserve.

"You'll be protected here and free to run," she said. "It's much too dangerous for you to stay with me. But you'll always be in my heart." Blinking back tears, Widow Tweed gave Tod a farewell hug. "Now, dear, don't you follow me." She gently placed him on the ground and then drove away.

It started to rain, then it poured. For a long time, Tod just sat in a puddle, shivering and watching the empty road.

It was dark when Amos saw Widow Tweed pull into her yard. "She's been gone all day," he said to Copper. "And she's come back alone. I'll bet she's dropped that fox off at the game preserve. But we'll get 'im. We'll get 'im!"

The next morning Big Mama flew to the preserve. "I'm gonna see how that little darlin's doin'," she said to herself. She thought she saw Tod sitting at the edge of a pond, but when she got closer, she saw that it was another fox that she knew. Her name was Vixey.

"Hi, Big Mama," said Vixey. "What brings you way out here?"

Big Mama settled down next to her. "I'm lookin' for a fox called Tod," she said. "He's new here—about your age and very handsome."

Vixey smiled. "Well, I'm not doing anything. I'll help you find him."

After a while, they found Tod sitting slumped in a ditch. "He seems so downhearted," said Vixey.

"Well," Big Mama sighed, "you can't blame him. He was dropped off here and left all alone. Honey, he needs cheerin' up. I'll tell you what we'll do. . . ." She whispered her plan in Vixey's ear.

A few moments later, Big Mama landed next to Tod. "Morning, Tod," she said brightly.

"Oh, hello, Big Mama," Tod said, trying to be cheerful but sounding very sad.

"Last night was pretty miserable for you, wasn't it," Big Mama said.

"It was terrible," Tod answered. "I couldn't find a dry spot to sleep in." Big Mama glanced over at Vixey, who was sitting by the pond, minding her own business. Tod followed her glance.

"Who . . . who . . . is . . . that?" he asked. "She's *really* pretty."

"Why don't you ask her her name?" suggested Big Mama.

"Good idea," Tod said, jumping up. He ambled down to the pond.

"Hi, there," he said to the fox, who became prettier the closer he came. "My name's Tod. What's yours?"

"Vixey," the other fox answered. "Did you know this pond is filled with fish?"

Tod's eyes lit up. "I'll catch some for you," he boasted. But it was the first time he'd ever fished, and he ended up falling in the water.

"That's the funniest thing I ever saw!" Vixey giggled.

Tod heaved himself out of the pond. "Go ahead and laugh," he sputtered. "You're just a silly female."

"You've got a lot of nerve," Vixey snapped. "Why don't you just grow up?"

Big Mama, who'd been watching from a tree, flew down to them. "Now look, you two, you like each other, so why not get along?" She shook her head at Tod. "That was no way to talk to Vixey. Just be natural and stop showing off, darlin'."

Tod looked ashamed. "Yeah, you're right," he said to Big Mama.

Vixey smiled prettily at him. "I just know you're going to love the forest. Come on, I'll show you around." They played together all day and by evening they were good friends.

Bright and early the following day, Amos Slade took Copper and drove up to the game preserve. He parked next to a tree with a sign that read NO HUNTING. "We're not doin' any of that," he grinned. "We're just gonna get us a no-good fox." He pointed toward the woods. "Now, get trackin', boy," he yelled to Copper. Copper sniffed his way into the forest, while Amos set traps. Soon he found the trail leading up to the pond.

"Good boy," said Amos. "That fox'll be comin' this way for water—only he won't be drinkin' any!" Carefully, he laid several traps on the ground. "Now we'll just relax and wait for him to show up."

A little later, Tod and Vixey appeared. "I sure am thirsty after all that walking," said Tod, heading toward the pond.

"Wait a minute!" Vixey warned, catching her breath. "Something's not right. It's too quiet." As Tod stopped short, he kicked a stone, which landed on one of the traps. It snapped shut, just missing Tod's foot. Instantly, Amos and Copper sprang from their hiding places.

"Quick, Vixey, run!" cried Tod. With Copper snapping at their heels, they headed into an open field and squeezed into an abandoned burrow. Copper clawed furiously at the entrance, but he was too big to fit inside.

"We can get out through the other end!" Vixey shouted. But Amos was already there. He lit a wad of dried grass on fire and shoved the flaming weeds into the narrow opening. Smoke poured into the burrow and choked the foxes. "Run through the fire," Tod gasped. "Run really fast. Maybe we won't get burned." They tore from the burrow and darted past Amos.

"I don't believe it," the old hunter growled. "Get 'em, Copper!" he yelled.

Tod and Vixey raced through the woods to the top of a rocky hill. Pausing to catch their breath, they looked back and saw an enormous bear lunge from the bushes. It attacked Amos just as he was loading his gun. The gun went flying in the air. Amos fell over backward and yowled—his foot

was caught in one of his own traps! Howling, Copper jumped between the bear and Amos. But with one swipe of his paw, the bear lifted Copper off his feet and sent him sailing through the air. He hit the ground so hard, he could barely get up.

Tod tore back down the hill. Copper saved my life once, he thought. Now I can pay him back. He sprang forward, landed square on the bear's back, and bit his ear. The enraged bear shook him off and chased Tod up a nearby cliff. With nowhere else to go, Tod backed out onto a fallen tree spanning a roaring waterfall. As the bear approached him, the tree suddenly gave way, sending them both crashing into the churning water below.

The bear was swept downstream. Tod managed to heave himself onto a floating log and push toward shore. Copper, shaking with fright, was waiting for him.

"Tod?" he asked. "Are you all right?" Amos limped forward, aiming his shotgun at Tod. At once, Copper stood over Tod and shielded him.

"Come on, Copper," said Amos. "Get out of the way."

Amos stared at Copper. Copper stared back at Amos—and slowly, Amos lowered his gun. "Well, all right, boy," he said, at last, "let's go home."

Tod watched his old friend head back toward the road. Then Vixey gently nudged him. "Let's go home, too," she said. And, together, the two foxes trotted into the forest.

The next day, just as Big Mama was settling down to sleep, Boomer and Dinky landed in the tree and began to search for another caterpillar. Then she heard somebody yell *Ouch!* Over on the farmhouse porch, Copper and Chief were watching Widow Tweed bandage Amos's foot.

"Well, well," Big Mama said, grinning. "Everythin's back to normal." Looking toward the woods, she saw that Tod and Vixey, side by side, were watching, too. "Yes, indeedy," said Big Mama, ruffling her feathers. "It surely is one fine mornin'!"

THE FOX AND THE HOUND
Behind the Scenes

Based on a book by Daniel P. Mannix, *The Fox and the Hound* began production in 1977 and was released in the summer of 1981. Veteran animator and producer-director Wolfgang "Woolie" Reitherman encountered the book while looking for new ideas for a movie. Remembering that his own son had once brought home a fox cub as a pet, Reitherman was so intrigued by the tale that he decided to bring it to the screen. The talented actors whose voices characterized the creatures in the film include Mickey Rooney as Tod, the fox whose best friend is a dog, and Kurt Russell as Copper, the dog who at first befriends and then nearly betrays Tod. Pearl Bailey lent her robust voice to Big Mama, and Tod's love interest, Vixey, was articulated by Sandy Duncan. With its pastoral backgrounds and muted color styling, the visual look of the picture was influenced by story sketches and impressionistic pastel drawings by Mel Shaw, an artist whose first project for Disney was *Bambi* and whose drawings influenced many of the Disney films made in the 1970s.

Copper and Tod meet for the first time in this pastel story sketch by artist Mel Shaw.

This story of a dog and a fox who did not know they were meant to be enemies was the final picture to feature the talents of Frank Thomas and Ollie Johnston. The last of the group of Disney artists known as the "Nine Old Men," these animators had worked with Walt Disney on the Studio's earliest feature films and were undisputed masters of their craft. The renowned pair left the film midway to work on their classic book about animation, *The Illusion of Life*. *The Fox and the Hound* was also the last film for Woolie Reitherman, who had worked on nearly every Disney animated film from *Snow White and the Seven Dwarfs* to *The Rescuers*, and who was Walt's hand-chosen successor as producer and director of all the Studio's animated features.

With that last bow of the first generation of Disney artists, a group of untried young animators took the stage. Most of the work on *The Fox and the Hound* was completed by artists drawn from a recruitment program established by the Studio in the late 1970s at California Institute of the Arts. The roster of raw talent working on the movie was formidable. Don Hahn, who would go on to produce the modern classics *The Lion King*, *Beauty and the Beast*, and *The Hunchback of Notre Dame*, served as assistant director. The dramatic bear fight sequence at the end of the film was animated by Glen Keane, who would later create the Beast, Aladdin, and Pocahontas. Tim Burton, the creator of *Edward Scissorhands*, *Beetlejuice*, and *The Nightmare Before Christmas*, animated Vixey. Henry Selick, who went on to direct *James and the Giant Peach*, also worked on the movie, as did the directors of *The Little Mermaid*, *Aladdin*, and *Hercules*, Ron Clements and John Musker. Mostly in their early twenties during the making of this film, these talented people were, in many cases, just acquiring command of their crafts. At the fingertips of these developing artists, a new era in Disney animation was quietly dawning.

Frank Thomas and Ron Clements discussing the animation of Tod.

CHRISTMAS CAROL

It was Christmas Eve in London. Large, fluffy snowflakes were falling from the darkening sky, and the chilly streets were bustling with towns-folk hurrying home to sit together with their families by the fire. But not old Ebenezer Scrooge. He was trudging back to work, glaring disdainfully at the festive crowds.

When he reached the counting house, his place of business, he used his cane to knock the snow from the sign above the door. It read SCROOGE AND MARLEY, but MARLEY had been scratched out. "Poor Jacob Marley," Scrooge murmured, referring to his old partner. "Dead seven years today. He was a good 'un—robbed the widows and swindled the poor." He chuckled to himself. "In his will he left me enough money to pay for his tombstone. But I had him buried at sea!"

The little bell on the door jingled as he opened it. "Cratchit!" he snapped to his clerk, who was tossing a piece of coal on the grate. "Wasting coal again?"

"N-N-No, sir," said Bob Cratchit. "I was . . . ah . . . just trying to thaw out the ink."

Scrooge jabbed the clerk with his cane. "Bah!" he cried. "You used a piece of coal last week. Now get back to work!"

Cratchit climbed back onto his high stool. "Speaking of work, Mr. Scrooge, tomorrow is . . . um . . . Christmas, and I was wondering . . . um . . . might I have the day off?"

"Oh, I suppose so," grumbled Scrooge. "But I'll have to dock you half a day's pay. Now let's see. . . ." He scratched some numbers on a piece of paper with his old quill pen. "I give you two and a half shillings a day. That's after the raise I gave you three years ago."

"Yes, sir," explained Cratchit, "that's when I started doing your laundry."

The door banged open. "Merry Christmas!" cried a young fellow, stamping the snow from his feet.

"And Merry Christmas to you, Master Fred," said Bob Cratchit with a friendly nod.

"Bah, humbug," muttered Scrooge. "And what brings *you* here, nephew?"

"I've come to invite you to Christmas dinner, Uncle," he said, handing him a wreath with a bright red bow.

"Will you be having plump goose with chestnut dressing?" asked Scrooge, tossing the wreath aside. "With plum pudding and lemon sauce? And candied fruits with spice sugar cakes?"

"Yup!" Fred said, beaming. "Will you come?"

"Are you daft, boy?" Scrooge cried. "You know I can't eat that stuff. Now, get out, out, OUT!"

Bob Cratchit covered his ears as Scrooge slammed the door behind his nephew. Seconds later, the door opened again. This time, two townsfolk, holding little collection cups, peeked timidly inside. "Alms for the poor, Mr. Scrooge?" one asked.

"If I gave to the poor," Scrooge retorted gruffly, "they'd no longer be poor, would they?"

"Well, ah . . . ," they stammered.

"Then you'd be out of a job, wouldn't you?" Scrooge continued. "Don't ask me to put you out of a job, especially not on Christmas Eve."

"Oh, we wouldn't do that, Mr. Scrooge," they replied and hurried out the door.

Scrooge emptied a large bag of shiny gold coins on his desk and, smiling, began to count to himself. When he heard Bob Cratchit closing his books for the night, Scrooge glanced up at the clock.

"That old clock is two minutes fast," he said, "but never mind, Cratchit. You may leave two minutes early—but don't forget my laundry!"

"Oh, you're so kind, sir," said Bob, grabbing his hat and scarf. He hoisted the bulky sack over his shoulder and staggered outside.

Scrooge continued stacking his money until the clock struck nine. He locked the door and tramped home through the wet snow.

As he unlatched the door to his house, he gaped in surprise at the door knocker. Before his very eyes, the brass lion head transformed into the face of his old partner. "Jacob Marley?" he gasped. "Is that you?"

"Scroooooge," wailed the ghostly knocker.

"No, that can't be," said Scrooge. He pushed open the door and raced upstairs to his bedroom. "I must be overworked," he thought as he bolted the door and collapsed into a chair. He jumped right back up when he heard a jangling noise. The ghost of Jacob Marley, draped in chains, appeared through the closed door, tripped over Scrooge's cane, and stumbled into the room.

"Scroooooge," the ghost moaned.

"Go away," cried Scrooge, cowering in his chair.

The ghost clanked toward him. "Ebeneeezer, I've come to warn you. For being mean and stingy all my life, I'm forced to carry these heavy chains for all eternity—maybe even longer. I'm doomed. Unless you mend your ways, Ebenezer Scrooge, the same will happen to YOU!"

Scrooge eyed the rusty chains with fright. "Help me, Jacob!" he begged. "Tell me what to do."

"Tonight you'll be visited by three spirits," said Marley's ghost. "Do as they say, or your chains will be heavier than mine."

The ghost drifted back through the closed door and fell clanking down the stairs. The sound of his chains vanished into the night.

"Gotta get some sleep," Scrooge muttered. He threw on his nightshirt and stocking cap and, before climbing under the covers, checked beneath the bed with a candle. By counting gold coins in his head, he managed to drift off to sleep.

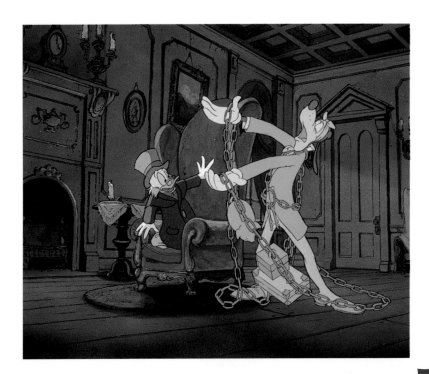

BRRRRINNNNG! BRRRRINNNNG! Scrooge bolted up in his bed. A little green chap in a top hat was standing on the nightstand. He was hitting the alarm clock bell with his tiny umbrella.

"Good, you're awake," he said.

"Who . . . who are you?" asked Scrooge, rubbing his eyes.

The creature bowed. "Why, I'm the Ghost of Christmas Past," he replied, and then hopped up to the open window. "Come on, Scrooge, let's go. We're going to visit your past."

"I'm not going out there," Scrooge protested. "I . . . I'll fall." But before he could say another word, Scrooge and the ghost were flying high in the dark sky over the snowy rooftops. They came to a landing in front of a familiar house. It was the old Fezzywig Tea Company.

Peeking through a brightly lit window, Scrooge cried out in surprise. "Why, it's Fezzywig playing his violin! He was my first boss, you know. And there are all of my very dearest . . . er . . . friends." He peered eagerly at the merry faces he once knew, recalling times he had long forgotten. "And there I am, sitting in the corner," Scrooge said quietly. "I always was a shy lad."

Suddenly he felt his heart jump. "There's lovely Isabel," he murmured. "She was my first and only love. This was the night I first kissed her under the mistletoe. How clearly I remember her pink silk dress and the satin ribbon in her hair." His face took on a sad and dreamy look. "I wonder where my dearest Isabel is now."

"Married to another," replied the Ghost of Christmas Past. "And it's all your fault. You loved your gold more than you loved her. And so, you lost her forever."

Scrooge covered his ears. "I know, I know," he sobbed. "Please, Spirit, take me home. I can't bear to watch any longer."

In a flash, he was back in his bed, weeping into a pillow. "Why, oh, why?" he sniffled, pulling the quilt over his face. "Why was I so foolish?"

"FEE, FI, FO, FUM," boomed a voice. "DO I SMELL A STINGY LITTLE ENGLISHMAN?"

Scrooge peeked out from the drapes covering his bed and was met by two enormous eyes staring back at him. They belonged to a giant who sat in the middle of the room. The giant, surrounded by dishes of scrumptious food, held up a slice of mincemeat pie. "I'm the Ghost of Christmas Present," he said to Scrooge. "Want a bite?"

Scrooge had never seen so many delicious things to eat. There were bunches of grapes, platters of roast meat, frosted cakes, and figgy puddings.

"Where did all this come from?" he asked.

"From the heart," said the ghost. "It's the Food of Generosity—something you've denied everyone you know."

"Bah, humbug!" said Scrooge. "Nobody's ever shown *me* generosity."

"You've never given them reason to," responded the ghost. "Yet there are some who find enough warmth in their hearts—even for the likes of *you*."

The ghost picked up Scrooge between his fingers and dropped him into his roomy pocket. With his gigantic hand, he pushed up the roof and stepped out among the lamp-lit streets. "Here we are," he said, placing Scrooge down in front of a small, shabby-looking house.

"Why did you bring me to this old shack?" demanded Scrooge, rubbing the frost from a window. "Well, what do you know, it's Cratchit's place." Inside, Bob Cratchit was helping his children hang popcorn on a scraggly Christmas tree. He watched Mrs. Cratchit place a measly portion of turkey on the table. "Surely they must have more food than that," he said. "What's bubbling in that big pot?"

"Your laundry," answered the ghost. "Look, here comes their youngest child, Tiny Tim."

A small, pale child, leaning on a makeshift crutch, hobbled down the stairs. When he reached the last step, Bob Cratchit picked up the tot, sat him at the table, and tucked a napkin under his chin. "Oh, Dad," cried Tiny Tim. "Look at the wonderful dinner! We must thank Mr. Scrooge."

"What's wrong with that kind lad?" Scrooge whispered to the ghost.

The ghost shook his head sadly. "Much, I'm afraid. If things remain as they are, I see an empty chair where Tiny Tim once sat."

Scrooge shuddered. "You mean to say—" But the Ghost of Christmas Present was gone, and Scrooge was left alone in the snow. "Don't go!" he pleaded. "Tell me about Tiny Tim."

The air grew thick with foul-smelling smoke, and Scrooge began to cough. He found, to his horror, that he was no longer at Cratchit's house but in the town graveyard. A fat fellow in a red hood stood in front of him, puffing on a big cigar.

"Are you the Ghost of Christmas Future?" Scrooge said, shivering with fear. "If you are, please tell me what will happen to Tiny Tim."

The ghost pointed to a freshly dug grave. The Cratchit family stood huddled around it. Sobbing, Bob Cratchit hugged Tiny Tim's crutch to his chest. Before walking away, he gently leaned it against the headstone.

"Oh, no!" groaned Scrooge, "I didn't want this to happen. Tell me this can all be changed."

Behind him Scrooge heard voices. Nearby, two grave diggers were digging another grave. "I've never seen a funeral like this one," said one. "No mourners or friends to bid the old bloke farewell. I think everybody was happy to see him go."

"Ah, well," said the other. "Let's go rest for a minute before we drop him in." Picking up their lantern and shovels, they ambled off.

Scrooge went over and peered into the deep hole. "Who . . . whose lonely grave is this?" he asked. The Ghost of Christmas Future struck a match on the headstone and lit a fresh cigar.

Scrooge gasped as he read the name. "It's *my* grave!"

The ghost laughed and slapped Scrooge hard on the back. "Help!" cried Scrooge, losing his balance and clutching wildly at the howling wind. Screaming, he tumbled headlong down, down into the bottomless grave.

"Spirit, let me out!" he pleaded. "I'll change!" The laughter and the howling stopped suddenly, and Scrooge found himself back in his bed once again, tearing wildly at the sheets.

Scrooge jumped up and flung open the window. The night had finally passed, and the sun was shining bright. Fresh snow sparkled in the streets, and church bells were ringing all over town. "It's Christmas morning!" he shouted. "The spirits have given me another chance!"

Throwing on his coat and hat, he scampered out into the street. The alms collectors were standing on the corner. "Something for you," said Scrooge. The two townsfolk stared in amazement as Scrooge dropped a handful of coins into their boxes. "Fifty gold sovereigns!" they gasped.

"What? Not enough?" Scrooge asked. He giggled and dug into his pocket

again. "Here's one hundred more!" He skipped down the street shouting "Merry Christmas" to everyone he passed. "Hello there, Fred," he said, running into his nephew. "I'm looking forward to that wonderful Christmas dinner."

"You mean you're coming?" asked Fred. "Really?"

"Of course," said Scrooge. "Be sure to keep it piping hot."

"I will, Uncle Scrooge," Fred replied. "And a very Merry Christmas to you."

Scrooge disappeared into the butcher's shop and the toy store. Toting two large sacks, he hurried to the Cratchits' house and rapped on the door.

"M-M-Mr. Scrooge?" stammered Bob Cratchit when he opened the door. "W-Won't you come in?" Then he saw the sacks. "More laundry?" he asked.

Scrooge stepped inside. "I've had enough of this day-off stuff, Cratchit," Scrooge shouted. "You leave me no alternative." He paused. "But to give you—a raise."

"A *raise*!" gasped Bob. "You mean it, sir?"

Scrooge nodded. "Yes, yes . . . I mean, no, I'm giving you a raise *and* making you my new partner!"

Then he ripped open the bag and pulled out a toy soldier. Smiling, he presented it to Tiny Tim.

"Oooh!" Tiny Tim gasped. "For me?"

"There's something for your brother and sister, too," said Scrooge. "In fact, this whole bag of toys is for you!"

The children all cheered together in delight. "Thank you, sir!" they exclaimed over and over.

With a little bow, Scrooge handed Mrs. Cratchit the other bag. "And for you, my dear. A nice plump goose."

Mrs. Cratchit beamed. "Oh, sir, how can we ever thank you?"

"You don't have to," said Scrooge. Bending down, he picked up Tiny
Tim in his arms. "We'll have this little fellow well in no time."

Tears filled Bob Cratchit's eyes. "A very Merry Christmas to you, Mr.
Scrooge."

Tiny Tim threw his arms around Scrooge's neck. "And God bless us," he
piped in his soft voice. "God bless us all, every one!"

MICKEY'S CHRISTMAS CAROL
Behind the Scenes

*M*ickey's Christmas Carol (1983) marked the first appearance of Mickey Mouse in a short animated film since *The Simple Things* had been released in 1953. Based on Dickens's classic tale about a miser who gets a dose of Christmas spirit, the film features the reunion of many Disney "stars" and was conceived as the first in a series of shorts starring the "Disney players." The classic Disney animated characters—Mickey, Donald, Goofy, and the gang—would star in playlets put on by their well-known troupe.

Animation began for *Mickey's Christmas Carol* in 1981. It was story artist Burny Mattinson's idea to create a short subject starring Mickey and his friends, and he was tapped as director of the project. The young animators who joined Mattinson on the picture found ample opportunity to hone their skills animating the classic Disney cast in a film meant to look and feel as if it could have been made thirty or forty years earlier, at the height of Mickey's popularity. Mark Henn, who later animated Ariel in *The Little Mermaid*, Belle in *Beauty and the Beast*, Jasmine in *Aladdin*, and young Simba in *The Lion King*, animated Mickey. John Lasseter, who would go on to direct *Toy Story*, did some of his earliest work as an animator, developing the sequence in which Jiminy Cricket lifts Scrooge McDuck out of his house and they fly across the city using the cricket's umbrella. "We were a small, young group, and we had a lot of fun animating Mickey and the gang for the first time in thirty years," says Henn.

Though the creative team wanted to emulate the look and feel of Mickey shorts from the golden age of Disney animation, when it came time to cast the voices, it became clear that this was a different era. "All the original voices were gone," explains Mattinson. "Walt Disney wasn't there any longer to do Mickey, and former sound effects man Jim Macdonald, who had voiced Mickey after Walt stopped, could no longer do the falsetto required." Ultimately, sound effects editor Wayne Allwine stepped in to fill Mickey's considerable shoes. Though at first it was thought that Clarence "Ducky" Nash, the original voice of Donald Duck, was in retirement, a desperate phone call from Mattinson brought an enthusiastic response. As the director recounts the story: "On the day of the recording session, Nash came to the Studio and the creative team held its breath as the elderly man walked to the stage. We looked at each other doubtfully as he adjusted his hearing aid. Then Nash opened his mouth to speak his first words in character and a collective thrill went through the room. Everybody looked at each other and thought, Wow, it's Donald Duck!"

OPPOSITE: *Clarence "Ducky" Nash—the voice of Donald Duck.*

THE GREAT
MOUSE DETECTIVE

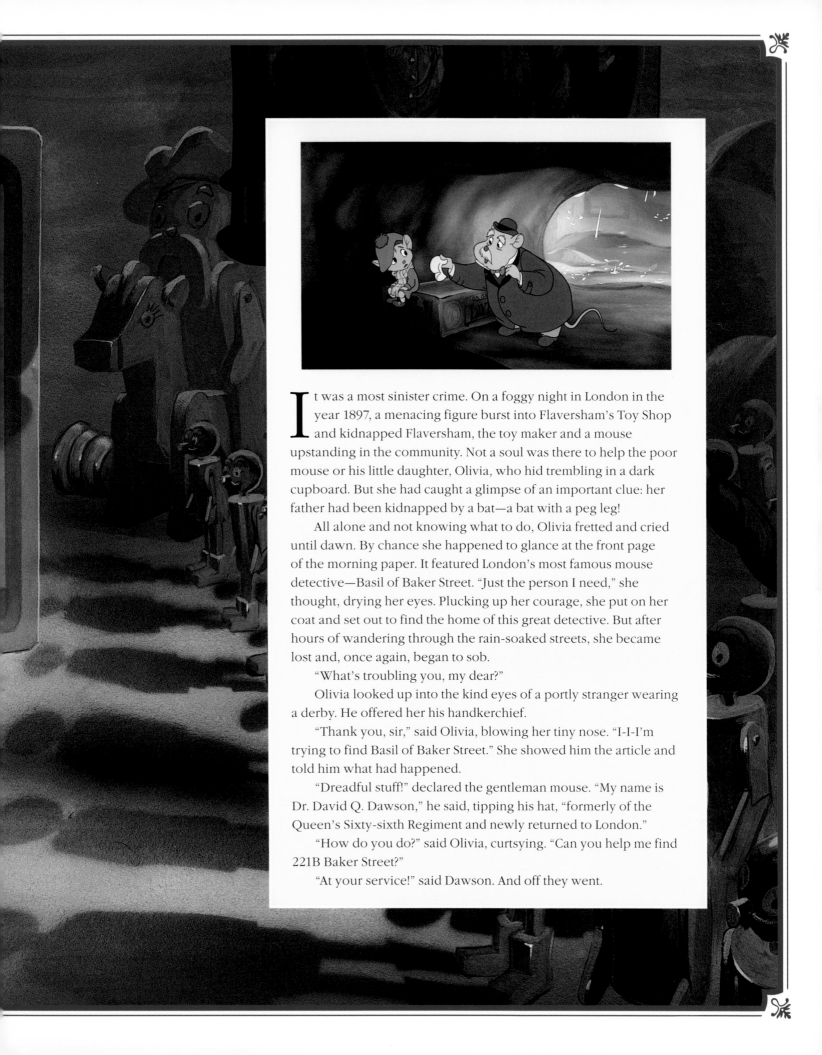

It was a most sinister crime. On a foggy night in London in the
year 1897, a menacing figure burst into Flaversham's Toy Shop
and kidnapped Flaversham, the toy maker and a mouse
upstanding in the community. Not a soul was there to help the poor
mouse or his little daughter, Olivia, who hid trembling in a dark
cupboard. But she had caught a glimpse of an important clue: her
father had been kidnapped by a bat—a bat with a peg leg!

All alone and not knowing what to do, Olivia fretted and cried
until dawn. By chance she happened to glance at the front page
of the morning paper. It featured London's most famous mouse
detective—Basil of Baker Street. "Just the person I need," she
thought, drying her eyes. Plucking up her courage, she put on her
coat and set out to find the home of this great detective. But after
hours of wandering through the rain-soaked streets, she became
lost and, once again, began to sob.

"What's troubling you, my dear?"

Olivia looked up into the kind eyes of a portly stranger wearing
a derby. He offered her his handkerchief.

"Thank you, sir," said Olivia, blowing her tiny nose. "I-I-I'm
trying to find Basil of Baker Street." She showed him the article and
told him what had happened.

"Dreadful stuff!" declared the gentleman mouse. "My name is
Dr. David Q. Dawson," he said, tipping his hat, "formerly of the
Queen's Sixty-sixth Regiment and newly returned to London."

"How do you do?" said Olivia, curtsying. "Can you help me find
221B Baker Street?"

"At your service!" said Dawson. And off they went.

They arrived at a stately old town house on a tree-lined street. "Why, I've heard of this place," remarked Dawson. "This is the home of Sherlock Holmes, the great human detective." Next to the entrance, down at the base of the building, they found another, much smaller, door.

"Oh, look!" cried Olivia. "This must be it."

A housekeeper, carrying an armload of books, answered their knock. "Mr. Basil isn't here at the moment," she said, "but you're welcome to come in and wait." After showing them into Basil's study, she scurried off to fetch some hot tea and cheese crumpets.

While Dawson made himself comfortable in a nice soft chair, Olivia gazed wide-eyed around the room. Tangles of glass tubes filled with bubbling chemicals were spread across tables, and pictures of oddly shaped footprints lay scattered all across the floor.

They spun around in surprise when the door sprang open and a masked mouse in a silk kimono rushed into the room. As Olivia and Dawson looked on astonished, the mouse whipped off his disguise and calmly put on a smoking jacket.

"Basil of Baker Street here," he said, introducing himself. "As you can see, I'm returning from a case."

"Please, sir," begged Olivia, "I need your help!"

Ignoring her, Basil studied Dawson. "You are a doctor," he declared, "and, um, just returned from military duty in Afghanistan. Am I right?"

A dumbfounded Dawson extended his hand and introduced himself. "How can you tell?" he asked.

"Elementary," explained Basil. "You've mended your cuff with the Lambert stitch—a stitch used only by a surgeon. And the thread is a pungent catgut found solely in the Afghan province." Basil picked up a violin from the shelf and began to play a melancholy tune. "Most relaxing," he explained dreamily.

Olivia tugged at his coat. "My daddy's gone."

"Miss . . . ?" said Basil.

"Flaversham," said Olivia. "Olivia Flaversham."

"Whatever," said Basil. "This is a most inopportune time. At present, I'm hot on the trail of a dangerous criminal. I simply don't have time to look for lost fathers."

"I didn't lose him," objected Olivia. "He was kidnapped by a bat."

Basil dropped the violin. "Did you say *bat*?" Olivia nodded. "Did he have a crippled wing?"

"I don't know," answered Olivia. "But he had a peg leg."

"Ha!" Basil shouted, leaping onto a chair and throwing up his arms.

"Do you know this bat?" inquired Dawson.

"Know him!" Basil announced. "That nonflying bat, one Fidget by name, is in the employ of the very fiend I am after—the nefarious Professor Ratigan." From over the fireplace, he took down a portrait that showed Ratigan posing in top hat and striped ascot and sporting a red carnation in his lapel. The professor's unshaven face and evil grin made Basil's guests shudder.

"The rat's a criminal genius," said Basil. "A Napoleon of crime. Who knows what he may be plotting, even as we speak. . . ."

Down near the city docks, Flaversham, the toy maker, was being held captive in Ratigan's dank, dark hideaway. The professor was displaying for him a robot he had created. It was designed to look just like the great Queen Moustoria. Wearing a metal crown on its head, the robot was jerkily pouring a cup of tea, which it spilled all over Ratigan's shoe.

"Quite an ingenious scheme, aye, Flaversham?" grinned Ratigan, shaking tea off his foot. "But, as you can see, not quite perfected. That's where you—the greatest of all toy makers—come in. You will have our little robot ready by tomorrow evening, just in time for our good queen's Diamond Jubilee!"

"The whole thing is . . . is monstrous!" sputtered Flaversham. "I . . . I won't have anything to do with it. Do what you want with me."

Ratigan raised his gold cigarette holder to his lips and calmly blew a large smoke ring right into Flaversham's face. "Oh, by the way," he said, "I've taken the liberty of having your daughter brought here."

"Olivia!" coughed Flaversham. "You . . . *wouldn't!*"

"Oh, wouldn't I?" Ratigan sneered. He pointed to the robot. "Finish it, or else!" Turning on his heel, he strode into the next room where a bat was hanging upside down, snoring loudly. "Wake up, Fidget!" he shouted, shoving a piece of paper at him. "Here's the list."

The bat read groggily. "Tools . . . Gears . . . Girl . . . Uniforms."

"You know where to go," said Ratigan. "And no mistakes!"

"Right, boss. No mistakes," mumbled Fidget, hobbling away.

Brushing ashes from his waistcoat, Ratigan walked through a pair of swinging doors into a room where all his gang members were throwing a noisy party. They waved their fizzy pink drinks in the air, welcoming their leader.

Ratigan smiled. "My friends," he said, "I'm giving this celebration because we're about to embark on a crime to top all crimes. Tomorrow evening, our royal monarch, Queen Moustoria, celebrates her Diamond Jubilee. With the help of Mr. Flaversham, it promises to be a night she'll never forget! And for once, that miserable second-rate detective, Basil of Baker Street, will not interfere with my plans!"

Everyone cheered in agreement. From the back of the room, one gang member raised his mug and toasted, "To Ratigan, the world's greatest rat!"

Everyone gasped.

"What did you call me?" hissed Ratigan.

"He didn't mean it, boss," someone called out. "He knows you don't like to be called a rat!"

"Silence!" Ratigan shouted. "You know what happens when someone upsets me." He took a little brass bell from his vest pocket and tinkled it. In seconds, a fat cat with gleaming teeth appeared. "Felicia, honey-bunny," cooed Ratigan. "I've a little tasty treat for you." The gang members covered their eyes as Felicia snatched up the doomed mouse and ate him.

Everyone shakily raised their glasses again. "To Ratigan," they shouted, "the world's greatest criminal mind!"

Back in the detective's sitting room, Basil puffed thoughtfully at his pipe and questioned Olivia for every last detail. "It's puzzling," he mused. "What would Ratigan want with a toy maker?"

Sitting next to the window, Olivia suddenly cried out. "There's a bat outside!"

Basil and Dawson dashed to the window but the bat was gone. They hustled through the front door and peered up and down the dark street. "No sign of the scoundrel," said Dawson. "But he left some rather unusual footprints."

"They're peg leg prints!" said Olivia, joining them at the door. "It must be the bat who took my father!"

Dawson picked up a ratty black woolen cap.

"Excellent work, old man!" cried Basil. "You've found his cap. Now all we need is Toby!"

Dawson and Olivia followed the detective back inside and through a hole in the baseboard. Staying close to Basil, they scrambled up inside the wall to the floor above. Peeking out from another hole, they saw a large, well-stocked pantry. Basil whistled to a dog stretched out on the floor. The big, bright-eyed hound bounded over to greet him. "Hello, Toby," Basil laughed as the dog sniffed around Dawson, who didn't seem to like it one bit. Next he licked Olivia, who broke into giggles.

Basil held the cap under Toby's nose. "Can you track down the owner of this cap for me?" Toby wagged his tail. "Good boy!" said Basil. The three of them climbed onto Toby's back. "Now, sic 'im, Toby!" the detective commanded.

Following the scent through the city, Toby led them straight to a toy shop. While the hound waited by the door, Basil led the others inside through an open window. "Hmm," he said, tiptoeing around the room. "How very odd. Those Royal Guard toy soldiers have all been stripped of their uniforms."

"And over here," added Dawson, "someone's removed the gears from these toys."

All of a sudden, the room erupted with noise as the other mechanized toys sprang into action. Basil and Dawson stared as the dolls, soldiers, and other toys spun, marched up and down, and whirred about the shop. They were so startled that neither of them noticed a shadow glide behind them. Then they heard Olivia scream.

"Gotcha!" sang out Fidget, stuffing her into a sack. He scrambled up a ladder and escaped through a skylight before Basil and Dawson could come to their senses. Fidget fled through the dark streets. He lugged the sack, with Olivia wiggling inside, back to Ratigan's secret hideout. With a big grin, he handed Ratigan his prize.

"Ah, Mr. Flaversham," laughed the professor, pulling Olivia out of the sack. "Allow me to present your charming daughter."

"Daddy!" Olivia flew into her father's arms. "I thought I'd *never* find you," she said, burying her face in his shirt.

Ratigan sighed. "Oh, how sweet. I just love tearful reunions." He yanked Olivia away and imprisoned her in a glass bottle. "We'll take good care of her," he said, looking Flaversham in the eye. "As long as you finish the robot by tonight."

"I . . . I'll finish it," Flaversham sputtered. "Just don't harm my daughter!"

Ratigan slammed the door behind him, bumping into Fidget. "Did you get everything else?" he snapped.

"Everything on the list," said Fidget, feeling in his pocket for the piece of paper. "Uh-oh," he mumbled. "I must've dropped the list."

"You fool!" Ratigan roared. "How could you lose it?"

"Well, ya see, boss," explained Fidget, "there was this dog . . . then Basil appeared . . . I wound up the toys to scare him off. . . ."

"What!" shrieked Ratigan. "Basil's on the case?"

Fidget gulped hard. Ratigan reached into his vest, pulled out the little bell, and rang it.

"Oh, no, boss!" squealed Fidget.

Felicia came trotting into the room. With a swoop of her paw, she popped the bat into her snaggle-toothed mouth. Just then Ratigan was struck by an idea.

"Oh, spit it out, dear," he said to Felicia, who obediently dropped the wet and tangled bat to the floor. "Fidget, old boy, you've given me a great opportunity. Basil's in for a big surprise!"

Dawson sat hunched on a stool in Basil's study. "Is there any chance we can get her back?" he asked meekly.

"There's always a chance, so long as we can think," said Basil, examining Fidget's list through a magnifying glass. "It's also fortunate that you found this clue. Aha! This paper's been gummed by a bat, smudged with coal dust used in sewer lamps, and saturated with seawater!"

"Meaning?" asked Dawson.

"This list comes from the area around the city docks," Basil patiently explained. "The exact spot where the sewer connects to the waterfront. There's no time to waste now. We've got some detecting to do."

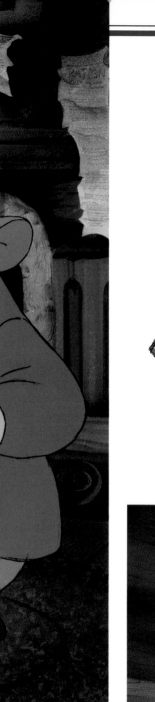

Within an hour, they were strolling into a seedy waterfront pub—Basil disguised as a sea captain and Dawson as a pirate. "I feel ridiculous," murmured Dawson, adjusting his eye patch.

"Just act natural," coached Basil. "We'll ask around for Ratigan, and if anyone questions us, just say he's an old friend of ours."

They wandered about as everyone watched the floor show. First there was a juggling octopus, followed by a salamander riding a unicycle. For the closing number, a blue-eyed mouse in a feathered dress sang love songs. Basil and Dawson tried, but not a soul in the joint would talk to them about Ratigan.

"Dear me," said Basil. "Is there no ruffian who'll help us?" He'd no sooner uttered these words than he was astonished to see Fidget parade past the piano.

"Dawson!" Basil cried. "After that bat!"

With Basil and Dawson in hot pursuit, Fidget raced down a foul-smelling alley and into an old sewer pipe. The pipe took many twists and turns before it led up to a rusty grate. Basil pushed it open and climbed into a dark room reeking of stale cigarettes. "We found it," he whispered, pulling Dawson after him. "Ratigan's secret lair!"

The gloomy room suddenly filled with light. A banner, with the words WELCOME BASIL on it, unfurled from the ceiling, and a flurry of bright balloons cascaded around Basil and Dawson.

"Basil of Baker Street—the greatest detective in all Mousedom," Ratigan greeted them with a burst of laughter. "I expected you to spot Fidget at least fifteen minutes earlier."

"Ratigan, so help me, I'll see you behind bars yet," growled Basil.

"I'd love to chat, but I do have an important engagement at Buckingham Palace," replied Ratigan. He snapped his fingers and three of his gang members sprang forward. Roughly, they tied Basil and Dawson onto a large rat trap. Ratigan placed a record player in front of the two captives. It was rigged, by a network of strings, to a revolver, an arrow, and an ax, all aimed directly at them.

"Ingenious, isn't it?" marveled Ratigan. "When the record's over, the string will tighten, the revolver will fire, the arrow will shoot, and the ax will drop on you. No need to worry, death will come instantly."

Olivia watched from inside the bottle as Ratigan switched on the record player. She desperately tried to signal to her friends, but they were too busy figuring out what to do.

Fidget reappeared and reported that all was ready. "Felicia just left for the palace," he said to Ratigan. "She's carrying Flaversham and the fellas dressed up in the Royal Guard uniforms. And the Queen's gift is already on the airship."

"Farewell, forever," Ratigan sang out to Basil. Waving, he and Fidget climbed aboard the professor's airship parked next to the fireplace. It rose up through the chimney into the sky and floated over the city

toward Buckingham Palace. As they drew closer they could see crowds of elegantly dressed mice promenading into the cellar of the palace where the festivities were scheduled to take place. As soon as they landed, Ratigan and Fidget sneaked inside and rapped on the door to Queen Moustoria's dressing chamber.

"A present?" said the Queen when she opened the door. She unwrapped the box. "How extraordinary!" she gasped. "A robot that looks just like *me!*"

Without warning, the robot began to chase the astonished Queen around the room. "Goodness gracious!" she cried, trying to flee.

But Ratigan's mice, disguised as her Royal Guards, blocked the door. They held her while the mechanical Queen glided down the hall and entered the throne room, which was packed with eager mice. Hidden behind a curtain, Flaversham sat at a control panel and guided the robot's movements. He spoke through a special tube, which made his voice sound just like the Queen's. The toy maker felt miserable doing it, but all he could think of was little Olivia.

"We are here," announced the mechanical Queen, "not only to commemorate my sixty years as your Queen, but to honor one of truly noble stature. May I present to you, Professor Ratigan—my new royal consort."

As the mice all murmured in shock and dismay, Ratigan strutted forward holding a long scroll. "Thank you, Your Majesty," he said and proceeded to read. "As your new royal consort, I'm placing a heavy tax on society's parasites and sponges—the ill, the elderly, and little children."

"You're mad!" shouted an elderly mouse. "You can't do that!"

"Oh, can't I?" said Ratigan. He turned to the Queen and bowed. "That is, with Your Majesty's permission."

There was a moment of silence followed by a little commotion behind the curtain. Then the robot began to speak. "You low-life scoundrel," answered the mechanical Queen. "You fraud, you impostor, you nincompoop!" Ratigan furiously clamped his hand over the robot's mouth and peered behind the curtain. Expecting to see Flaversham at the controls, he was astonished to find Basil calmly sitting in the toy maker's place.

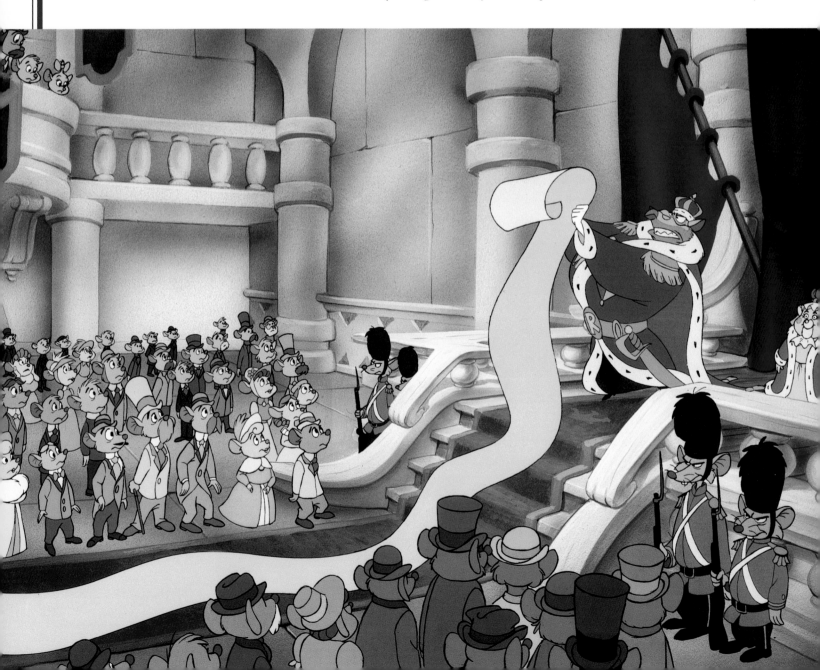

"How did—" Ratigan began.

"I escape?" finished Basil, grinning. "Elementary. By pulling the string when the record was only half over. Your entire mechanism was thrown completely off. We rescued Olivia and caught a ride on Toby straight to the palace. We arrived right behind you."

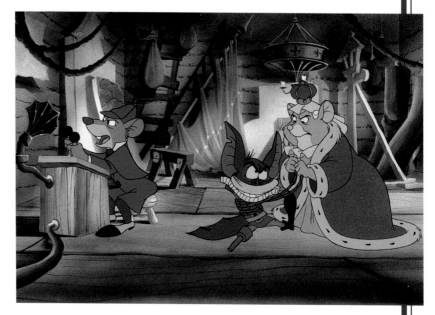

"But where *is* my Olivia?" Flaversham whispered to Dawson.

A shrill whistle pierced the air. Everyone looked up at the balcony and saw Fidget clutching Olivia under his one good wing. Ratigan immediately appeared next to them. "Stay where you are," he called down to the crowd, "or the girl dies."

The crowd froze in terror as Ratigan and Fidget disappeared with Olivia through a hole in the wall. A loud whirring sound told Basil they were escaping in the airship. The detective quickly sized up the situation. "Dawson, gather up the helium balloons," he said as he pulled the British flag from a pole. "And Flaversham, fetch me a matchbox." Within moments, he'd created a flying contraption by tying the four corners of the flag to the matchbox and then stuffing the balloons under the flag.

"An air balloon!" marveled Dawson, as they guided it outside. They all climbed in and quickly rose into the air, floating past Green Park, Lord Nelson's statue, and Tower Bridge. "It looks like they're heading for Big Ben!" Basil shouted as he steered toward the clock tower.

Fidget was pedaling madly, trying to keep the airship aloft. "They're catching up," he wheezed. "Ya gotta lighten the load, boss." He glanced knowingly at Olivia.

Ratigan grabbed Fidget from his seat. "Enough whining," he said and tossed the surprised bat overboard.

"No, not me! I can't fly!" Fidget yelled. Ratigan grinned as he watched the flailing bat make a tiny splash in the Thames River far below. He jumped into the driver's seat and started pedaling fast. But by now Basil was right behind.

"Keep it steady, Dawson," Basil instructed, leaning out toward Ratigan. With a brave leap, he threw himself onto the airship's rudder. Ratigan immediately lost all control and crashed straight into the face of Big Ben.

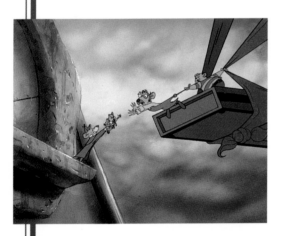

Basil landed in a heap inside the clock tower. He could barely stand, but when he saw Ratigan dragging Olivia away, he pulled himself together and chased after them. After wresting her from Ratigan's grasp, Basil pulled Olivia onto a narrow ledge.

"Over here, Dawson!" called Basil. Dawson managed to steer the air balloon closer. Holding his breath, Basil held Olivia in midair while Flaversham stretched out his arms.

"Daddy, I can't reach!" she cried. With a frantic move, the toy maker snatched his daughter and pulled her aboard. A gust of wind caught the miniature air balloon and blew it away from the tower.

All of a sudden Ratigan sprang out and chased Basil back inside the clock tower. They scrambled in and out of the turning gears and spinning wheels as Basil barely escaped the professor's razor-sharp claws. After several more close calls, Basil found himself backing up along the ledge with nowhere to go and Ratigan approaching.

Suddenly, Big Ben struck the hour. The vibration of the great bell knocked Basil and Ratigan right off their feet. Everyone in the balloon screamed as they watched Ratigan plummet to the ground. Basil, it seemed, had also met his end.

"It's all over," Dawson sobbed. "Our brave friend is gone."

"No, he isn't! Look!" cried Olivia, pointing toward Basil, who was merrily pedaling along on what was left of Ratigan's airship. He drew alongside and Dawson pulled him safely aboard. Olivia threw her arms around the detective's neck and kissed him.

"Well, now," Basil said, patting Olivia's head. "I say it's high time we all go back home."

"Sounds awfully good to me," agreed Flaversham. "This has been quite an adventure. And thanks to you, good chap, we've lived to tell the tale."

"Right-o!" agreed Dawson. He offered his hand to Basil. "It's been a pleasure working with you."

Basil took Dawson's hand. "I was hoping you'd join up with me. I could use a trusted associate. There are bound to be many more crimes to solve."

Dawson smiled. "At your service!"

On that firm handshake, the world's most famous crime-fighting team was formed—Dr. David Q. Dawson and the great mouse detective, Basil of Baker Street.

THE GREAT MOUSE DETECTIVE
Behind the Scenes

Burny Mattinson, Melvin Shaw, Pete Young, and Joe Hale first proposed, or "pitched," the idea for a picture based on Eve Titus and Paul Galdone's children's book *Basil of Baker Street* (1974) with a single piece of art. To illustrate their idea, the artists simply took a background of a little town setting from *Mickey's Christmas Carol* and changed the foreground characters to mice. Over the next few years, the creative team working on *The Great Mouse Detective* generated heaps of development and early story sketch work. They made a presentation board—a storyboard that describes in a few visual sketches the idea of the story—and received an okay to begin producing the picture. Four years and mountains of drawings later, they found they would have to sell their ideas all over again to a new management team running the Studio. They showed their presentation board—no reaction. They showed some storyboards—still nothing. Then they showed the barroom sequence—the one section of the story they had put on film. "They loved it," says producer Burny Mattinson. The project was green-lighted a second time.

Don Hahn, production manager on the film, calls *The Great Mouse Detective* "a *real* new beginning." Explains Hahn: "In addition to seismic shifts at the top, there was an influx of young artists and a change of location from the old animation building in Burbank to a Glendale warehouse. There was a sense that if animation was going to survive we'd have to reinvent the wheel and understand how it works again." In Hahn's view, "The positive fear associated with that prospect helped make *The Great Mouse Detective* a good little movie."

The Great Mouse Detective was in many ways a developmental proving ground for the artists of Feature Animation to establish and refine their technique and then to define their own style. The film about a detective mouse who lives at 221B Baker Street, right under the feet of Arthur Conan Doyle's legendary sleuth,

Sherlock Holmes, was the first directed by this new generation of artists, and their fresh, contemporary ideas are everywhere in evidence. Among the four directors of the movie, first-timers John Musker and Ron Clements had a particular talent for finding humor in situations and characters, lending a playful wit to the film.

Animator Mike Gabriel, who later directed *The Rescuers Down Under* and *Pocahontas*, recalls animating a basset hound and studying the animal to get to know it. Eric Larson, an early master of Disney animation who served as an animation consultant on the *The Great Mouse Detective*, saw Gabriel's animation and complimented the vitality and humor of the work. Gabriel recalls: "Something came to life working on that character. It came to my mind just then that if you're going to do an animal or any creature in a film—study that animal. Get the essence. And if you can capture it to the point where you think like that animal and put across the emotion with behavior natural to that animal that will spark a lot of entertainment."

Among the many creative directions that had their roots in *The Great Mouse Detective* was the use of the computer in animation. Though it was not the first time computer-generated imagery appeared in a Disney animated film, the chase through the interior of Big Ben, the famous clock tower in London, represents the first use of computer graphics to show part of the action in an integrated, seamless way. With what would now be considered very simple, low-tech methods, Big Ben's intermeshing gears were created inside a computer and printed out a frame at a time using a plotter. From such humble beginnings, many extraordinary scenes have since sprung. Such memorable moments as the title characters' dance through a romantic three-dimensional ballroom in *Beauty and the Beast*, the fearsomely dramatic wildebeest stampede in *The Lion King*, and the epic crowds of *The Hunchback of Notre Dame* can trace their origins to the clock tower scene in *The Great Mouse Detective*.

A final frame from the climactic chase scene inside Big Ben.

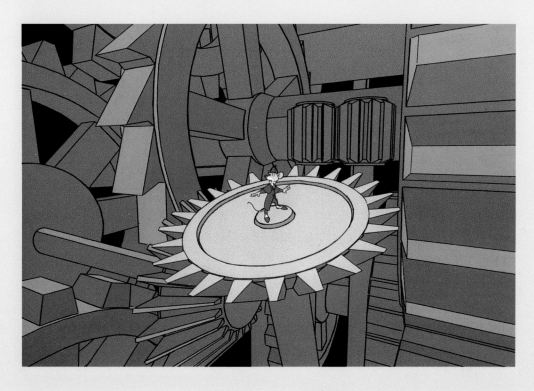

A s the late afternoon sun sank behind the skyscrapers towering over New York Harbor, a little barge with a bent TV antenna bobbed alongside an abandoned dock.

Inside, an English bulldog was watching a television rerun of Shakespeare's *Macbeth*. A Chihuahua named Tito sat at his feet, pawing expectantly through an old wallet he'd found on the street. Finding it empty, he tossed it into the gang's loot box, already piled high with discarded toasters, broken telephones, and a wide range of old sneakers.

"Frankie, man," Tito piped up, "what'chu watching? Does he get the girl?"

"Quiet, you nincompoop!" the bulldog snapped back, "And my name is Francis. Not Frank. Not Frankie. *Frawn-cis*."

The door banged open. Einstein, a gangly old Great Dane, trotted in, gripping a broken tennis racket between his teeth. "Look what I got," he said, dropping it on the floor.

"Good show," Francis said. "Now all we need is the court and the net."

Rita, a leggy Afghan hound with long silky ears, looked glum. "Fagin won't be happy about this," she told them. "Today's the day he's supposed to pay back Sykes." Tito reached back into the loot box. "Ain't got no money," he informed her, "but, hey, check out this primo wallet!"

Francis examined Tito's teeth marks. "It's a beauty," he observed. "Genuine shredded leather."

Rita glanced out the window. "Here comes Dodger. Maybe he's had some luck."

A friendly looking mutt with a lopsided grin strutted into the room. "Whoa! Cool it, Dodger fans," he announced, wearing a string of sausages wrapped around his neck. "I'd like to introduce you to . . . dinner! Hot dogs à la Dodger!"

Francis was so happy to see food that he could barely maintain his composure. "Thank you, Dodger," he declared. "You remain our preeminent benefactor."

"Yeah, and you're okay, too," added Einstein. "So how did you do it?"

"Let me tell you, it was tough!" Dodger explained. "Only *I* could have done it. Picture the city. Eighth and Broadway . . . crowds are hustling . . . hot dogs are sizzling. Enter Dodger, one bad puppy. Along comes a greedy, ugly psychotic monster with razor-sharp claws, dripping fangs and—"

An orange kitten fell through the barge's rotting roof and dropped into the middle of the dogs. Surrounded, he explained, "I followed a dog here. I . . . I just wanted some of the sausages I helped him get."

"Hey, kitty," Dodger said, "what took you so long?"

Francis observed the newcomer. "I assume this is the psychotic monster with dripping fangs?"

"Yeah, come on, Dodger," teased Tito. "Let's see this big bad kitty fighter in action."

Rita gently nosed the kitten. "Enough kidding around, guys. He's so little. I wonder where his mother is."

"You got a name, cat?" Tito asked.

The kitten shook his head. "I was left for adoption in a box on the sidewalk. My brothers were all taken yesterday and I was left all alone. Then Dodger came along." He narrowed his eyes. "He said we'd be pals."

Out on the dock, a makeshift motor scooter screeched to a halt. Startled, Oliver jumped into the loot box as a frazzled-looking man stumbled inside. Fagin, a good-hearted thief, pulled a box of dog biscuits from inside his coat. The five dogs jumped on him all at once, grabbing for the biscuits. Einstein gave him a big slurpy kiss.

"Okay, okay!" Fagin laughed. "No licking!" But he didn't laugh long. "Sykes is right behind me," he informed the gang, "and he's here for his money. Did anyone have any luck?"

Fagin scrounged around inside the loot box and pulled out Oliver. "How're we ever going to pay Sykes off with a . . . pussycat?"

A car door slammed outside. Sykes's huge Dobermans, Roscoe and DeSoto, shoved their way into the barge. They bared their teeth and snarled at Fagin.

"Look who's here, kids," said Fagin, trying to act casual. "Nice doggies!"

Picking up the loot box, Fagin sauntered out to the big black car parked on the dock. He squinted in the bright glare of the headlights.

Sykes rolled down the window. "Where's the dough?" he growled, sticking out his pudgy hand.

"Actually," replied Fagin, "I've got some luxury items here that should make a considerable dent in my debt to you."

"I don't want your garbage, Fagin," Sykes snapped. "I'll give you three more days. If you don't have the money by then, well, I hate to think what's going to happen . . . to you and your little gang." He honked the horn to round up his Dobermans.

Inside the barge, DeSoto was having too much fun to notice. He'd just discovered Oliver.

"Look what I found," DeSoto chuckled, yanking Oliver out from under a sheet of newspaper.

"Forget it, DeSoto," Roscoe urged his comrade. "We gotta go."

"But I like cats," insisted DeSoto. He leaned down close to Oliver and licked his lips. "I like to eat them."

Oliver winced in fear and took a wild swipe at DeSoto's nose.

"Yowww!" howled DeSoto. "The little creep scratched me!"

The two Dobermans advanced toward Oliver, backing him against the wall. Dodger stepped in front of them. "That's enough!" he growled.

"Run along," Rita chimed in. "Your master's calling."

Roscoe looked Dodger in the eye. "Just because we gotta go doesn't mean we're finished here. You guys are gonna pay for what that cat did."

The Dobermans bounded out the door, passing Fagin on his way inside.

"It's hopeless," sobbed Fagin. "My days are numbered—and the number is three." Then he brightened up a bit. "Say, who scratched DeSoto's nose?"

Dodger gently nudged Oliver forward. Fagin looked down at the kitten and chuckled. "We've never had a cat in our gang before," he said, picking Oliver up and scratching his chin. "But we can use all the help we can get!"

Dodger gave Oliver his very own sausage. "You did all right, kid," he told him. Oliver gobbled it right down, curled up next to Dodger, and went to sleep. He'd had a really big day.

The next morning Oliver tagged along as the gang meandered down a crowded sidewalk. "Grab what you can," Tito instructed Oliver. "It's easy."

"You gotta use your head to survive," Einstein added. *THUNK!* A loaf of pumpernickel fell off a passing bakery truck and hit Einstein on the head. "See what I mean?" he grinned, snatching up the bread.

"But to pay back Sykes," pointed out Francis, "we need to find something really big."

A shiny limousine turned the corner. "Like a CAR!" yipped Tito. "It's time for the chauffeur shuffle!" He positioned himself next to Oliver. "Stick with me, kid. I'll show you how it's done."

As the limousine slowed down for a red light, Einstein bumped his head hard against the front fender and wobbled away in a daze. Francis jumped into place. He let out a dramatic groan and flopped down with his tongue hanging out.

"Oh, poor thing," cried the distraught chauffeur, jumping out. "What have I done?" While a crowd gathered around Francis, Tito hopped into the driver's seat and started fiddling with the wires under the dashboard.

"What'cha doin'?" asked Oliver.

"Don't bother me," Tito mumbled. "I'm startin' the car without a key."

Oliver looked closer. "But Tito," he said, "the key's right here." He turned the key and the motor started, sending Tito flying out the door with a tremendous electric shock. In a panic, Oliver covered his ears with his paws. To his surprise, a little girl leaned forward from the backseat and picked him up.

"You poor kitty," she exclaimed.

When Francis saw Tito zip out the window in a shower of sparks, he jumped up and dashed away with his pals.

"You scoundrels!" shouted the chauffeur, shaking his fist in the air. He climbed back into the limousine.

"Look, Winston!" piped up the little girl. "I've got a new friend!"

From the rearview mirror, Winston saw Oliver cuddling in the little girl's lap. "Now, Miss Jenny," he said, kindly, "I don't think your mother and father would like you to bring home a dirty little street kitten. And I'm certain Georgette wouldn't want another pet in the house."

"But he's half-starved," Jenny protested. "Besides, Mummy and Daddy will be away for my birthday next week, and the kitty will keep me from getting lonely." Winston had to agree. He started the car and drove uptown along Park Avenue. Dodger and Tito hopped on top of a taxi and followed close behind.

As soon as Jenny was home, she took Oliver into the pantry to find some food. Georgette, a snooty French poodle, glanced up from her gourmet doggy brunch. "A cat!" she snorted and stalked off in a huff.

"Don't be like that, Georgette," Jenny called after her. But Georgette had left to sulk in her private room.

Jenny had hoped Georgette would be a bit more friendly toward Oliver, but what could she expect? Georgette was a dog and Oliver was a cat. Georgette had quite a nice life for a dog, and now Jenny would see to it that Oliver was taken care of as well. That afternoon, she bought him a silver pendant to wear around his neck that read OLIVER 1125 FIFTH AVENUE, and gave him his very own crystal bowl.

Early the next morning, Dodger and the gang huddled behind a newsstand and watched Jenny leave her town house and board a school bus.

"Okay," Dodger cried, "let's go!"

Einstein trotted up the stone steps, pushed the doorbell with his nose, then hid behind a shrub. When Winston answered the door, he found Francis lying on the steps looking sick.

"AHA!" cried out Winston. "It's you again!" He charged down the steps and chased Francis across the street.

With Winston gone and the door wide open, the rest of the gang sneaked into the house. In the parlor, they came face to face with Georgette. "Help! Intruders!" she shrieked.

"Relax," Dodger reassured her. "We don't want any trouble. We'll leave just as soon as we get back our cat."

"Your cat?" asked Georgette, breaking into a smile. "Follow me." She led them to Jenny's room, where Oliver lay snuggled up on the bed, sound asleep.

"Look at him, Dodger," Rita whispered. "He looks so peaceful. Let's just forget it."

"You can't do that," Georgette insisted, frantically. "The poor dear's simply traumatized. He misses you all terribly."

"No kidding?" said Dodger, brightening up. "Then we'll take him."

Without waking Oliver, they put him into a pillowcase. Dodger carefully picked up the tiny bundle with his teeth and carried Oliver back to the barge.

When he woke up, Oliver was shocked to see the old gang staring down at him. "What's going on?" he asked.

"It was the rescue of the century," bragged Tito. "Frankie was awesome."

"I *was* rather good, wasn't I?" Francis agreed.

"But I have another home now," said Oliver, "and someone who loves me."

"What do you mean, kid?" asked Dodger. "We risked a lot to get you. You're in the gang—and gang means family."

Oliver's eyes filled with tears. "But guys, I was happy there. I like every one of you but . . . there was a little girl . . . I just want to go back."

"This place not good enough for you? Don't want to mix with the riffraff? There's the door," said Dodger abruptly. "No one's stopping you."

Just then Fagin moseyed in. "Hey," he said to Oliver. "You're back!" He squinted at the pendant around Oliver's neck. "Oliver 1125 Fifth Avenue," he read aloud. "So that's where you've been. Your new owner must be worried sick about you. Alone in that big house with only his millions and millions of dollars to . . ." Fagin's eyes lit up. "That's it!" he hooted. "We're saved!" He found a scrap of paper and a stubby pencil.

He began writing, "Dear Mister Very Rich Cat Owner Person . . ."

When Jenny got home from school, she hunted all over for Oliver. "Here kitty, kitty," she called. "Have you seen him, Georgette?" Pretending to look concerned, Georgette shook her head. When Jenny opened the front door to look outside, she noticed a wrinkled piece of paper stuck in the mail slot. She pulled it out and found a scrawly note and a hand-drawn map. As she read, her eyes grew big. "And if you don't bring the money," she said aloud, "you'll never see your cat again."

"Oh, Georgette," Jenny cried. "Oliver's been kidnapped! We have to get him back!"

On a street corner across town, Fagin called Sykes from a pay phone.

"So, Fagin," asked Sykes, "do you have something wrinkly and green to make me happy?"

"Not yet," Fagin answered, "but I've got an airtight kitty plan. I've kidnapped a rich cat, uh, I mean a cat from a rich family. They're coming tonight with the money I owe you."

"I think there's hope for you yet," said Sykes. "Remember, you've got twelve hours, and this is your last chance."

"Not to worry," Fagin assured him. As he hung up, he could hear Roscoe and DeSoto snarling in the background.

After dinner, Jenny told Winston she was taking Georgette for a walk. Cautiously, she made her way down to the docks. Georgette kept pulling at her leash, looking worried. "Stay close," Jenny whispered. "It sure is creepy here." She turned the note sideways, then upside down. "This map's really hard to follow," she said in a shaky voice. "I think we're lost!"

Not far away, Fagin paced up and down, waiting. "What's keepin' Mr. Moneybags?" he muttered, nervously. "That was a perfectly good map I drew."

He squinted into the darkness and saw a little girl and a French poodle peering out from behind a rusty oil drum. "Hey, little girl," he said, approaching her. "What're you doing out here? This is a tough neighborhood."

"I'm lost," Jenny explained, trying hard not to cry. "I'm supposed to meet somebody to get my kitty back."

"Your kitty?" Fagin gulped.

Jenny nodded. "His name's Oliver and he's been kidnapped," she explained. "Look, I even brought this to pay them." She pulled a pink piggy

bank from a paper bag. "It's all the money I have. Four dollars and seventy-six cents. Do you think it's enough?"

"Aw, gee," murmured Fagin, feeling awful.

"What kind of a person would steal a kitty?" Jenny sobbed.

"A poor desperate man at the end of his rope who owed someone a lot of money?" Fagin answered.

Jenny started to walk away. After hesitating

only a moment, Fagin put his hand in his pocket and gently pulled out
Oliver. "Hey, little girl!" he called after her. "Look what I just found—a kitty!
Maybe it's yours."

"Oliver!" cried Jenny, running back. "You found him!"

Just as Oliver leaped into her arms, a big black car slowly cruised
toward them. The door popped open, and a big, meaty hand reached out
and grabbed Jenny. Georgette barked frantically as Oliver fell to the ground.

"Sykes! You can't do that!" Fagin protested.

"Keep your mouth shut and you won't owe me a thing," Sykes yelled.
"I'll get all I need from this kid's father!" He slammed the door, and the car,
with its tires squealing, careened around the corner.

Dodger and the rest of the gang came rushing up. "What happened?"
Dodger asked Oliver.

"Somebody took my Jenny!" he cried. "You have to save her!"

"Don't worry," Dodger promised. "We'll get her back."

Later that night, the gang and Georgette picked their way across a trash-strewn shipping yard toward Sykes's warehouse.

"Sykes is tying Jenny to a chair," gasped Georgette, peering through a window into a smoke-filled office.

"Shhh," Tito warned her. "Roscoe and DeSoto might be outside."

Francis tiptoed around, checking the doors and windows. "They're all locked," he whispered. "But there's an open window on the third floor."

"That's just great," Dodger mumbled, kicking a discarded football helmet lying at the bottom of a trash pile. "Too bad dogs can't fly." He examined the helmet, looked up at the window, and eyed the trash heap. "Hmmm . . . dogs can't fly," he grinned, "but I know a cat who's going to!"

The gang watched, puzzled, as Dodger balanced a long board, like a seesaw, on top of the trash pile. Carefully, he slid Oliver into the helmet and set it on one end of the board. He motioned to Francis. "Jump down on the other end!"

Francis climbed up the pile and jumped. The other end shot straight up, sending Oliver and the helmet whizzing high in the air and through the open window. "Don't worry," Dodger assured his pals. "Everybody knows that cats always land on their feet!"

THUDD!!! In his office below, Sykes looked up, startled, at the ceiling. "Somebody's upstairs," he said to Roscoe and DeSoto. "Let's go see who it is."

While Sykes and the dogs looked around upstairs, Oliver crept downstairs and let the gang in. They quickly found Jenny and untied her.

"I thought I'd never see you again, Oliver," Jenny cried, holding him close.

Fagin zoomed up in his motor scooter. "Let's get out of here!" he yelled as everyone clambered aboard.

Behind them they heard the roar of another motor starting up. "It's Sykes!" Jenny shrieked. "He's after us!"

Fagin careened around a corner on one wheel with Sykes and the Dobermans close behind. "I'll head for the subway!" he shouted. "He'll never follow us there!"

They bounced down the wide concrete steps. Fagin steered the scooter along the platform, breathing a sigh of relief, until he saw the car slamming through the turnstiles after them.

"Hold tight!" hollered Fagin, as the scooter shot onto the tracks and caromed down the winding tunnel. Reaching the end, they found themselves racing over a suspension bridge crossing the river. Fagin and the gang all gasped—a subway train was coming straight at them!

The scooter veered sharply to the right and narrowly scraped past the speeding train. Behind them, Sykes was not as lucky.

Car parts shot in all directions. Standing at the edge of the bridge, Fagin and Jenny watched silently, as bits of crumpled metal and shattered glass sank in the river, far below.

"One thing's for sure," Fagin said quietly, gazing down at a floating hubcap. "We'll never have to worry about Sykes again."

The next week, Winston invited Fagin and the gang over to celebrate Jenny's birthday.

"Anyone want some cake?" sang Jenny happily. "Okay," she said as Einstein's eyes lit up, "but not the whole thing."

"Jenny," Winston said, "Don't forget to thank your new friends for the lovely gifts."

"Oh, yes. Thank you. It's what I've always wanted: a broken tennis racket, an old wallet, and a half-eaten loaf of pumpernickel bread."

As the gang was getting ready to leave, Jenny hugged everyone good-bye. "This is my nicest birthday ever. Mummy and Daddy will be home tomorrow. I've got some new friends, and Oliver is back safe and sound."

Dodger leaned close to Oliver. "You're okay . . . for a cat!" he whispered. "We'll keep a spot open for you in the gang. Vice president, uptown chapter."

Oliver gave him a playful scratch on the nose.

OLIVER & COMPANY

Behind the Scenes

With an all-star cast of primarily four-footed characters voiced by the likes of Bette Midler, Billy Joel, and Cheech Marin, *Oliver & Company* is a decidedly contemporary retelling of Charles Dickens's well-known novel *Oliver Twist*. Set in New York City, the 1988 film boasts songs performed by pop artists Joel, Midler, Huey Lewis, and Ruth Pointer of the Pointer Sisters, among others. "The vocal personalities really brought this film to life," says Mike Gabriel, who worked on *Oliver & Company* as a story artist, a supervising animator, and a character designer.

Although Disney artists would seem to be naturals for representing the thoughts and feelings of the animal world, the last Disney film to portray four-footed creatures with any degree of accuracy in their movement had been *The Fox and the Hound* (1981). Many of the artists working on *Oliver* found animating dogs and cats with a degree of realism a brand-new challenge. In order to help prepare them for the assignment, regular classes in dog anatomy were held, and a steady stream of dogs were brought to the Studio for the animators to study as models. In cases where animators wanted to study a particular walk or run more closely, video footage was shot and examined frame by frame.

Making New York City an animated character in its own right was largely the responsibility of artists in the newly formed computer animation department. Taxicabs, buses, subway tunnels and trains, elaborate cityscapes, and a fully rendered Brooklyn Bridge all contribute to the sense of movement, rhythm, and action of a bustling metropolis. For the first time, a team of people (including art director Dan Hansen and production stylist Guy Deel) went on location to do research, taking hundreds of pictures of New York City streets and buildings from a dog's-eye level.

To complement the hip voice talent, modern urban setting, and contemporary storytelling, the creative team for *Oliver & Company* worked with a distinctly modern style of animation. Director George Scribner wanted the look and feel of the film to reflect New York City's graphic quality, energy, and edge. The movie features bold patches of color and rough, solid black outlines for both the character animation and the backgrounds, displaying a modern sensibility.

Though influenced in its style by two classic Disney films, *101 Dalmatians* and *Lady and the Tramp*, *Oliver & Company* represents the first time the young team of artists, animators, and directors had the opportunity to make a film from original vision to final print. "The question became, What kind of movie would we have a ball doing?" says Andreas Deja, who was responsible for many of the major character designs. The result was a movie "a little gutsier and a little naughtier" than many of the recent films.

Tina Price animates Fagin's cart with the use of a computer.

THE

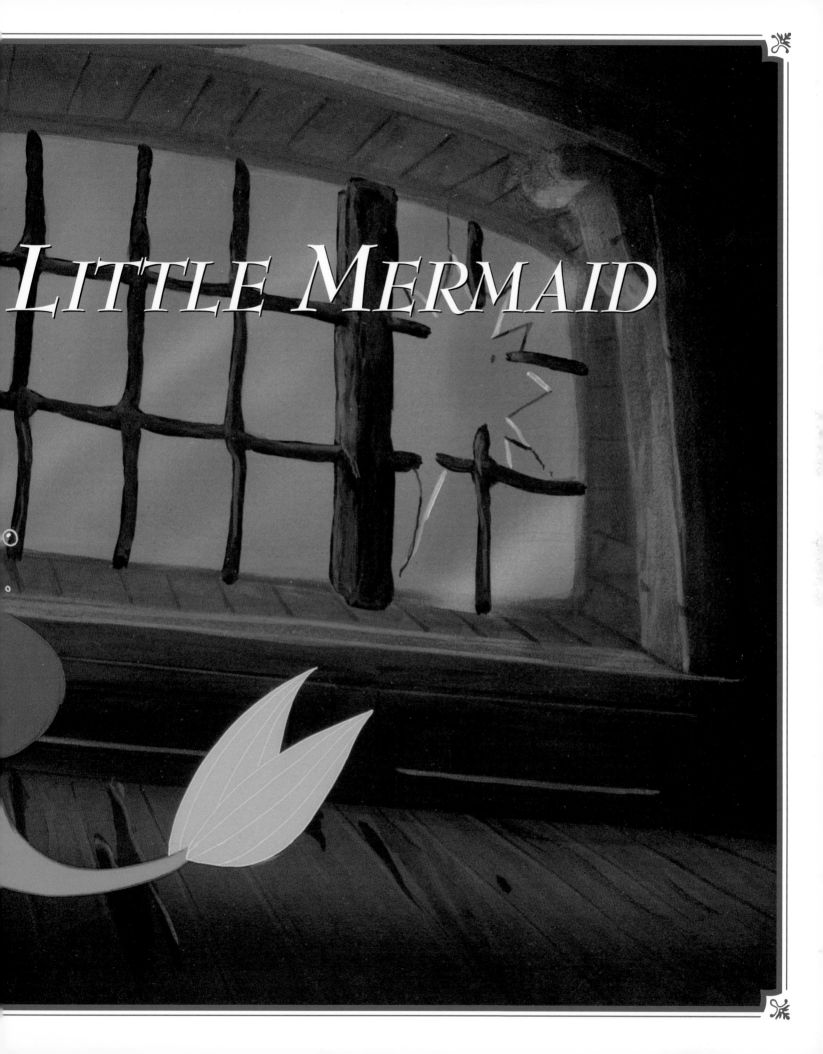

LITTLE MERMAID

T he enchanting merpeople, half fish and half human, dwelled in a shimmering kingdom at the bottom of the sea. Their ruler, King Triton, was the father of seven daughters. The youngest was named Ariel. She had a beautiful voice and loved to sing. Although Ariel disobeyed her father now and then, he loved her with all his heart.

Ariel and her best friend, a fish called Flounder, spent most of their time exploring sunken shipwrecks. Whenever they found a human treasure, like a worn belt buckle or rusty oil lamp, Ariel would add it to her collection, which she kept hidden in a cave.

One day Ariel came across two objects she'd never seen before—a silver fork and a pipe. "Flounder, look!" she said. "Maybe Scuttle can tell us what these are." They swam to the water's surface to find the seagull. Spotting them from his rocky perch, Scuttle gave out a cheerful squawk.

Ariel showed Scuttle her new treasures. "Hmmm," he said, examining the fork. "I do believe this is a dinglehopper. Humans use it to comb their hair. Here, I'll show ya." He twirled the feathers on his head into a fluffy hairdo. "And this," the gull continued, pointing to the pipe, "is a snarfblatt, which humans blow in to make music."

"Music!" Ariel cried. "I completely forgot. I'm supposed to sing at the royal concert today! Sorry, Scuttle, but I've got to go."

Flounder trailed after Ariel as she dove down to her father's palace. "What am I going to do with you, Ariel?" asked King Triton. "You have the most beautiful voice in the kingdom yet you missed the concert." He gestured toward a disappointed-looking crab. "Poor Sebastian was beside himself when you didn't appear."

Sebastian, the court composer, scurried up to her. "Princess Ariel," he said, shaking his claw at her, "because of your forgetfulness, the entire program was ruined."

"It wasn't Ariel's fault," Flounder said. "It took Scuttle forever to figure out about the dinglehopper and the snarfblatt."

"You visited that seagull?" King Triton asked, glaring at Ariel. "How many times have I told you not to travel to the surface! You might have been seen by one of those horrible humans. Do you think I want my youngest daughter snared by some fish eater's hook?" Knowing it was no use arguing, Ariel apologized and swam off with Flounder.

Sebastian edged forward and cleared his throat. "Your Majesty, if I may suggest something. I think Ariel needs constant supervision. You know, someone to watch over her."

Triton beamed. "A fine idea, Sebastian," he declared. "And you're just the one to do it."

Sebastian followed Ariel into her cave of treasures. "How do I get myself in these situations?" he crabbed. "I should be writing symphonies." Sebastian's eyes goggled. Piled high along the walls were pocket watches, mirrors, eyeglasses, vases, telescopes, paintings, and pots—human treasures of every kind! Ariel carefully placed the fork and pipe among them.

"Father must be mistaken," she told Flounder. "How could humans be bad when they make such wonderful things?"

She held up an old teapot. "I'd like to meet these humans. I'd like to trade in my fins for a couple of . . . feet! If I could only have one day on land, I'd run around and—oh, Sebastian!"

"Ariel!" he scolded. "If your father heard you talking that way, he'd flip out."

Suddenly, a large form floating on the surface cast a dark shadow on the sea floor. "What do you suppose that is?" Ariel said. Before Sebastian could stop her, she rose to the surface.

Ariel had never seen such a sight! Silhouetted against the full moon was a huge ship. The night sky thundered with bursts and cascades of brilliant color.

KABOOM!

"Jumping jellyfish!" exclaimed Sebastian.

Scuttle came flying over. "What's all the racket?"

Ariel swam to the side of the ship and pulled herself up to the edge of the deck. The crew was having a rousing party, dancing and shooting fireworks. A shaggy dog, barking happily, bounded among the men's prancing feet.

"Calm down, Max," an elderly gentleman called to him. "It's time for Prince Eric's surprise." With a flourish, he unveiled a life-size statue of the prince, bravely drawing his sword. "Prince Eric," he said, "may I, as your humble valet, wish you a most happy birthday."

Eric grinned in embarrassment. "Thank you, Grimsby, but, er, you really shouldn't have."

Ariel stared dreamily at the prince. "He's so handsome," she whispered.

Sebastian gave Ariel's tail a little pinch. "Will you please get your head out of the clouds and back in the water where it belongs."

A black misty curtain drifted across the moon.

"Hurricane a-comin'!" a sailor shouted down from the crow's nest. "Secure the rigging!"

The ship began to pitch and roll in the whistling winds. With an ear-splitting crack, a bolt of lightning struck the mast, setting the ship afire. "Abandon ship!" ordered Eric, and, at once, the men lowered the lifeboats over the sides.

As Eric rowed away, he realized Max was missing. He dove back into the water and, climbing aboard the flaming ship, tossed Max to safety. Before he could leap from the deck, the ship's powder kegs blew up, and Eric was thrown, unconscious, into the sea.

Ariel dove into the fiery debris to save Eric. Using all her strength, she swam with him toward shore and pulled him onto the sand. She pushed back his damp hair and sang softly to him. With the first light of dawn, Eric weakly opened his eyes and smiled. When Ariel heard voices approaching, she vanished back into the water.

"Prince Eric!" cried Grimsby. "Thank heavens you're safe!" Max waggled over and happily licked his master's face.

"A girl rescued me," Eric murmured, as if in a dream. "She held me in her arms and sang with the most beautiful voice I've ever heard."

"I think you swallowed too much water," Grimsby said, picking seaweed from Eric's jacket.

On some nearby rocks, Sebastian scolded Ariel. "We're going to forget this ever happened," he said. "Your father must never know." But all Ariel could do was gaze at the prince in the distance, limping away with Grimsby toward his castle.

"Ariel," said Flounder, bobbing up next to her. "Come see what I just found."

Ariel followed her friend along the coral-covered sea floor. As they approached her secret cave, she saw a tall form shining in the sun's slanted rays.

"It's Eric's statue!" cried Ariel. "This is the greatest treasure of all!"

Meanwhile, in a dark grotto close by, Ursula, the cruel sea witch and enemy of King Triton, gleefully watched Ariel through her shimmering magic bubble.

"So little Ariel's in love with a human prince," she said to her underlings—a pair of snickering moray eels called Flotsam and Jetsam. "Triton's daughter would make a fine addition to my little garden." With her long, black tentacles she gestured down toward the shriveled gray souls of her merpeople victims ensnared in the weeds.

"Who knows?" she continued. "The little mermaid's disobedience may be the key to my defeating Triton."

A few days later, King Triton called for Sebastian. "Ariel's been acting very peculiar," he said. "You know, mooning about and singing to herself. I suspect she's in love. Have you been keeping something from me?"

"I tried to stop her," Sebastian cried. "I *told* her to stay away from humans."

"Humans?" Triton gasped. "What about humans?"

"Uh, who said anything about humans?" Sebastian asked sheepishly.

Triton glared. "Maybe you'd better tell me what's going on."

When King Triton heard everything Sebastian had to tell, he stormed over to Ariel's cave. He found her inside, singing softly to Eric's statue.

"I consider myself a reasonable merman," Triton thundered, "but contact between the merworld and the human world is strictly forbidden. Why did you disobey me and rescue that human?"

"I had to—he would have died," protested Ariel.

"One less fish eater to worry about," her father roared.

Ariel admitted the truth at last. "Daddy, I love him."

Triton was stunned. "I'm going to get through to you," he said, raising his trident, "and if this is the only way—so be it!"

"Daddy, no!" begged Ariel.

Bolts of lightning shot from the trident, shattering all of Ariel's treasures one by one. Finally, Triton leveled the staff at the statue and completely destroyed it. Ariel fell to the cave floor and sobbed.

After Triton had gone, Flotsam and Jetsam slithered out from behind a rock. "Poor, sweet child," said Flotsam. "You have a serious problem."

"But we know someone who can help," added Jetsam. "Someone who can make all your dreams come true."

Ariel looked up at the eels uneasily. "I don't understand."

"Ursula . . . has great powers," Flotsam said slyly.

"The sea witch?" Ariel asked, horrified. "No, I couldn't possibly . . ." Ariel paused when she looked down and saw what remained of Eric's statue. Flotsam and Jetsam crept closer.

"Imagine," they said, "you and your prince . . . together . . . forever!"

Outside the cave, Flounder and Sebastian were startled to see the eels swim past followed by Ariel.

"What are you doing with this riffraff?" Sebastian demanded.

"I'm going to see Ursula," Ariel replied. "Why don't you tell my father? You're good at that!"

Tagging along fearfully, they followed Ariel to the dark grotto and were revolted by the sight of the gray wormy creatures reaching out to them for help.

"Come right in, angelfish," said Ursula, ushering Ariel into her lair. "I hear you're in love with a human. Well, dearie, the solution to your problem is simple. *You* must become human, too!"

Ariel gasped. "Can you do that?"

"Of course," Ursula chuckled. "It's what I do. I confess I've been nasty in the past, but now I live to help poor needy merfolk—like you."

Ursula wrapped Ariel in one of her long tentacles and squeezed her close. "Here's the deal. I'll make you a potion that will turn you into a human for three days. If dear old Princie kisses you before sunset on the third day, you will be human forever. But if he doesn't," she said, squeezing tighter, "then you'll turn back into a mermaid and belong to *me*!"

"But if I become human," Ariel realized with alarm, "I'll never be with my father or sisters again."

"That's right, but you'll have your man," Ursula persisted. "Life is full of tough choices, isn't it? And there's one more thing, sweet cakes. We haven't discussed payment."

"But I don't have anything," Ariel protested.

"Oh, it's just a token, a trifle. You'll never even miss it. What I want . . . is your voice!" Ursula whipped out a golden scroll. "Just sign here."

Ariel wavered with the fish bone quill in her hand. Then she cringed and quickly signed her name.

"A wise decision!" said Ursula.

She bent over a black cauldron and, stirring the potion, recited a magic spell. A great cloud rose and enveloped Ariel. The little mermaid's voice was sucked from her throat in a swirling golden mist, which floated straight into a shell necklace hanging around Ursula's flabby neck. Laughing maniacally, the sea witch waved her arms over the cauldron. A bright light flashed and suddenly Ariel's tail was transformed into two legs.

Ursula gestured toward the entrance. "Now you are free to go to your prince!" she said.

Ariel found she could barely swim, so Sebastian and Flounder helped push her to the surface.

"Oh, what a soft shell I'm getting to be," muttered Sebastian. "I know I should report this to King Triton at once, but little Ariel is so happy."

Every day since the storm, Prince Eric had wandered along the shore searching for the beautiful girl who had rescued him.

"Be reasonable," Grimsby told him again and again. "You must have imagined her."

"I tell you she's real," the prince replied. "And when I find her, I'll marry her."

One morning, as Eric strolled along the beach, Max ran ahead, bounding right up to a girl relaxing on the sand.

"I hope he didn't scare you," Eric said to Ariel. "Say, you seem very familiar to me." He peered into her eyes. "Haven't we met?" Ariel smiled. "I knew it!" he cried. "You're the one I've been looking for. What's your name?"

Ariel's smile faded as she tried to talk. She put her hand to her throat and shook her head sadly. Eric was crestfallen. "You couldn't be who I thought you were," he said. "She had a beautiful voice." Believing Ariel had been washed ashore from a shipwreck, he took her to the castle to rest.

Instead of resting, the little mermaid spent the day wandering around the castle, marveling at all the treasures. That evening, one of the servants showed Ariel to her chamber and gave her a gown to wear to dinner. It fit her perfectly and, as she entered the dining room, the prince smiled at her.

Grimsby leaned forward and whispered, "Isn't she a vision? And she's *real*!"

Ariel sat down and noticed a dinglehopper next to her plate. She picked it up and started to comb her hair. Eric burst out laughing. "What a funny girl," he commented to Grimsby. "Combing her hair with a fork!" But he thought she was charming and enjoyed her company very much.

Eric and Ariel spent the next day exploring the village together. Ariel had never imagined life on land could be so wonderful. And Eric began to forget all about the girl with the beautiful voice.

Late in the afternoon, they went rowing and floated into a sparkling lagoon turning gold in the late sun. Sebastian, Scuttle, and Flounder hid among the tall reeds and watched closely.

"If only you could speak," Eric said, gazing fondly at Ariel. "I'd love to know your name." He closed his eyes and tried to think of a name to suit her. As they passed by, Sebastian perched on a cattail and whispered to the prince: "Her name is Ariel."

Eric opened his eyes. "I know. It's Ariel!" She nodded. "What a lovely name," murmured Eric. Slowly, he leaned forward to kiss her. But just as their lips were about to touch—*SPLASH!* The rowboat tipped over.

Peeking out from behind the overturned boat, Flotsam and Jetsam snickered and swam off. From her shadowy lair, Ursula watched through the magic bubble.

"Nice work, boys," she chortled.

By the time Flotsam and Jetsam slithered back into the cave, Ursula was beside herself with rage.

"The little tramp! At this rate he'll kiss her before sunset tomorrow for sure," she screamed at them. She reached into a large clamshell containing her potions. "It's time Ursula took matters into her own tentacles. Triton's daughter will be mine, and then I'll make him writhe."

Before the eels' eyes, the sea witch transformed herself into a beautiful young woman with shiny, black hair. The shell around her neck began to glow, and she sang in Ariel's clear, melodious voice. "Call me Vanessa," said Ursula, winking slyly at her two lackeys.

Eric stood on his balcony watching the moon rise. He was thinking about Ariel and their wonderful day together when he became aware of the sound of someone singing. He could hardly believe his ears. It was the girl who had rescued him! He ran downstairs and out toward the garden where Ursula, disguised as Vanessa, was waiting for him. Prince Eric was so swept away by the sound of her voice that all thoughts of Ariel vanished. At dawn, he woke Grimsby to tell him he planned to marry Vanessa that very day.

When Ariel heard the news, she was brokenhearted. She sat by the water's edge thinking of her father and regretting the deal she'd made with Ursula. She looked up sadly as the wedding ship sailed away toward the setting sun.

"This is terrible," Sebastian whispered to Flounder. "I wonder who the prince is marrying so suddenly."

Out of the blue, Scuttle landed next to them all in a dither. "Listen to this," he said, panting for breath. "I just peeked in the porthole and saw the bride in her cabin. She's really Ursula, the sea witch, in disguise. And she's singing with a stolen set of pipes."

Sebastian sprang into action. "Ariel," he said, knocking a barrel, with a rope attached to it, into the water. "Tie the rope around Flounder and hold on to the barrel. He'll tow you out to the ship." He turned to Scuttle. "You must stall the wedding. I'll go and warn the king that something terrible is about to happen."

Swimming as fast as his fins could carry him, Flounder finally reached the ship. As Ariel climbed over the rail, she saw that the ceremony had already begun. Vanessa and Prince Eric were standing side by side before the Royal Minister.

"Do you, Eric," he asked, "take Vanessa to be your—"

Without any warning, a group of squawking birds, led by Scuttle, flew in from all directions. The alarmed guests scattered, covering their heads, as Max barked at their feet. Flapping wildly, Scuttle dove at Vanessa. He snatched away the shell necklace and it dropped to the deck. The sea witch let out a shriek. A golden mist streamed from the broken shell into Ariel's throat. Overwhelmed with joy, she began to sing. Hearing her, Eric rushed to take her in his arms. "It was you all the time," he said. Then he kissed her.

"Too late!" Vanessa declared triumphantly and pointed to the horizon. "The sun has already set. Ariel's mine!"

The terrified guests recoiled in horror as Vanessa changed back to her true hideous self. Ariel tried to run but fell—she was a mermaid once again. Helpless, she was dragged by Ursula back into the sea.

King Triton emerged from the depths and confronted the sea witch. "Let her go!" he demanded.

"Not a chance, Triton. She made a deal," Ursula explained, showing him the golden scroll. "It's legal, binding, and watertight. But," she added, "I might be willing to make an exchange . . . for you!"

Knowing the decision he must make, King Triton pointed his glowing trident at the scroll. With a blinding bolt, Ariel's name changed to his own.

"At last!" Ursula cried, grabbing the trident and placing his golden crown upon her head. "I'm the ruler of all the seas!" Triton fell at her feet and slowly began to shrivel up.

"Daddy!" Ariel screamed. As she leaped at Ursula, she saw Eric swimming underwater toward them, aiming a harpoon. Before Ursula could react, he struck her in the arm.

"You little fool!" she yelled. With a roaring gush, Ursula grew to an enormous size and burst through the water's surface. She stirred the sea with the trident into a raging whirlpool that swept Eric away and sucked Ariel to the bottom. Above, a violent storm broke out and the sky turned black.

The swirling water caught Eric's sunken ship and spun it toward the surface. Like a drawn dagger, the broken mast surged upward. Eric grabbed hold of a rope dangling over the ship's side and pulled himself aboard.

Ariel clung to a rock at the bottom of the whirlpool. "Good-bye, sweet cakes," Ursula said, aiming the trident at her.

Throwing his weight against the wheel, Eric steered straight at the sea witch looming before him. The ship lurched forward on a great wave, impaling her on the mast. At the same instant, flashes of lightning struck the golden crown on her head. There was a blinding explosion. In seconds all that was left of Ursula was a charred tentacle floating on the water.

The sea witch's spell was broken. All of her captives turned back into mermen and mermaids. As the trident settled down near Ursula's cave, Triton snatched it up. Once again he took his place as ruler of the underwater world.

The following day, King Triton summoned Sebastian to his throne room. "I see now that Ariel and Prince Eric truly love one another," he said. "I've decided to make her human and let her go."

"A good choice, Your Majesty," said Sebastian. "I always say children have to be free to live their own lives."

Triton laughed. "Oh, is that what you say? The only trouble," he added sadly, "is how much I'm going to miss her."

At sunset, before the wedding ship sailed, Ariel said good-bye to Flounder, Sebastian, and Scuttle. "I'll never forget you," she told them. One by one, she hugged her six sisters. King Triton blinked back tears and smiled. Ariel threw her arms around his neck and kissed him. "I love you, Daddy," she whispered.

As all the merpeople waved farewell, Ariel felt truly happy. She would miss them all, but now she would hold their memories in her heart and treasure them forever.

THE LITTLE MERMAID
Behind the Scenes

Roger Allers was finishing up the detail work on some storyboards for *Oliver & Company* when he found himself being distracted by music wafting through the walls of his Flower Street office. Right next door, Howard Ashman and Alan Menken were working on the songs for an upcoming animated feature based on Hans Christian Andersen's "The Little Mermaid." Allers was so taken by the infectious energy of those songs that, upon reading the story treatment, he volunteered to work on *The Little Mermaid*.

The engaging songwriting and delightful score for *The Little Mermaid*, Disney's 1989 release, inspired nearly all the artists who came to work on the film. Lyricist Ashman and his partner, composer Menken, brought the spirit, craft, and form of a classic Broadway musical, along with boundless talent, energy, and ideas, to the world of animation. Early in the production, Ashman, who coproduced the film with John Musker, spoke to the Disney artists about the relationship between the forms of the animated film and the classic musical comedy. Ashman talked about the significance of different kinds of songs and how they could be used to drive the action. Menken studied the scores of earlier animated classics to get a better feel for how the music worked with the animation. The result was a score full of memorable and integrated musical numbers ranging from mermaid Ariel's longing to be "Part of Your World" to Sebastian's Calypso-influenced counsel to stay "Under the Sea," and from villainous Ursula's sarcastic lament "Poor Unfortunate Souls" to the playfully animated love song "Kiss the Girl." The close collaboration among songwriters, directors, and story artists harked back to the early days at Disney, when the director's office was known as the "Music Room" and songs were sometimes written before storyboarding began.

The idea for the first animated classic fairy tale since *Sleeping Beauty* released thirty years earlier, came from director Ron Clements, who had found the story while browsing in a bookstore, hunting for projects. He and John Musker share both the directing and writing credits for the film. Among the many people who contributed to the early visual development of *The Little Mermaid* were cartoonist Rowland B. Wilson, two-time Caldecott medal winner Chris Van Allsburg, and Disney layout artist Ken O'Connor. Pastel drawings created by sketch artist Kay Nielsen in the 1940s for a treatment of the classic tale, which was never made, also helped inspire the contemporary group.

The unforgettable songs created by lyricist Howard Ashman (left) and composer Alan Menken inspired all who worked on The Little Mermaid.

The artists worked to create both a convincing illusion of underwater reality and an emotionally believable set of characters. For inspiration in creating the fantastic undersea world, an aquarium was installed in the animation building. To emulate the movements of mermaids, a larger tank was built for live-action model Sherri Stoner to swim in. "Watching seals was helpful, since they are mammals with definite spines and bone structure," says Mark Henn, the supervising animator for Ariel. Yet the difficulty of creating believable underwater animation paled compared to the task of bringing life to Ariel on dry land. "During the second half of the picture she's not speaking," explains Henn. "She has to communicate her feelings without saying a word, which for an animator is the greatest challenge."

Codirectors Ron Clements and John Musker led *The Little Mermaid* team to produce a film with a strong story and values yet modern appeal. The immediacy of the central theme, that we have to let children grow up and be who they are, resonated with audiences, and *The Little Mermaid* became the most successful animated film made to that point. It attracted both children and adults for repeat viewings with its combination of a memorable classic tale, playfully witty story-telling, and unforgettable songs. People could feel, emanating from the screen, the energy that began in the room next door to Roger Allers's office.

Ariel and Sebastian in a development piece by artist Rowland B. Wilson.

THE PRINCE AND

THE PAUPER

Long ago, in the little kingdom by the sea, things were going from bad to worse. The King, a kind and fair man, became ill and lost touch with much that was happening. The Captain of the Guard, a ruthless and greedy man, took advantage of this unfortunate situation. He fattened his own pockets at the expense of the poor. Worst of all, he did it in the King's name.

One snowy day, outside the walls of the castle, a hungry pauper named Mickey was trying to make ends meet by selling firewood to passersby.

"Buy some kindling?" he called out. "Keep the home fires burning!" But nobody stopped. His friend, Goofy, who stood a few feet away, wasn't doing any better.

"Snow cones!" he shouted. "Get yer tasty snow cones!" Goofy jumped out of the way when a huge wagon rattled by. "Look, Mick," he said, licking his lips. "That's the royal food wagon delivering food to the castle." Mickey's dog, Pluto, saw a sausage hanging from the rear of the wagon and dashed after it.

"Pluto, come back!" Mickey cried out, chasing him right through the castle gates. The gatekeeper stepped aside as Mickey charged by. "Y-Your Highness?" he stammered.

The Captain of the Guard sauntered over from the castle and grabbed Mickey by the collar. "What's going on?" he asked the gatekeeper. "Why'd you let this raggedy peasant in here?"

"He's no peasant, Captain," explained the gatekeeper. "It's His Highness, the Prince."

The Captain looked closely at Mickey. He pointed to a figure staring down from a castle window. "Well, then, tell me, you fool—who's that?!"

The Royal Tutor joined the Prince at the window. "You must get back to your lessons, Your Highness. Do not concern yourself with that beggar boy below. The Captain of the Guard will take care of him."

The Prince ignored his tutor and leaned out the window. "Captain," he called, "stop manhandling that citizen. Even the lowliest subjects of this kingdom should be treated with respect. Have him brought up to me at once."

The Captain scowled. "The Prince wants to see you," he barked at Mickey.

"Stay, Pluto," Mickey said, patting him on the head. "I'll be right back."

"I'll watch your dog," said the Captain. But as soon as Mickey entered the castle, he tossed Pluto back into the street.

Mickey wandered down a long hall lined with shiny suits of armor. "Wow!" he said. "What swell duds!" Suddenly, his feet shot out from under him. He skidded down the highly polished floor and crashed into the metal suits, knocking them over, one after another. A helmet with a purple plume toppled off and landed square on Mickey's head. Hearing the commotion, the Prince rushed out, only to have a helmet land on his head, too.

The Prince and the pauper removed the helmets, blinked, and stared at each other. "AHHH!" they both exclaimed. "You look just like *me*!"

Mickey gulped. "Gosh, Your Royal Highness," he said. "W-We could be twins." Remembering his manners, he bowed low. "My name's Mickey. Mickey Mouse. I hope I haven't, uh, disturbed you."

The Prince smiled. "Actually, you saved my life. I was about to die of boredom when you interrupted my lesson. Do you have any idea what it's like to be the Prince?"

"It must be fun!" said Mickey.

The Prince shook his head. "I never have a moment to myself. Breakfast at seven—"

"Breakfast?" said Mickey, his mouth watering.

The Prince nodded. "Lessons until lunch. Fencing until tea time. A banquet every night. Bedtime at nine. . . ." He sighed. "How I envy your freedom!"

"You envy me?" Mickey said, perplexed.

"Sure I do," said the Prince. "You don't have to study dreary books, you can stay up as late as you like, eat anything you want—" He stopped short. "You've given me a wonderful idea!"

"I have?" asked Mickey.

"Don't you see?" said the Prince. "We'll switch places for a day! Nobody will be able to tell the difference. I'll take your place with your friends in the streets. And you shall be the Prince, here in the castle."

Mickey's mouth dropped. "Me? Prince?" he gasped. "H-H-How do I act? W-W-What do I say?"

"Don't worry about it," said the Prince. "I'll be back in the wink of an eye. And if there's any trouble, all will know me by this." He held up his ring, emblazoned with the royal crest. "Quick, we'd better switch clothes before my tutor comes looking for me."

Moments later, the Prince, wearing Mickey's rags, was climbing down a vine along the castle wall. He reached the ground, only to find the Captain waiting for him.

"Well, my athletic little peasant," the Captain said with a nasty grin, "did you have a nice visit with the Prince?"

"Peasant?" the Prince said, laughing. "I've fooled you, Captain. I am the Prince!"

The Captain laughed back. "And I am the King!" He grabbed the Prince by the scruff of his neck and threw him over the castle wall, into the street.

The Prince felt a big, wet tongue licking his face. It was Pluto, happy to see his master, until he realized—*PHTOOEY!*—it wasn't his master at all. He trotted away with a distasteful look on his face.

"There you are, Mickey!" Goofy cried, rushing over and dusting off the Prince. "Where'd you go?"

The Prince sprang to his feet. "I did it!" he cried, skipping down the street. "I'm free!"

"Mickey?" Goofy called after him. "Are you okay?" But the Prince was already out of sight.

The Prince wandered carefree through the bustling town until a snowball came sailing through the air and smacked him in the face. Then came another, and another. Giggling, a bunch of children jumped up from behind a snowbank and scampered off. "This is no fun," thought the Prince. "Life outside the castle isn't so easy after all!"

Meanwhile, back at the castle, Mickey yawned as the Prince's tutor quizzed him on geography. "What country's capital is Constantinople?" asked the tutor.

But Mickey was much more interested in the aroma of food that drifted into the room. His stomach gurgled as he smelled bread pudding, mashed potatoes, and roast—

"Turkey!" shouted Mickey, jumping out of his seat.

"Correct!" said the tutor.

Mickey dashed into the hallway. He grabbed a turkey leg from the food cart passing by.

"You can't do that!" said the kitchen maid. "It's not lunchtime yet."

"Oh, yes I can!" shouted Mickey. "I am the Prince!"

That afternoon, as the Prince passed an alley, he heard a commotion. "Help! Help me!" a young maid cried out. The Prince saw her struggling with a guard from the castle. He was trying to yank a chicken from her grasp. A curious crowd had gathered to watch.

"Relax," said the guard, grabbing the chicken at last. "We're taking this to the castle for the King's dinner."

"Please don't take it," the maid pleaded. "It's all my children have to eat!"

"Unhand that hen!" demanded the Prince. "As your royal Prince, I command you to obey."

"I think you forgot your crown," the guard snickered. Laughing, he wandered off with the chicken squawking under his arm.

"Thanks for trying to help," the maid said to the Prince. "This happens all the time. The castle guards take everything we have."

The Prince was shocked. "That's terrible! Imagine, stealing in the King's name. Well, I'll see to it that it doesn't happen again."

The royal food wagon came rumbling up the street.

"Halt!" the Prince shouted. "I am the King's son."

"And I'm the Queen's mother," the driver quipped.

The Prince displayed his royal ring. The confused driver jumped down from the cart and ran off to find some guards. Hopping onto the wagon, the Prince began handing out food to the hungry townspeople.

Just then, Goofy wandered by. "Gawsh, Mickey," he said, "have you flipped your wig?"

The crowd parted as the driver rushed up, accompanied by two guards. "He's the one who showed me the ring," he said, pointing to the Prince.

"You there!" the guard shouted. "You're under arrest."

"C'mon, Mickey!" cried Goofy. He pulled the Prince off the cart and grabbed a ham bone. "Let's get out of here!"

Later, in the castle cellar, a guard was telling the Captain about the afternoon's events.

"I may be losing my mind," he reported, "but when that guy jumped off the wagon, I'm sure I saw the royal ring."

"The ring!" exclaimed the Captain. "So it *was* the Prince I booted out."

"You threw out the Prince?" gasped the guard. "Oh, are you gonna get it."

The Captain puffed on his cigar and blew smoke in the guard's face. "Not if he doesn't come back alive," he said.

"A great idea!" the guard agreed. "And I think I know where to find him. I saw him run off with a local lad by the name of Goofy. . . ."

Upstairs, Mickey was practicing fencing. "Knave! Villain! Take that!" he said, slicing the air with his sword.

"Excuse me, Your Highness," interrupted the Royal Tutor, entering the chamber. "You must come right away."

Mickey shook his head. "I'm not going anywhere. I've been running around since breakfast—hunting with blood-thirsty falcons, sitting through two hours of geography lessons, and experimenting in the chemistry lab, I—"

"But it's your father, the King," insisted the tutor. "He's in his last hours and wishes to see you at once—before it's too late."

Mickey jumped to his feet. "Oh, uh, we'd better tell the Prince."

"*You* are the Prince, sire," said the tutor, a little surprised.

"Oh, uh, I've been meaning to talk to you about that," said Mickey.

The tutor beckoned him toward the door. "I'm afraid there's just no time. Your father is gravely ill."

Reluctantly, Mickey put on his slippers and, with a heavy heart, followed the tutor to the King's bedside. The King weakly raised his hand. "My son," he said, "soon you will be King. You must promise that you will rule the land from your heart, justly and with compassion for all."

"I p-p-promise," said Mickey. He couldn't bear to upset the dying King.

"And I wish you to be crowned right away—this land must not be without a ruler. . . ." The King's voice faded away.

Mickey paced up and down the hall outside the King's chamber. "This is just awful," he thought. "I've got to find the Prince."

He was about to go outside when the Captain grabbed him by the collar.

"Good day, my phony Prince," he said, dragging Mickey to the window. "Now that our dear departed King is out of the way, you're going to do everything I say, because if you don't . . . ,"—he pointed to Pluto, who was tied to a post in the courtyard—"your little doggie will pay for it!"

Near the docks on the far side of town, the Prince was hiding out in Goofy's house. Around midnight, the church bells began to toll. The Prince opened the shutters and listened to their mournful sounds.

"Say there!" he called down to a passing townsman. "Has something happened?"

"The King is dead," the man called back. "And the Prince is to be crowned in the morning."

The Prince lowered his head. "Father," he said softly.

"Soup's on!" called out Goofy from the fireplace. He ladled a big bowl of floating ham bits and set it on the table. "Here ya are, Mickey—I mean, Your Majesty." Goofy winked.

The Prince walked past him in a daze. "Now it's up to me," he murmured, "to right the wrongs I've seen. Children going hungry, corruption everywhere. . . ."

As the Prince was pulling on his gloves, Goofy noticed the royal ring.

"G-Gawsh!" he stuttered. "You really are the Prince, ain't yah?"

The Prince smiled at his new friend. "You saved my life and this will not be forgotten. Come, we must return to the castle at once."

"Or to the dungeon!" guffawed the Captain of the Guard, throwing the door open wide. He nodded to his men. "Get 'em, boys."

In a panic, Goofy stumbled backward and fell out the window into a pile of soft snow. The guards surrounded the Prince and led him back to the castle.

"This is an outrage!" the Prince cried, as he was thrown into a cell.

The Captain grinned at him. "After the pauper's crowned, it will be adieu for you."

The Prince shook the bars but they wouldn't budge. He slumped to the floor and sat with his head buried in his hands. How could he have gotten into such a mess? Changing places with the pauper had been a big mistake. Now his poor father was dead and Mickey was going to be crowned King!

A sudden fanfare of trumpets made him jump. The coronation was about to begin.

"Psssst," hissed a voice. "Over here." The Prince hurried over to the bars and peered into the gloom. Out of the shadows a figure slowly crept toward him. It was Goofy!

"Your Majesty," Goofy whispered. "Look at what fell out of the guard's pocket." Smiling toothily, he held up a key. "Just sit tight and I'll have you out in a jiffy."

The Great Hall was mobbed with townsfolk, waiting excitedly to see the crowning of their new king. Mickey squirmed nervously on the throne.

"Your Highness," said the Archbishop, holding a crown above Mickey's head, "please stop wiggling." But Mickey kept dodging out of the way.

The Archbishop cleared his throat and addressed the crowd. "It is both my duty and pleasure to crown you . . . to crown you . . ." The Archbishop sighed with frustration. "Stay still," he whispered to Mickey.

Suddenly, Mickey's face brightened. "Look," he said loudly, for all to

hear. "I'm the Prince, right? And whatever I order must be done."

The crowd murmured in agreement. Mickey jumped to his feet and pointed to the Captain of the Guard. "Seize him!" he ordered. "He's nothing but a selfish scoundrel."

The Captain drew his sword and advanced toward Mickey. "This man is not the Prince!" he announced.

"But I am!" a voice proclaimed. Everyone turned toward the balcony and saw a young lad dressed in rags, wielding a shiny sword.

The Prince, grabbing hold of a large chandelier, swung across the Great Hall and landed in front of the Captain. With a flourish of skilled swordplay, he backed the Captain against the wall. "Guards," commanded the Prince. "Take him away."

The Prince then joined Mickey at the throne. The confused Archbishop looked first at Mickey and then at the Prince. "Good Heavens, you're identical," he said. "Which of you shall I crown?"

The doors of the Great Hall burst open. Pluto scrambled down the aisle with several guards at his heels. He raced straight up to Mickey and licked his face.

The Archbishop patted Pluto. "Thank you, my little friend. Now I know who to crown king." He held the crown over the Prince's head. "With the powers vested in me," he pronounced solemnly, "I crown you King."

"Long live the King!" roared the people.

From that day on, the King, with his loyal companions Mickey and Goofy at his side, ruled the land from his heart—with justice and compassion for all.

THE PRINCE AND THE PAUPER
Behind the Scenes

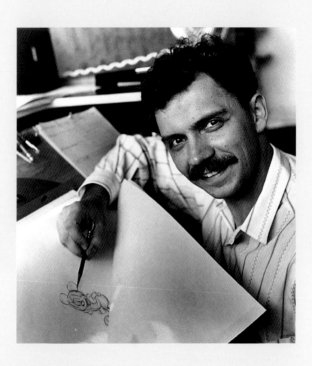

When it comes to animating the classic Disney characters, "it's not just how they look or move, but what is in their *souls* that makes them so incredibly appealing," says supervising animator Andreas Deja. *The Prince and the Pauper*, a short film released along with the feature *The Rescuers Down Under* in 1990, presented a tremendous challenge for the animators: to bring to life characters that people already feel close to and think they know. Directed by George Scribner, who also directed *Oliver & Company*, and produced by Dan Rounds, *The Prince and the Pauper*, like *Mickey's Christmas Carol* (done seven years before), combines Disney's classic characters and animation style with contemporary storytelling.

Because the look of characters such as Mickey, Donald, and Goofy had evolved over the years, the artists working on *The Prince and the Pauper* went back to Disney shorts from the 1930s and 1940s to design their characters. *Mickey and the Beanstalk* (1947) provided the visual basis for Donald and Goofy, and *Brave Little Tailor* (1938) was the model for Mickey. Says Deja, who animated Mickey as both pauper and prince: "We wanted to make *The Prince and the Pauper* a miniature classic and animate [Mickey] a bit like classic Disney animator Freddie Moore did way back in the 1930s. We wanted to bring that early Mickey personality to life."

The impulse to make a film reflecting the look and feel of the early shorts extended beyond the character designs and animation. Says background artist Natalie Franscioni-Karp: "The desire was to create an environment where Mickey looks natural and at home. We wanted to create backgrounds to suit his proportions, make him the star of the film." The artists of the background and lay-out departments, led by art director Thom Enriquez, worked to re-create the style of the backgrounds in such early films as *Brave Little Tailor, Dumbo,* and *Pinocchio.* The settings have a decidedly old-world look—bold, rounded, and three-dimensional. The transparent painting style the background artists adopted, using acrylic on board, emulates the rich watercolors of earlier films. The edges of the backgrounds were darkened as they were in the old days to focus attention on the characters.

While the art direction and animating style celebrated the golden age of Mickey shorts, the tone of the writing, editing, and camera work, reflected current filmmaking techniques. According to director Scribner, "The attempt here was to take the very best of the old and combine it with an up-to-date attitude and approach to filmmaking."

Mickey Mouse in the 1938 short Brave Little Tailor.

THE RESCUERS
DOWN UNDER

Cody sat straight up in bed. He heard something. Wait—there it was again. He ran to the window and listened to the deep droning sound. Faloo, the kangaroo, was sending a distress signal to him. One of the animals must be in trouble! As fast as he could, he got dressed, yanked on his hiking boots, and tossed a few biscuits into his knapsack. He was already out jogging through the scrubby underbrush when his mom called after him, "Coooody, be home for supper!"

"No worries!" Cody shouted back and sprinted across the dry, rocky outback. He followed Faloo's call and found her at the foot of a high cliff. She was blowing into a hollow tree limb, sending out the alert.

Cody dashed up to her. "Faloo! Is someone caught?"

"You don't know her," the kangaroo answered in her gentle voice. "Her name is Marahute, the great golden eagle. The poor thing's in a poacher's trap." Faloo nodded toward the cliff. "She's up there—on top," she told him. "It's a very steep climb. Be careful, little friend."

Cody patted Faloo's head. "I'll get her loose," he said.

At the foot of the cliff, Cody reached around for a good place to grab onto, jammed his boot into a narrow toehold, and started up. Bit by bit, he pulled himself up the steep rocky wall. When, at last, he peeked over the top of the ridge, he saw Marahute, lying hopelessly tangled in heavy ropes. As soon as she saw Cody, she let out a terrified screech.

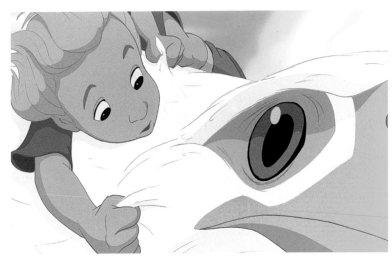

"Calm down, Marahute," Cody said softly, pulling himself onto the wide flat rock, "I'm not going to hurt you." But when he flicked open his sharp pocketknife to cut the ropes, she thrashed about in a panic. One by one, Cody sliced through the ropes. Then he jumped up and waved his arms. "You're free!"

Marahute rose to her feet and stretched her wings. But Cody was standing too close and she knocked into him. He stumbled backward and, wildly waving his arms and legs, vanished over the cliff. Marahute plummeted after him, scooped him up in midair, and flipped him onto her back. Flapping her enormous wings, she soared toward the sky. "Higher!" hooted Cody, holding on tight.

Marahute carried Cody over the mountains and swooped down across the forest. As she wheeled high above a grove of gum trees, Cody whooped at the top of his lungs. Several koalas, nibbling on eucalyptus leaves, glanced up in surprise. Marahute rose sharply and flew loops in the sky over the desert. Running on his hind legs, a frilled-neck lizard skidded to a stop and watched. "More!" yelled Cody.

But it was time for Marahute to return home. She flew to a high rocky ledge and set Cody down in her nest of feathers and grass. "Thanks, Marahute," he said. "That was really something!"

The golden eagle pushed back the grass to show Cody three huge speckled eggs. "You're a mother!" he said, smiling. "Where's their daddy?" Marahute drooped her head and looked away. "I'm really sorry," Cody told her. "My dad's gone, too."

A hot breeze sprang up and a golden feather floated from the nest. Marahute caught it with her beak and gave it to Cody. "Thank you," he said as the feather glinted in the sunshine. "It's lovely." Carefully, he tucked it into his knapsack.

"I'd better go now," he told her. "Mom'll wonder where I am." Marahute carried Cody down to the ground. As he was racing home, he passed by a spice bush and heard a jingling sound. A mouse was dangling from a string, tied to one of the branches. A tiny bell was attached to the branch, and whenever the mouse struggled, the bell rang.

"Don't worry, mate," Cody told the exhausted mouse. "I'll get you loose."

"Stay away!" squeaked the mouse. "It's a trap!"

Cody stepped closer and began to untie the string. All at once, the ground caved in, and he and the mouse dropped into a deep pit. "It's a poacher's trap!" Cody gasped, rubbing his skinned knee.

"His name's McLeach," explained the mouse. "He's real nasty. And he's got a huge lizard—a six-foot goanna named Joanna. She's as mean as he is." The mouse pricked up his ears.

"What's that rumbling noise?" Cody asked him.

"It's McLeach's bushwhacker," cried the mouse, scrambling up Cody's back and into the knapsack. "He's coming to check on me."

A couple of minutes later, they heard McLeach drive up and slam on the brakes.

"Hey, Joanna, we got something!" the poacher shouted, hopping out. "Maybe it's a dingo or a big ol' razorback hog." He peered into the pit. "A boy??" he cried out in surprise. Joanna slithered over to take a look and flicked her long forked tongue at Cody.

"Uh, sorry for this big hole, kid," McLeach said, holding a branch down toward Cody. "My lizard, Joanna, keeps digging 'em."

Cody grabbed the end of the branch and pulled himself up. "This is a trap and you set it," Cody said, glaring. "You're trapping animals and selling them for money. And you were going to use that poor little mouse as bait."

The mouse poked his head out of the knapsack. Hissing loudly, Joanna sprang onto Cody's back. "Stop it! Get off me!" shouted Cody.

Joanna yanked the knapsack away and poked her head inside. Rummaging around, she pulled out the golden feather. McLeach snatched it from her and smiled at Cody. "Say, where'd you get this pretty feather, boy?"

Cody shook his head. McLeach pulled another golden feather from his hat band and held it under Cody's nose. "You see," he said. "I already got the father. Now, you tell me where mama eagle and those little eggs are."

"It's a secret," Cody said, stubbornly.

"Well, we'll just see about that!" said McLeach, sticking both feathers back in his hat band. He grabbed Cody around the waist and carried him to the bushwhacker.

"Hey! Lemme go!" cried Cody, kicking his feet and trying to punch McLeach. "I'll get the rangers after you."

"Oh, no, not the rangers," said McLeach. "Whatever will I do?" Hooting with laughter, he dumped Cody into a big metal cage on the back of the truck. "So, boy, how're you gonna call the rangers now?"

As soon as the bushwhacker rumbled away in the dust, the mouse crept out of Cody's knapsack and scampered off into the underbrush. He speeded through a long hollow log and hurried toward an old half-pint milk carton hidden in the weeds. There was a small door and a neatly lettered sign that read R.A.S. TELEGRAPH OFFICE.

The mouse poked his head inside. "Rescue Aid Society?" he shouted. "Anybody here?" An elderly mouse looked up from his lunch. After hearing what had happened to Cody, he tapped a message on the telegraph: URGENT . . . BOY KIDNAPPED IN AUSTRALIA . . . RELAY THIS MESSAGE TO NEW YORK.

The alert was relayed across the Pacific Ocean to the coast of the United States, where it was picked up and sent by mice operating R.A.S. stations from San Francisco to Denver to Washington, D.C., and to its final destination— the basement of the United Nations headquarters in New York City.

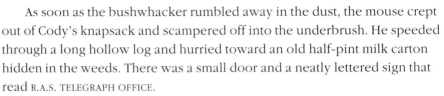

Although the message arrived during the worst blizzard in history, the Chairmouse from England immediately called an emergency session.

"I must apologize for getting you out in this weather," said the Chairmouse, as the mice filed to their seats, "but there's been a kidnapping in Australia and a young boy needs our help."

"It sounds like a job for Bianca and Bernard," the delegate from Spain declared. The other members all agreed. They turned toward two seats, marked HUNGARY and UNITED STATES. But they were empty.

"Where in the world could they be?" asked the Chairmouse.

"I think they went out to dinner," piped up the delegate from Morocco.

In a posh restaurant several blocks away, Bianca raised a glass of champagne. "To my dear Bernard," she toasted, "and to our wonderful partnership."

Bernard clinked his glass against hers. "There's something . . . uh . . . that I want to . . . uh . . . ask you," he stammered. He reached into his pocket

and pulled out a tiny box, which he kept hidden under the table. As he opened it, an engagement ring bounced out and rolled across the floor. "Would you excuse me for a moment?" he asked, jumping up.

While Bernard crawled from table to table, François, the headwaiter, handed Bianca a telegram. "It's from the R.A.S.," he said in a low voice. "You and Mr. Bernard have been chosen for a dangerous mission to Australia."

Bianca read the telegram. "Where's Bernard?" she asked. "I must tell him at once."

François bowed. "Allow me, I'll let him know." He found Bernard on the other side of the restaurant. "Sir," the headwaiter informed him, "I have a message for you."

Bernard was so preoccupied, he didn't hear

a word François said. Snatching up the ring, he hurried back to Bianca.

"Did you talk to François?" she asked.

"Yes," answered Bernard, "but there's something—"

"I know exactly what you're going to say," Bianca interrupted, thinking Bernard was talking about the message. "François told me."

Bernard blinked. "He did?"

"I think it's a marvelous idea," Bianca said, putting down her glass.

Bernard gulped. "You do?" he asked. "Well, how does next April sound?"

"Darling, we must act right away," declared Bianca. "Tonight!" She hopped off her seat and scampered off to get her coat.

Bernard trailed after her. "Don't you at least need a gown or flowers or something?"

"Just a pair of khaki shorts and hiking boots," Bianca answered.

"Hiking boots?" said Bernard, a little taken aback.

Bianca led Bernard back to the United Nations headquarters basement, where the members were all waiting for them. "Delegates," she announced, "Bernard and I have decided to accept the mission to Australia."

"Australia?" Bernard mumbled to himself. And he'd thought they were going to get married!

Later that night, Bianca and Bernard rushed through the blinding snow to a rooftop heliport. A big birdhouse stood shuddering in the wind. ALBATROSS AIR was painted on the roof. Bernard peeked into the frosty window. "Thank heavens," he said. "The light's on."

They straggled inside and set their luggage down on the floor. An albatross, wearing a headset, was listening to music and dancing around. Bianca tapped him on the foot. "Excuse us for interrupting," she said. "We're Miss Bianca and Mister Bernard, from the Rescue Aid Society. We need to charter a flight to Australia."

The albatross made a sweeping bow. "The name's Wilbur," he replied. "At your service. Now, when do you want to go? Mid-June would be nice."

"Now," said Bianca. "Tonight."

"What??" squawked Wilbur. "Have you looked outside? Sorry, no go."

"But a little boy has been kidnapped," Bernard pleaded.

"K-K-Kidnapped?" Wilbur sputtered. "Nobody's gonna take a little kid's freedom away while I'm around. Okay, storm or no storm, let's go! Just gimme a second to loosen up the ol' back."

Wilbur stretched out with a few quick squats and push-ups. Bianca and Bernard buckled themselves into a sardine tin strapped to his back.

"Is this a nonstop flight?" Bianca asked.

"Whad'ya think I am?" Wilbur said, adjusting his goggles. "A jumbo jet? We'll be making a connection with a bigger bird. Ready for takeoff?"

Bianca nodded enthusiastically. Next to her, Bernard shut his eyes and held on tight. Madly flapping his wings, Wilbur tore across the rooftop and, after a couple of slips and slides, took off into the whirling storm. Thoroughly worn out, he touched down at Kennedy Airport, where they stowed away safely in the wheel well of an Australia-bound plane.

Twenty-two hours later, as the plane circled the Sidney airport, Wilbur swooped out of the wheel well. "Next stop, Mugwomp Flats in the outback," he announced, leveling off and heading away from the city. "Did we lose anyone back there?"

"Miss Bianca," Bernard said, a bit woozy, "from now on, can't we just take the train?"

They were soon flying over the rugged countryside. When they landed at Mugwomp Terminal, Wilbur collapsed exhausted on the ground. A kangaroo mouse in a bush pilot's outfit came out to meet them. He smiled when he saw Bianca.

"G'day, ma'am," he greeted her. "Welcome to Australia, or as we call it, the Land Down Under! My name's Jake. Let me get that bag for you."

"Hey," cried Bernard. "I've got a lot of luggage, too."

"Here, I'll help you, pal," Wilbur said, struggling to his feet. "OW!" he groaned. "My aching back."

"Got just the right thing for ya, mate," Jake assured him. He called on a

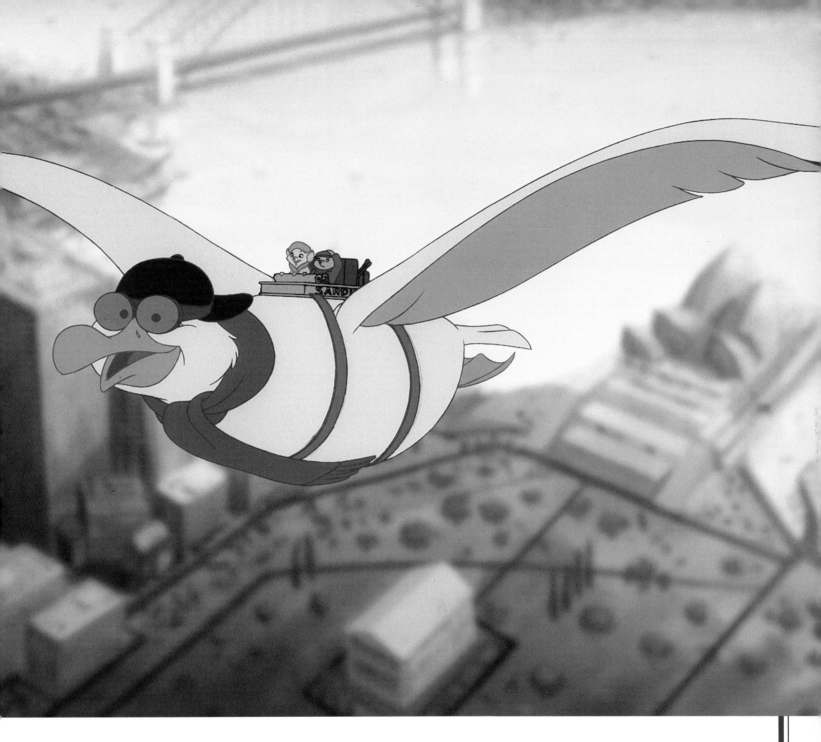

doctor and some nurses to care for Wilbur. Then he sauntered back to
Bianca and Bernard. "I hear you've come to rescue that boy McLeach nabbed."

"How did you know?" Bianca asked, very impressed.

Jake winked at her. "It's tough keeping secrets in the outback," he told her.
"He's probably got him stashed away in one of the old mines. So, which way
are you taking? Suicide Trail through Nightmare Canyon or Dead Dingo Pass?"

"Suicide Trail?" Bernard gulped.

"Good choice," agreed Jake. "More snakes but less quicksand. But you'll
need my help. Most of this place is unmapped territory." He whistled
through his teeth, and a flying squirrel glided over from a nearby tuckeroo
tree. "This is how we travel Down Under," Jake said. "Hop aboard!"

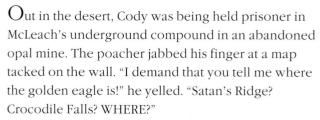

Out in the desert, Cody was being held prisoner in McLeach's underground compound in an abandoned opal mine. The poacher jabbed his finger at a map tacked on the wall. "I demand that you tell me where the golden eagle is!" he yelled. "Satan's Ridge? Crocodile Falls? WHERE?"

"I don't remember," Cody replied.

McLeach's eyes grew dark with rage. "You'd better remember soon," he said, "or I'll feed you to the crocs! That bird's worth a fortune and I'm going to be rich."

He dragged Cody down a winding tunnel to a room stacked high with cages. "Get in," he ordered, locking him inside a cage already occupied by a frilled-neck lizard. Before leaving, McLeach hung the key ring on the wall. Cody squinted in the dim light. He was shocked to see that the cages were filled with animals.

"Fancy that," observed an elderly koala named Krebbs. "Now McLeach is trapping his own kind!"

"There's gotta be a way out," Cody said, fiddling with the lock.

Krebbs smiled thinly. "Oh, there's a way out," he agreed. He gestured toward a kangaroo and a platypus crammed together in a dirty cage. "Red, over there, will go out as a wallet, and Polly will end up a nice belt. And your lizard cagemate, Frank, he'll go as a lovely lady's purse."

Frank burst into sobs. "I don't want to be a purse," he cried, and clutched Cody's shirt. "Please, don't let them do it."

"Don't worry, mate," Cody assured him. He peered closely at the lock. "This is pretty simple. We just need something to pick it with."

Frank's eyes lit up. "I know! I'll use my tail!"

Krebbs rolled his eyes. "Oh, this I've got to see."

"You'll thank me when you're free," said Frank. He inserted the tip of his tail into the lock. "Let's see now, I push it a little further in . . . pull it back a bit . . . now turn it this way. . . ."

"Aw, Frank," Red groaned, "give it a rest."

Bianca and Bernard sat on a tree root alongside a riverbank. "Jake's been gone a long time," Bernard said, glancing at his watch.

Bianca fluffed up her fur. "Don't worry, darling," she said. "He'll be back. He's arranging for our next mode of transportation."

Bernard plucked up his courage and got down on one knee. "Now that we're alone, dearest Bianca," he began, "I would be most honored if you—"

"LOOK OUT!" Jake yelled as he leaped out from behind a tree, twirling a rope. Bianca and Bernard watched in astonishment as the bush pilot darted along the bank and lassoed a python swimming past.

"I've been looking all over for you, Twister," Jake said to the gigantic snake. As Twister struggled to free himself, Jake yanked hard on the rope and wrapped it tight around the python's jaws. "We've got a long way to go, and you're taking us there without any trouble. RIGHT?"

Twister nodded.

"Climb on," Jake called out, offering his hand to Bianca. "Don't worry. Twister's harmless now that he knows who's boss."

Jake sat down beside Bianca on Twister's head while Bernard barely managed to hold on to the snake's slippery tail. Twister swam swiftly, winding his way down the muddy river.

Just before they reached Crocodile Falls, Jake steered Twister over to the side, and the three mice jumped off. They set out in the direction of the opal mines. Before long they came upon some bushwhacker tracks, which they decided to follow. The tracks led straight to McLeach's compound.

Inside, Frank was still frantically trying to open the lock with his tail. "Forget it," said Krebbs, "you're just making your tail sore."

But just then the lock gave way and the door flew open. "I did it!" whooped Frank. "We're free! We're free!"

"Shh!" Cody warned him. "McLeach'll hear you." He scrambled out of the cage and grabbed the key. "I'll have you all out in a minute," he whispered to the animals. He squatted in front of Krebbs's cage and fit the key in the rusty lock.

"Surprise!" yelled McLeach, grinning, in the doorway. He yanked Cody to his feet. "Say good-bye to your friends," he said. "This is the last you'll ever see of them."

He pushed Cody outside into the bright sunshine. Bianca, Bernard, and Jake hid behind a boobialla bush.

"Look, Bernard," Bianca whispered. "It's the boy."

"Now git," McLeach told Cody. "It's all over. Someone shot your bird right out of the sky. Bang! Now she's dead."

Cody's eyes got big. "I don't believe you."

"Yep," said McLeach. "I heard it on the radio." He pushed Cody away. "Go home."

Cody started to go. He noticed that the bushwhacker, parked at the entrance, was now outfitted with a large crane, attached to the back. Before he was out of earshot, he heard McLeach speaking to Joanna in a loud voice. "Too bad about those golden eagle eggs," he told her. "They'll never survive without their mother." Joanna's eyes gleamed at the thought of fresh eggs.

Cody changed directions and ran.

"Bingo!" laughed McLeach. "It worked. The kid thinks the bird's dead and he's worried about the eggs. Now, all we have to do is follow him to the nest!" He started up the bushwhacker while Joanna slithered into the passenger seat. As McLeach pulled away, the three mice hopped onto the back of the truck.

McLeach followed just far enough behind Cody to keep him in sight. He trailed the boy to the edge of a cliff and saw Cody climb down over the side.

McLeach roared in delight to Joanna. "That's where the bird must be!" He drove the bushwhacker close to the edge and dragged out a large net, which he attached to the end of the crane.

"He's going to drop the net over the eagle!" Jake whispered to Bianca and Bernard. "We've got to get down there and warn Cody."

Bernard peered over the edge of the steep cliff. "No worry, mate," Jake told him. "Just don't look down."

Bianca smiled brightly at Bernard. "Come on, darling," she urged him, following Jake. Bernard gulped and climbed down after her.

Down below, Cody was kneeling in Marahute's huge nest.

"Oh," he murmured, touching the eggs, "they're still warm!" Carefully,

he covered each one with soft feathers.

"Cody!" a tiny voice called out. A lady mouse was tugging at his sock.

"Who are you?" he asked, smiling at Bianca.

"There's no time to explain," she said, hastily. "You are in grave danger."

From the corner of his eye, Cody saw a golden eagle flying toward them. "She's alive!" he cheered. He jumped up and down and waved his arms. "Marahute!" he yelled. "It's me!"

"McLeach is on the cliff!" Bernard cried out to Cody.

The boy looked up and saw the bushwhacker's crane poking out over the top of the cliff. "Marahute," he screamed, "turn back! It's a trap!"

As Marahute hovered over the ledge about to land, McLeach dropped the net. Hopelessly entangled, she thrashed about while the crane slowly began to pull her up.

"She's mine!" cried McLeach.

Cody jumped off the ledge and grabbed hold of the net. Dangling, he tried to cut the ropes with his pocketknife.

Jake whirled his long rope and lassoed Cody's foot. He tossed the other end over to Bianca and Bernard. "Hold tight, you two. We're going for a ride!" he called as he was pulled up after Cody.

The three mice rose in the air, but the rope slipped from Bernard's grasp and he tumbled back onto the ledge.

When the net reached the top, McLeach was surprised to see Cody clinging to it. "That meddling brat," he muttered. "I'll have to get rid of him for good." Before Cody could untangle himself, McLeach hoisted Marahute over the bushwhacker and dropped her, along with Cody, Bianca, and Jake, into a cage.

McLeach peered in through the bars and gloated. "I'm gonna be rich," he said to himself. "I've got the rarest bird in the world. And now, she's about to become even rarer." He looked around. "Joanna, get over here."

Joanna slithered out from beneath a bush.

"How about some great big, triple-A jumbo eagle eggs?" McLeach asked. Joanna hungrily whipped her long tongue from side to side. McLeach tied a rope around the lizard's belly and started to lower her toward the nest. "Finish every one of the eggs!" he ordered. "And I mean every one!"

When Joanna reached the nest, she snatched up the closest egg. She chomped down eagerly and cried out in pain. The shell was as hard as a rock. Furious, she tried the other two, but she couldn't break them either. She had to do something or McLeach would have a fit.

Joanna nudged the eggs out to the edge. Swinging her tail like a golf club, she knocked them one by one over the side. McLeach would never know the difference. She tugged on the rope, and he pulled her up.

As McLeach drove off in the bushwhacker, Cody slumped against the side of the cage. Bianca jumped up onto his shoulder.

"Now, Cody," she said. "We mustn't lose hope. Bernard is still out there."

"That's right," snorted Jake. "If anyone can get us out of this, it's ol' Berno."

Bianca smiled at Jake. "You don't know Bernard. He'll think of something."

Bernard peeked out from under the nest. "Joanna fell for it! She thought the rocks were eggs!" As he was uncovering the real eggs, which he'd piled high with grass, an albatross flew flapping by.

"Wilbur!" Bernard cried, scampering along the ledge. "Boy, am I glad to see you!"

Wilbur landed on the ledge and almost crashed into Bernard. "Sorry," he explained. "My back's fine now, but I'm still having a little trouble with touchdown. Where's Miss Bianca?"

Bernard told Wilbur what had happened. "It's up to us to get everybody out of this mess," the mouse said. "But I need you to stay here and sit on these eggs. You know, keep them warm."

Wilbur backed up. "You gotta be kiddin'."

"But we need your help!" Bernard begged him.

Wilbur rolled his eyes. "Oh, all right. I'll do it."

Before he set out, Bernard made sure that the eggs were safe under Wilbur. He scrambled to the top of the cliff and began running along the bushwhacker's tracks in the dirt road. He went for miles and miles before he collapsed, ready to give up.

Right behind him, a ferocious razorback boar lay snoozing next to a log. Bernard gathered up his courage, stood on his tiptoes, and yelled, "Excuse me!" The boar squinted bleary-eyed at Bernard and snorted. Bernard reached up and gave the razorback a good pinch on the snout.

"I've got a long way to go," he informed him, "and you're taking me there. RIGHT?"

The razorback nodded. Bernard swiftly climbed aboard. "Now, git!" he cried, and they were off.

"You ready, boy?" McLeach shouted. "The crocs love live bait!"

Bianca and Jake watched helplessly from the cage as McLeach tied Cody to the end of the crane and dangled him over Crocodile Falls.

"Oh, please hurry, Bernard," Bianca prayed. Laughing, McLeach pulled the lever and started to lower the crane. Suddenly the motor died, and Cody came to a stop inches above the water.

"What the blazes is going on!" muttered the poacher. Hearing a loud scuffling in the bushwhacker, McLeach whipped around. An enormous razorback bounded out of the driver's seat.

"Joanna!" he roared. "Get 'im!" But after taking one look at the razorback, Joanna hid under a bush. Fuming, McLeach leaned inside the truck and discovered the keys were missing.

"Well," he muttered, reaching for his rifle, "there's more than one way to skin a cat." He strode over to the edge of the falls and aimed at the rope.

"No!" screamed Cody. McLeach fired and the rope began to fray.

Bernard wiggled out from under the bushwhacker's foot pedal and hurried toward the cage with the keys.

"It's Bernard!" cried Bianca. "See, Jake, I told you he would rescue us."

"Way to go, mate!" Jake said.

Bernard tossed the keys to them through the bars and rushed off.

"I hope I know what I'm doing," he murmured to himself. He ran up to Joanna, stuck out his tongue and bounded away.

The bloodthirsty lizard shot after him. Bernard headed straight for McLeach, who was getting ready to fire again. The mouse darted between the poacher's legs. Joanna slammed right into McLeach and the two of them toppled into the water. Joanna managed to swim to the far shore but McLeach was swept, screaming, over Crocodile Falls.

The rope holding Cody snapped and the current pulled him away. Bernard ran onto a dead branch jutting out over the water. Desperately, he reached down and grabbed the end of the rope as it swept past.

"Help," cried Cody, plunging over the edge of the waterfall. Marahute, with Jake and Bianca on her back, swooped down and caught him before he disappeared into the thundering falls. The great eagle soared through the mist into the night sky.

Bianca greeted Cody with a sigh of relief. "But where's Bernard?" she asked.

Looking around, Cody saw the rope hanging over the side, and he began pulling it up. Bernard was clinging to the end of it with his eyes tightly shut.

"Thanks, little mate," Cody said.

Bianca hugged Bernard. "You were magnificent. You're the hero of the day."

Bernard got down on his knees and took a tiny box from his pocket.

"Before anything else happens," he asked, "will you marry me?"

Bianca patted his head. "Of course, darling," she answered. "I thought you'd never ask!"

THE RESCUERS DOWN UNDER
Behind the Scenes

"We felt the size of an ant in a huge world," Maurice Hunt, art director of *The Rescuers Down Under* once said of the research mission to the Australian outback that he, producer Thomas Schumacher, directors Hendel Butoy and Mike Gabriel, and story supervisor Joe Ranft took in preparation for making this first-ever animated action adventure film. In the vast, isolated landscape of Australia, the filmmakers discovered a world both immense and sublimely beautiful. The drama and impact of the exotic setting inspired them to push the scope, scale, and spectacle of *The Rescuers Down Under* beyond what had traditionally been done in animation. The result: the further adventures of Miss Bianca and Bernard, the stars of the first *Rescuers* movie (1977), became the setting for an adventure of the filmmakers' own.

Animator Glen Keane studies eagles in order to bring Marahute to life on screen.

"*The Rescuers Down Under* was the first movie ever to be entirely digitally produced," says Thomas Schumacher, Executive Vice President of Feature Animation, who served as producer of the 1990 film. "Not one frame of that movie was photographed by a camera." The computerized postproduction system known as CAPS (computer animation production system) was originally conceived to take the steps of inking and painting—tasks that by hand had long been completed painstakingly cel by cel—and perform them using a computer instead. It soon became clear that it was possible to use the system to achieve far more.

In addition to being able to take advantage of a nearly infinite palette of colors and to add greater dimension to shadows and other tonal effects, the filmmakers were suddenly free to take huge leaps in terms of camera angles, spectacle, multiple layering, and visual depth. "The CAPS system completely liberated the way we use the camera," asserts Schumacher. From the breathtaking opening scene, which compresses a thousand miles of Australian terrain seen from a bug's-eye view to the powerful, majestic flight of Marahute the eagle, the artists looked for every opportunity to include perspectives and camera angles that would emphasize the awe-inspiring scope of the world their characters inhabited. They stretched themselves and the new technology as far as they possibly could.

"We were able to create shots we had not been able to before," explains director Gabriel. "Marahute's flight is an example of the amazing things we were able to do—taking people on great flights of fancy. Story artist Chris Sanders created original storyboards for this breathtaking scene, and Glen Keane, who animated Marahute, took a pass at those boards and added great details and phenomenal stagings. Layout artist Rasoul Azadani took Glen's drawings and made incredible layouts from them. And then they were scanned into the computer and put together in a way that permitted tremendous depth and scale."

Working with the unfamiliar and untested postproduction system was not an easy undertaking. "Every frame of that film was an adventure," asserts Schumacher. "Not only had we never done it before, but I do not think that at the time people knew what it would ultimately yield." Through their willingness to experiment and push the boundaries of this new technology, the pioneering group who created *The Rescuers Down Under* achieved a milestone in visual expression that has had an impact on every Disney animated film since.

Storyboard sketches from the sequence in which Marahute takes Cody for a breathtaking ride over the outback.

Once upon a time, in a faraway land, a young prince lived in a splendid castle deep in the forest. He had everything his heart desired. But despite his wealth and possessions, he was spoiled, selfish, and unkind.

One bitter winter night, an enchantress, disguised as an old beggar woman, appeared at the castle gate and asked for shelter from the cold. In return, she offered the prince a single beautiful rose. Repulsed by her haggard appearance, the prince told her to go away. "Do not be deceived by appearances," she told him, but he refused to let her in. As punishment for his selfishness, the enchantress transformed him into a hideous beast and placed a powerful spell on the castle and all who lived there.

Before leaving, the enchantress handed the rose to the prince. "This rose will bloom until your twenty-first year," she said. "During that time, you must learn to love another. If you also earn her love by the time the last petal falls, the spell will be broken. If not, you will remain a beast forever!"

The prince concealed himself in his castle, hiding his ugliness from those outside. Alone and friendless, his only means of seeing the world around him was through a magic mirror.

As the years passed, the prince fell into despair. For who could ever learn to love a beast?

One morning, in a village beyond the forest, a beautiful girl named Belle skipped down her cottage steps and strolled into town to the bookseller's shop. "Do you have any new books?" she inquired.

The shopkeeper laughed. "Not since you asked me yesterday," he said, taking a book from the shelf. "But you may have this one to keep. I believe it's your favorite."

"Oh, thank you!" Belle said. "It's a wonderful story about far-off places, magical spells, and a prince in disguise."

As Belle walked down the street with her nose buried in her new book, the townspeople gossiped. "Belle is very nice," said the butcher. "And she certainly is a beauty," whispered the fishmonger. But everyone agreed that she was very odd. "But what can you expect—with a crazy father like Maurice!" the baker explained.

Belle heard them talking but she didn't care. "They're right," she thought. "But I'm glad I'm different."

"Hello there, Belle," said a tall, handsome young man with a deep voice.

"Oh, hello, Gaston," Belle said, trying to ignore him.

Gaston snatched the book from her. "How can you read this?" he asked. "There are no pictures!" Belle grabbed the book back. "You should get your head out of books," he said, patting her shoulder, "and pay attention to important things—like me. Think about becoming my wife. After all, I am the strongest, most handsome—"

"Vainest man around," interrupted Belle. "Please go away, Gaston. I have to get home to help my father. He's getting one of his inventions ready to show at the fair."

"That crazy old loon," Gaston said, laughing. "Your father needs all the help he can get!"

KABAAAM! Clouds of smoke billowed from Belle's cottage.

"Papa!" she called, rushing home and peering into her father's workshop. "Are you all right?"

Maurice climbed out from beneath a strange contraption with a shiny hatchet attached on top. "I've done it, Belle!" he declared. "Watch." He flicked a switch, and the hatchet began chopping up and down in a frenzy. Splinters and wood chips flew everywhere as the machine tossed neatly cut logs into a stack nearby.

"It works, Papa!" cried Belle. "You're sure to win first prize."

She helped her father lug the wood chopper outside and strap it to their wagon. Maurice hitched the cart to Phillipe, their devoted horse, and climbed into the saddle. "This invention will bring a new life for us, Belle," he said, leaning down and kissing her good-bye.

"Good luck, Papa," she called out as he rode away.

Maurice traveled through the forest for hours before he realized he was lost. "Dear, dear," the old man muttered, glancing about nervously. "This doesn't look right to me." All of a sudden, Phillipe stopped short.

"What is it?" asked Maurice. Out of the darkness crept a pack of snarling wolves. They rushed at the frightened horse and snapped at his flanks. Whinnying, Phillipe reared and charged forward. "Whoa!" Maurice shouted, but he was thrown and landed sprawling in the mud. Phillipe galloped off with the wolves close behind.

Scrambling to his feet, Maurice fled through the forest. With several wolves at his heels, he came upon an iron gate and, squeezing through, found himself in the courtyard of a great castle. As he stumbled toward the entrance, it began to pour. Shivering, Maurice pulled his soaked cape around him and began pounding on the door. To his surprise, it opened a crack.

Maurice poked his head inside. "Hello?" he called in a shaky voice. "I don't mean to intrude, but I've lost my horse and I need a place to stay for the night." As he wandered about the gloomy chamber, a candelabrum and a wooden mantel-clock watched from the shadows.

"Not a word, Lumiere," the clock whispered. "Maybe he'll go away."

But the candelabrum, ignoring the clock, called out to Maurice. "Over here!"

"Incredible," Maurice said, squinting across the room. "A talking candelabrum!"

The clock, known as Cogsworth, stepped forward. "I am sorry," he announced to the dumbfounded Maurice, "but you'll have to leave. The master doesn't like uninvited guests."

Lumiere pushed past Cogsworth. "Of course you are welcome to stay," he said. "Cogsworth can be a bit stuffy." He led

Maurice to an armchair in front of a crackling fire. "Please, sit down and
relax. Mrs. Potts will be here in a moment with some hot tea."

"Not the master's chair!" Cogsworth sputtered. A footstool scurried over
and tucked itself under Maurice's feet.

"Thank you," Maurice said. He leaned back and sighed. "You are most kind."

Cogsworth tried to head off Mrs. Potts, a teapot, in the hall. "No tea!"
he ordered. "This has gone far enough. Remember who's in charge of
the household."

Mrs. Potts bustled right past him, with a little teacup at her side. "Would
you like some tea?" she offered Maurice.

"It will make you feel warm and cozy," the teacup piped up. "Won't it, Mama?"

Mrs. Potts smiled at him as she poured from her spout. "Yes, Chip," she
answered. "A spot of tea will fix him right up."

Just as Maurice raised the cup to his lips, he heard pounding footsteps.

"It's the master!" Cogsworth gasped.

Maurice stared in horror: a fearsome beast, more terrifying than any
creature he had ever seen, stood snarling in the doorway. "Who's this
stranger?" the Beast roared.

"I-I-I," Maurice babbled, "was lost and—"

"Are you staring at me?" the Beast demanded. Maurice shook his head
frantically, but he couldn't take his eyes off the hideous figure before him.
The Beast yanked him out of the chair, dragged him to the castle tower, and
locked him in a dark cell.

In the forest, Phillipe barely managed to outrun the wolves. He raced back to the cottage yard.

"Phillipe! Where's Papa?" Belle cried out anxiously. She unhitched the wagon and mounted the exhausted horse. "You must take me to him, at once!"

Phillipe cautiously retraced his steps through the forest. They came up to the castle, where they found a hat lying near the gate. "It's Papa's!" Belle gasped. She dismounted and, leaving Phillipe in the yard, entered the castle.

"Hello?" she called softly. "Papa, are you here?" Not even Lumiere dared to answer this time. Hearing a faint cry, Belle climbed a winding staircase that led up to the tower. "Papa?"

"Belle? Is that you?" her father called. Shaking with fever, he reached out to her.

"Papa!" Belle sobbed, grasping his cold hands through a barred window. "Who did this to you?"

"No time to explain," said Maurice. "You must get out of here!"

The Beast came storming down the hall. Belle recoiled at the sight of him. "Who are you?" the Beast growled.

"I'm Belle, and I-I've come for my father," she said, trying to keep her voice steady. "Please, let him out. Can't you see that he's ill?"

"He never should have trespassed!" the Beast replied.

"Please! I'll do anything," pleaded Belle.

"There's nothing you can do. He's my prisoner," said the Beast, turning away.

Belle held his arm. The touch of her hand startled him. "Wait, take me instead."

The Beast was astounded. "You? You would take his place? You wouldn't run away?"

"No, Belle! Don't do it!" pleaded her father. Belle only nodded. "You have my word."

"Please, let me stay," the old man begged as the Beast carried him down the stairs. "I've lived my life. Spare my daughter!"

Out in the courtyard, the Beast shoved Maurice into a carriage. "Take him home," he commanded. Obediently, the enchanted carriage sped through the gate and was gone.

The Beast stormed back into the castle and was met by Lumiere. "Your Grace," he said nervously, "since the girl is here to stay, you might want to offer her a comfortable room."

The Beast growled in response and returned to the tower. There, he found Belle sobbing.

"You didn't even let me say good-bye," she cried.

"Come," said the Beast. "I'll show you to . . . your room."

"My room?" Belle asked surprised.

"The castle's your home now," he said, leading her to a spacious room. "You may go anywhere you please, but . . . you must never set foot in the west wing." He paused at the door. "You will join me for dinner tonight. It's not a request. You'll come!"

Belle threw herself on the bed and sobbed into a pillow. Soon she heard a gentle knock on the door. Mrs. Potts, with Chip behind her, stepped in. "I thought you might like some tea," she said softly.

"A talking teapot!" Belle exclaimed.

Chip giggled. "She's pretty, Mama."

Mrs. Potts poured tea into Chip. "That was a very brave thing you did," she said.

At that, the wardrobe spoke up. "We all think so."

Belle stared back in amazement.

"Here, let me help you dress for dinner," continued the wardrobe, opening her doors. "I have lots of ravishing gowns from which you may choose."

Belle gently closed the doors. "You're very kind," she said, "but I'm not going to dinner."

In the royal dining room, the Beast paced back and forth. "What's keeping her so long?" he shouted at the servants.

"Be patient with her," urged Mrs. Potts. "And try to act polite. She's lost her father and her freedom all in one day."

"Have you thought that if you and this girl fall in love, the spell will be broken?" Lumiere asked.

"Of course I have," the Beast snapped. "But look at me! She'll never see me as anything but a monster."

"But, Your Eminence, the rose—" Lumiere began.

Cogsworth appeared at the door. "Your Highness," he said nervously. "Don't get upset, but . . . uh . . . she's not coming."

"WHAT?" ranted the Beast. He charged up the stairs to Belle's room. "Come down to dinner NOW!" he bellowed at her closed door. Then, remembering Mrs. Potts's suggestion, he lowered his voice. "Please. It would give me . . . great pleasure."

But Belle refused to leave her room.

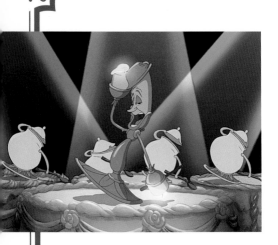

Later that night, having grown quite hungry, Belle cautiously found her way down to the kitchen.

"Splendid to see you," said Cogsworth. "You must be famished."

"Why, yes," replied Belle. The servants immediately began rushing about, grabbing pots and pans and setting the table. In no time at all, they presented Belle with a sumptuous dinner. She had never eaten such wonderful food.

"That was quite a feast," she said, patting her mouth with an embroidered napkin. "You certainly are generous to your guests." She rose from the table. "And now I'd like to see the castle, if you don't mind."

Cogsworth spoke right up. "Lumiere and I will show you around." They escorted her on a tour, pointing out the tapestries and furnishings. After a while, Belle was unable to contain her curiosity. She slipped away and ventured straight to the west wing. Reaching the end of a dark hall, she opened a door and found a room in shambles. A painting that had been clawed to shreds hung crookedly over the mantel. Looking closely, Belle saw it was a portrait of a young prince. His blue eyes were the color of the summer sky.

On a table in the center of the room, a single rose bloomed beneath a crystal dome. Enchanted by its brilliant glow, Belle reached out to touch it.

"NO!" roared the Beast, coming up behind her suddenly. "I ordered you to stay away from here. Now, get out!"

Belle fled down the stairs and out the door. "I don't care if I gave my word," she said to herself. "I'm not staying here another minute." She found Phillipe waiting patiently in the courtyard. She leaped on his back and rode off into the night.

It was snowing hard, and Phillipe stumbled in the deep drifts. Four hungry wolves appeared from behind a thicket. Belle's heart filled with terror. Their fangs bared, the animals sprang at Phillipe. The terrified horse slipped, throwing Belle to the ground. Just as a wolf was about to spring at her throat, the Beast appeared in the blinding storm. He snatched the wolf away while several others attacked him. They fought fiercely until the wolves slunk off, defeated. Exhausted, the Beast collapsed.

Belle rushed to his side. "You . . . saved my life," she said shyly.

Helping the Beast onto Phillipe, Belle led them back to the castle.

All the following days, while Belle cared for the wounded Beast, she worried about her father and wondered if he was safe at home. Back in the village, Maurice was growing frantic. He begged the townspeople to help him rescue his daughter, but they all laughed at his fantastic story about a great hairy beast in a castle. "Maurice, the old loon," they chuckled. "He really is crazy!"

But Maurice was determined to rescue his daughter, even without their help. "Poor child," he thought. "She must be miserable."

Oddly, Belle came to like living in the castle. The Beast gradually changed as well. He didn't lose his temper as often. At times, he was even gentle and sweet. "It's so strange," thought Belle. "I'm beginning to grow fond of him."

One morning at breakfast, the Beast told Belle that he had a surprise for her. He led her deep into the castle to a room she'd never visited before.

"A library!" Belle exclaimed in delight. "I've never seen so many books."

"They're all yours," the Beast said, but he was surprised to see her eyes suddenly fill with tears.

"Is anything wrong?" he asked.

"Everything would be so nice if only I could see Papa again, just for a moment," she said. "I miss him so."

The Beast smiled. "You can see him," he told her, taking her hand and leading her to the forbidden room in the west wing. He held up the magic mirror. "This will show you anything you wish to see."

But Belle gasped when she looked into it and saw her father wandering lost in the forest, calling her name. Suddenly, he collapsed on the ground.

"Oh, Papa!" Belle sobbed. "He's in trouble. He may be dying. I must go to him."

The Beast studied the rose on the table. It had begun to droop, and he sighed as one more petal fell. Then he turned to Belle and gently stroked her hair.

"I will set you free," the Beast said. He handed her the magic mirror. "Take it with you so you'll always have a way to look back and remember me."

Blinking back tears of joy, Belle hugged him. "I will never forget you," she said.

The Beast and his servants watched Belle ride away on Phillipe. "How could you let her go?" Cogsworth asked in amazement.

"Because . . . I love her," the Beast said simply and walked away.

"He's fallen in love!" Lumiere shouted. "The spell will be broken!"

"That's not enough," Mrs. Potts reminded him. "She has to love him in return."

Belle found her father lying unconscious. Using all her strength, she managed to lift him onto Phillipe. When they reached home, she put him to bed.

"I thought I'd never see you again," Maurice murmured, opening his eyes. "How did you escape?"

"I didn't escape, Papa," Belle said. "The Beast is different now. He let me go. Look what he gave me."

As she took the mirror out of her bag, Chip tumbled into her lap. "A stowaway!" Belle exclaimed.

"Did you leave because you don't like us?" Chip asked.

Belle set the little teacup on the night table. "Of course not—"

There was a knock at the door. Belle found Gaston standing outside.

"Hello, Belle," said Gaston. "I'm here to take your crazy father to the asylum. He thinks he's seen a beast."

"My father isn't crazy," Belle said angrily.

"Of course he is," said Gaston. "But I can save him from the asylum—*if* you'll marry me!"

Belle pushed past him and found a crowd of people in the yard. "To the asylum!" they shouted.

"My father's telling the truth," Belle declared. "Look!" She held up the magic mirror. When the Beast's image appeared, everyone drew back in horror. He was standing on the balcony, roaring in anguish.

"He's a monster!" cried a woman. "Our children won't be safe."

"I say let's kill the Beast!" shouted Gaston.

"But he's not dangerous," Belle pleaded. "He's kind and gentle."

Gaston pushed Belle into the cottage and locked her and Maurice in the workshop. "Now you can't warn your beast friend," he said. Riding in front of the angry mob and using the magic mirror to guide him, Gaston led the way to the castle. "Kill the Beast!" they chanted.

After they'd gone, Chip tumbled down from the night table and peered outside. "Ah!" he said when he saw the shining hatchet on top of Maurice's wood-chopping machine. He toddled across the yard, climbed up, and flipped the switch. It rattled forward and—chop, chop, chop—right through the workshop wall. Belle and Maurice rushed out to find Phillipe.

Outside the castle, Gaston dismounted and boldly thrust his way through the door. He rushed to the tower and found the Beast gazing sadly out the window. Gaston slipped an arrow into his bow and aimed carefully. He struck the Beast in the shoulder and then shoved him out onto the balcony. "What's the matter, Beast?" jeered Gaston. "Too kind and gentle to fight back?"

The Beast, despite his pain, was silent. Since Belle had gone, he no longer cared what happened to him. Gaston broke off a chunk of stone railing and raised it over his head.

"No!" screamed Belle from the courtyard below. She rushed through the door and up the stairs. The sound of Belle's voice aroused the Beast from his despair. He grabbed Gaston and pinned him against the wall.

"Let me go," begged Gaston. "Don't hurt me!"

The Beast glared at him. "Leave!" he ordered.

But as soon as the Beast's back was turned, Gaston pulled out a dagger and stabbed him. The Beast swung around in agony and knocked Gaston off balance. Screaming, Gaston plummeted to the courtyard far below. The Beast fell back mortally wounded.

Belle took the Beast in her arms. He managed a smile. "You came back," he whispered. Then he closed his eyes. Inside the room, the last remaining rose petal trembled, ready to fall.

"Oh, please don't leave me." Belle pleaded. She rested her head on his chest and sobbed. "I love you."

Suddenly, as if by magic, a glowing light swirled about the Beast's body, gradually transforming him from a beast into a man. When the light faded away, a handsome young prince lay in the Beast's place. When he opened his eyes, Belle saw they were as blue as a summer sky.

"Belle," he said, rising to his feet, "it's me."

She gazed into his eyes. "It *is* you," she said. Behind her, glowing magically, the rose was in full bloom.

Belle and the prince embraced and kissed. The delighted servants cheered, and then they, too, were transformed back into people. Mrs. Potts brushed off her apron and hugged her little boy.

"Mama," asked Chip, "are they going to live happily ever after?"

"Of course, my dear." She smiled. "Of course."

BEAUTY AND THE BEAST
Behind the Scenes

ABOVE: *Rough animation of the Beast by Glen Keane.*

On January 18, 1992, *Beauty and the Beast* was awarded the Golden Globe for best comedy/musical of 1991. The film, which was the first animated feature directed by Kirk Wise and Gary Trousdale, was also the first animated feature ever to be nominated for best picture by the Academy of Motion Picture Arts and Sciences. *Beauty and the Beast* was admired for its artistic achievement and its impeccable crafting as a piece of entertainment, but even more, the film was and continues to be beloved for its heart.

Asked to explain its appeal, producer Don Hahn points to the movie's sincerity. "*Beauty and the Beast* strikes an emotional chord with people," says Hahn. "People relate to the Beast's character, they want to know more about him. The enchanted objects are charming, and people want to know more about *them*, and the settings—the French farmyard, the enchanted castle, and the forest—are extremely appealing and inviting."

At the emotional core of *Beauty and the Beast* is the wonderfully conceived cast of characters, led by the magnificent Beast. Supervising animator Glen Keane built a Beast of disparate parts—taking from the lion his mane, from the buffalo his beard and head structure, from the boar his tusks and nose bridge, and from the gorilla his brow. The animator placed this frightening countenance atop the body of a bear and the legs and tail of a wolf to create the Beast's singularly imposing physical appearance.

Interpreting the Beast involved far more than developing a set of external characteristics; Keane needed to show the Beast's nature both inside and out. "The eyes are the windows of the soul," says Keane. "When Belle looks into the Beast's eyes, she must see his human heart and soul. She must see sincerity and believe that she can truly love this creature. This had to come across in our animation."

Beauty and the Beast has no external evil for the hero to overcome. Asserts Don Hahn, "The Beast's greatest obstacle is his own nature, and his success depends not on his conquering a villain but on dealing with negative aspects of himself."

The *Beauty and the Beast* team relished the chance to devise a story line that would turn some well-worn clichés inside out. The Beast is clearly, in Belle's words, "no Prince Charming," yet Gaston, the nominal villain of the piece, has the look of a typical leading man. If the Beast is a transformation of the traditional Disney hero, Belle is a departure from the classic heroine and a far cry from the passive girl in the fairy tale. In the original tale, the young woman simply follows her father's instructions to go to the Beast's castle. In the animated film, Belle's own decision to find and rescue her father sets the story in motion. The original character evolved in the artists' minds to become the independent, smart, courageous Belle, strong enough emotionally to give up her own world in order to save her father.

The strength of the characters extends beyond the major players. It was executive producer and lyricist Howard Ashman's inspiration to present the enchanted objects in the castle as animated characters with unique personalities. His practical need for a set of characters that could further the story in song resulted in a cast of animated objects truly compelling and fascinating to watch.

Supervising animators for the enchanted characters (left to right): Will Finn (Cogsworth), Nik Ranieri (Lumiere), and Dave Pruiksma (Mrs. Potts and Chip).

"No one really knows how an enchanted object moves," asserts Nik Ranieri, supervising animator of Lumiere, so the animators had a great deal of freedom in their drawing. "You can get away with anything as long as the character has weight and volume," adds Ranieri. Yet getting away with *anything* was not really the intention of the animators. The challenge and fun in animating Cogsworth, Lumiere, Mrs. Potts, Chip, and the rest was to allow each personality to come through distinctly while preserving the integrity of the objects. Cogsworth's affectation and stuffiness are personified in the limitations of his enchanted state as a wooden clock, while Lumiere's suave and devil-may-care manner shines through his incarnation as a candelabrum. Mrs. Potts's transformation into a teakettle seems to embody her nurturing personality.

As Belle's supervising animator Mark Henn explains: "The goal was to create strong performances. We tried to understand each character's situation or predicament and create a believable personality that would come across, so people would forget that they were looking at drawings and painted backgrounds. We wanted the audience to be as caught up in the drama as the characters themselves seemed to be."

ALADDIN

Agrabah was an enchanting city—a lush, tree-filled oasis in the desert, where date palms grew and waters flowed like silver in the twilight. It was also a place of mystery and danger, where knives flashed in the dark and blinding sandstorms choked one's breath.

One chilly night under a bright crescent moon, a lone man sat astride his steed. The man's name was Jafar—Royal Advisor to the Sultan. Perched quietly on his shoulder was a red-and-blue parrot, called Iago. Together, they waited in silence for the thief. At last, a panting horse bearing a man in rags galloped up to them.

"A thousand apologies for my lateness," the thief said, "but I have found the treasure you seek." He held up a piece of a golden ornament, decorated with a scarab, the sacred beetle.

Jafar reached inside his robe and pulled out the other half of the ornament. The instant he joined the halves together, a crash of thunder shook the still air. The scarab glowed and leaped from Jafar's hand. Surrounded by a blinding light, it streaked across the dunes.

"Give chase!" Jafar shouted, spurring his horse. "It will lead us to the Cave of Wonders . . . and the LAMP!" Jafar and the thief raced after the magical scarab, which split apart and lodged into the sand. With a roar, the huge head of a tiger-god rose from the trembling dune, its scarab eyes burning like coals. It opened its cavernous mouth to reveal a stairway winding endlessly downward.

"At last!" breathed Jafar. "After all my years of searching—I have found the Cave of Wonders!" He pushed the thief toward the tiger-god's gaping maw. "Now, bring me the lamp," he charged, "and the rest of the treasure is yours. But remember, the lamp . . . is mine."

"WHO DISTURBS MY SLUMBER?" demanded the tiger-god.

"Er . . . it is I, your most humble Gazeem," replied the thief.

"KNOW THIS! ONLY ONE MAY ENTER HERE. ONE WHOSE WORTH LIES FAR WITHIN. THE DIAMOND IN THE ROUGH!"

The thief hesitated. "Go on!" Jafar urged him. "What are you waiting for?" Fearing the worst, the thief approached the stairway and peered into the unknown depths. The instant the thief shakily trod on the first step, the tiger-god let out an earsplitting roar. The thief vanished, his cry cut off in midscream. And then there was silence.

The Cave of Wonders began to dissolve back into sand. Its voice fading, the tiger-god spoke once again: "SEEK THEE OUT . . . THE DIAMOND IN THE ROUGH."

Jafar stared in bewilderment—the Cave of Wonders was gone! Iago poked at the scarab halves, lying dull in the sand. "We're never going to get hold of that stupid lamp," he squawked. "We got a problem here, a big—"

"Patience, Iago," mused Jafar. "The thief was obviously less than worthy. It seems only one may enter. Now I must find this one . . . this diamond in the rough."

Late one afternoon in the marketplace, a poor peasant named Aladdin was running for his life. The royal guards were after him again. "All this for stealing a loaf of bread?" he asked himself as he scrambled up a wall. He leaped from the rooftop, grabbing hold of a clothesline, and tumbled down right in front of Razoul, the Sultan's head guard.

"Gotcha!" cried Razoul, seizing Aladdin. But, at that moment, a scrappy little monkey jumped from an awning and pulled the guard's turban over his eyes.

"Perfect timing, Abu!" said Aladdin. "C'mon, let's get out of here." They darted through the city, dodging the guards at every turn. At last, they dropped to safety behind a high wall. "And now," Aladdin said to Abu, taking the bread from inside his shirt, "we feast!"

Two little street urchins stood watching him with hungry eyes. Aladdin sighed and held out the bread to the children. "Here, go on," he told them. "Take it."

As the children ran off to eat, they crossed in front of a richly dressed man on horseback, heading toward the Royal Palace. "Out of my way, you filthy brats," he barked.

"Look at that, Abu," said Aladdin, shaking his head in disgust. "Another worthless prince has come to town, seeking Princess Jasmine's hand in marriage." He shivered and rubbed his arms. "Wind's blowing in from the east. We'd better go home."

Keeping to the shadows, they made their way to the edge of Agrabah. They climbed into an old burned-out building, where Aladdin lived with all his possessions—two straw mats, a small stove, and a tin cup. He pushed back a ragged curtain and watched the twilight settle over the city.

"Someday, Abu," said Aladdin, "we'll be rich and live in a palace. . . ."

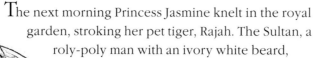

The next morning Princess Jasmine knelt in the royal garden, stroking her pet tiger, Rajah. The Sultan, a roly-poly man with an ivory white beard, watched his daughter in dismay. "Rajah has frightened away another suitor," he said. "This must stop."

Jasmine smiled sweetly. "He was just playing with him, Father. Weren't you, Rajah?" The tiger nuzzled her and purred with a low rumble.

"You've got to stop rejecting every suitor who comes to call," the Sultan scolded her. "The law says you must be married to a prince by your next birthday—merely three days away!"

"Father, I'm not going to be forced into marriage," protested Jasmine. "If I ever do marry, it will be to a man I love. I know you want to protect me, but try to understand. You've never let me do a thing on my own. I've never even been outside the palace walls!"

The Sultan rolled his eyes toward the heavens and waddled back into the throne room. Jafar stepped from the shadows. He was carrying his staff, adorned with the head of a serpent.

"Ah, Jafar, my most trusted advisor, what am I to do?" asked the Sultan, wringing his hands. "Jasmine refuses to choose a husband."

Jafar smiled. "Perhaps there's a solution to this thorny problem. But it would require the use of a mystic blue diamond. . . ."

"You mean, my ring?" asked the Sultan, looking at his hand. "But it's been in the family for years. . . ."

Jafar held up his staff and slowly waved it back and forth before the Sultan. The serpent's eyes glowed bright. Transfixed, the Sultan slowly removed his ring. "Take . . . it . . . Jafar," he said in a dazed voice. "Whatever you need . . . will be fine."

The Royal Advisor, bowing low, backed out of the throne room. Quickly, he stepped into a hidden passage and climbed a staircase to a secret chamber.

"Now we shall see!" Jafar murmured to Iago. He hastened across the room to a brass hourglass. Holding his breath, Jafar inserted the Sultan's ring into a groove on top.

"Sands of time!" Jafar intoned, as he turned the hourglass over. "Reveal to me the one who can enter the cave!" Before his eyes, a sandstorm whirled

within the glass and the image of a young man appeared. It was Aladdin.

"There he is!" Jafar exclaimed to Iago. "My diamond in the rough! Let's have Razoul extend this boy an invitation to the palace, shall we?"

Out in the royal garden, Jasmine, concealed in a hooded cloak, was saying good-bye to Rajah. "I'll miss you," she said, stroking his neck. "But I can't stay here and have my life lived for me." Without looking back, she climbed a tree next to the wall and dropped down on the other side. She hurried from the palace grounds and found herself, for the first time in her life, wandering about the crowded streets of Agrabah.

"Sugared dates! Pistachios!" the merchants in the marketplace called out, hawking their wares. "Would the lady like a silver necklace?" "Try this melon—your taste buds will dance and sing!"

Jasmine saw a little boy staring at a mound of ruby red fruit. "You must be hungry," she said and chose the ripest apple for him. When she started to turn away, the vendor was furious. "You'd better pay for that!" he cried.

"Pay?" Jasmine said, surprised at his anger. "But I don't have any money. Please, if you let me go to the palace, I'll get some money from the Sultan."

"Do you know what the penalty for stealing is?" the vendor threatened, grabbing her hand and unsheathing his dagger.

Aladdin, who had been watching from nearby, leaped forward. "I've been looking all over for you!" he said loudly to Jasmine. Then he whispered in her ear. "Trust me!" He shook the merchant's hand. "I'm so glad you found her. My sister's a little crazy."

The vendor was suspicious. "She says she knows the Sultan," he told Aladdin.

"She thinks this monkey is the Sultan," said Aladdin, pointing to Abu.

Jasmine knelt before Abu. "O wise Sultan," she said, trying not to giggle. "How may I serve you?"

"Get her out of here," the vendor told Aladdin.

Aladdin led Jasmine through the market up to his dwelling. "Is this where you live?" she asked.

Aladdin gestured to a gaping hole in the wall. "It's not much, but it's got a great view." He gazed over the rooftops at the palace, shimmering in the hot sun. "I wonder what it's like to live there?"

Jasmine murmured to herself. "People tell you what to do and when . . ."

"Where're you from?" Aladdin asked. "I've never seen you in the marketplace before."

Jasmine shrugged. "It doesn't matter. I ran away and I'm not going back. My father is forcing me to get married."

Without warning, Razoul and his guards burst into the room. "Run!" Aladdin yelled, but the guards were too quick.

Jasmine threw back her hood. "Unhand him!" she commanded. "By order of the Princess."

Aladdin was stunned. She was dressed in the finest silks and a gleaming jewel adorned her hair.

"P-P-Princess Jasmine," Razoul stammered. "What are you doing outside the palace?"

"That's not your concern," she replied. "Release him at once."

"My orders come from Jafar," Razoul explained, dragging Aladdin away. "You'll have to take it up with him."

When they reached the palace, Jasmine summoned Jafar. It was several moments before he arrived. "I cannot honor your request to release this boy," he lied. "He was convicted of kidnapping you. The sentence was carried out immediately—death by beheading."

It was cold and dark in the palace dungeon. Aladdin sat slumped with his wrists shackled to the damp wall. "I can't believe she was the Princess. I must have sounded so stupid to her," he said aloud.

As soon as it was night, Abu peeked through the bars of the window high above Aladdin's head.

"Abu," Aladdin whispered. "See if you can get me out of here." Abu swung down by his tail and, in a few minutes, managed to undo the locks.

"Wait," wheezed a shaky voice. Jafar, disguised as a crippled beggar, limped out of the shadows. "There is a Cave of Wonders filled with treasures beyond your wildest dreams," he said. "If you want to impress your princess, you'd be wise to listen."

"But she has to marry a prince," Aladdin said, warily. "What good would a treasure be to *me*?"

"You've heard of the golden rule," said Jafar. "Whoever has the gold . . . makes the rules."

Aladdin's eyes widened. "So why would you share all this treasure with me?"

"I need a pair of strong young legs to get it," said Jafar, extending his bony hand. "Do we have a deal?" Aladdin looked uneasily at Abu as he shook hands with the beggar. Jafar pushed against a stone in the wall and it slid back, revealing a staircase. "Let us go!"

Late that night, out in the chilly desert, Aladdin stood amazed as the Cave of Wonders emerged from the sands. "Fetch the lamp," Jafar urged, pushing him forward, "and you shall have your reward."

"WHO DISTURBS MY SLUMBER?" demanded the tiger-god.

Aladdin gulped. "Uh, it is I, Aladdin," he answered.

"PROCEED. TOUCH NOTHING BUT THE LAMP."

Aladdin made his way down the winding steps and found himself in an enormous cavern piled high with mountains of gold coins and sparkling emeralds, rubies, and sapphires.

"Look at this place, Abu!" Aladdin said. As he began to search about, he felt Abu yank his trousers. Chattering wildly, the monkey pointed to a gold-tasseled carpet. It was sneaking up behind them.

"A Magic Carpet!" gasped Aladdin. "Maybe you can help us," he said to the little rug. "We're looking for a lamp."

The Magic Carpet rose, spun in a circle above their heads, and soared across the cavern. Aladdin and Abu chased after it and ended up in a shadowy chamber. Rising from the center, a huge pillar of rock stood in a shaft of light, filtering through a crack in the ceiling. Aladdin spied a small object resting on the very top—it was the lamp!

"Wait here, Abu," Aladdin said. "Whatever you do, don't touch anything!" He climbed the pillar and grabbed the lamp. As he stuck it under his shirt, he saw Abu pick up a shining jewel. "No, Abu!" yelled Aladdin.

At once, the tiger-god's voice echoed throughout the chamber. "YOU HAVE TOUCHED THE FORBIDDEN TREASURES. NOW YOU SHALL NEVER AGAIN SEE THE LIGHT OF DAY."

The cavern walls began to rumble and shake. Molten lava flowed from cracks in the stone floor and bubbled up in a boiling pool beneath Aladdin. Clutching the pillar, Aladdin slipped toward the fiery liquid. At the last second, the Magic Carpet swept beneath him. Zooming down, they plucked up Abu and rose toward the opening of the cave. Jafar was waiting for them with outstretched arms.

"Give me the lamp!" he ordered, snatching it from Aladdin and hiding it under his cape. He pulled a sharp dagger from his sleeve. "Now for your reward!"

Abu shrieked and sprang at Jafar, who cried out as the monkey, baring his teeth, bit him hard on the hand. Writhing in pain, Jafar struggled to free himself. He shoved Aladdin and Abu backward down into the depths. When they landed, the ground quaked and the cave sealed shut.

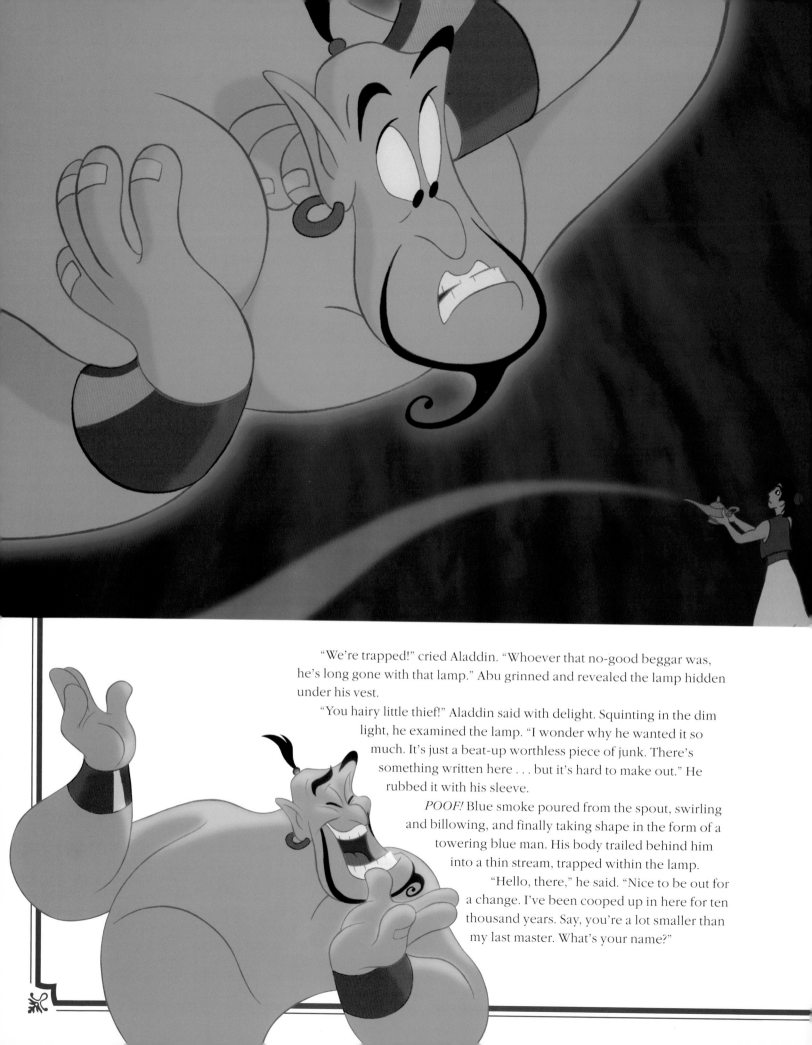

"We're trapped!" cried Aladdin. "Whoever that no-good beggar was, he's long gone with that lamp." Abu grinned and revealed the lamp hidden under his vest.

"You hairy little thief!" Aladdin said with delight. Squinting in the dim light, he examined the lamp. "I wonder why he wanted it so much. It's just a beat-up worthless piece of junk. There's something written here . . . but it's hard to make out." He rubbed it with his sleeve.

POOF! Blue smoke poured from the spout, swirling and billowing, and finally taking shape in the form of a towering blue man. His body trailed behind him into a thin stream, trapped within the lamp.

"Hello, there," he said. "Nice to be out for a change. I've been cooped up in here for ten thousand years. Say, you're a lot smaller than my last master. What's your name?"

"A-A-Aladdin," he stammered. "Wait a minute—I'm your master?"
The blue man nodded. "Hey, what you rub is what you get! I'm the
Genie of the Lamp—all set to grant you three wishes."
Aladdin scratched his head. "I must be dreaming. . . ."
"So, what'll it be?" the Genie asked him.
"Remember, though, a few no-can-dos: You can't
wish for.more wishes. I can't kill anybody. I can't make
anybody fall in love. And I can't bring people back from
the dead. That's it. Anything else—it's yours!"
Aladdin turned his head and winked at Abu. "Some all-
powerful Genie," he said. "I don't know, Abu, he probably can't
even get us out of this cave."
"Did you listen to me?" asked the Genie. "You're getting your
wishes—so have a seat!" He grabbed Aladdin and Abu and leaped onto the
Magic Carpet. "Yo, Rugman! Gimme some tassel!" In a blinding flash, the
cavern ceiling cracked open wide and the Magic Carpet rose into the early
morning sky. They floated across the hot desert and landed in a shady oasis.
"Doubt me, will you?" said the Genie with a big smile. "Now, you've got two
wishes left. What'll they be?"

"Three wishes," Aladdin corrected him. "I never actually wished to get
out of the cave. You did that on your own."

The Genie rubbed his chin. "All right, you baaaad
boy! But no more freebies."

"I want these wishes to be good," said Aladdin.
"Give me an idea. What would *you* wish for?"

"Freedom!" said the Genie.

"You're a prisoner?" Aladdin
asked surprised.

"It's part of the whole Genie gig," he
explained. "Phenomenal cosmic powers,
itty-bitty living space. The only way for me to be
free is for my master to wish me out. But let's get real.
It's not gonna happen."

"I'll do it," promised Aladdin. "After I make two wishes, I'll use my third
one to set you free."

The Genie looked doubtful. "Well, here's hoping. Now! Let's make some
magic! What is it you want most?"

"Well, there's a girl I like a lot," Aladdin told him, "but she's the Princess.
So, for my first wish, Genie, I wish to become a prince!"

"No problem," said the Genie. With a double *POOF!* and a twist of
smoke, he transformed Aladdin into a prince, garbed in a white turban and
elegant robes.

"Ooh, I like it! But now you'll need to make a grand entrance." With a
snap of his fingers, he changed Abu into an elephant. "Talk about your trunk
space! But we're not through yet. Hang on to your turban, kid. We're gonna
make you a STAR!"

That afternoon, Jafar rushed up to the Sultan. "O Great Ruler," he announced, unrolling a long scroll, "there's a solution to your problem. It says right here . . . if the Princess hasn't chosen a husband by her sixteenth birthday, the Sultan shall choose for her."

"But," stammered the Sultan, "how can I choose for her? She's hated all the suitors so far."

"Listen, there's more," Jafar continued. "In the event a suitor isn't found, the Princess shall wed . . . the Royal Advisor!"

"Oh, I don't know," said the Sultan. "You're so . . . old." A sudden blare of trumpets made him jump. "Something's going on in the streets," he said, running to the balcony. "Look, Jafar—there's a prince riding an elephant. He's coming toward the palace!"

"Make way!" shouted the Genie, darting through the excited crowd. "Make way for Prince Ali Ababwa!" The whole city welcomed the mysterious prince as he rode through the palace gates in front of a grand procession.

"Your Majesty," Aladdin said to the Sultan, "I, Prince Ali Ababwa, wish to seek your daughter's hand in marriage."

"I'm delighted to meet you," replied the Sultan. "May I present Jafar, my Royal Advisor. We both agree you've made a most impressive entrance." He nudged Jafar. "You might not have to marry Jasmine after all."

"No, no," cautioned Jafar, eyeing the Prince suspiciously. "I must advise against this. This man is not for the Princess."

"Oh, I'm sure I'll like her," insisted Aladdin, wondering where he'd seen Jafar before. "Just let me meet her. I'll win her over."

Unnoticed, Jasmine entered the throne room. "How dare you! All of you," she cried. "I'm not a prize to be won." Turning on her heels, she stormed out to the royal garden.

Day passed into night. Aladdin watched Jasmine as she stood on her balcony gazing at the stars. The Genie floated behind him. "What'll I do?" Aladdin asked.

"Just be yourself," advised the Genie. "Tell her the truth."

Aladdin frowned. "That's the worst thing I could do. She'd never marry a street rat like me." Clutching his turban in his hands, Aladdin called up to her: "Princess Jasmine, please give me another chance."

"Just leave me alone," she replied coldly. At that moment, the moon, emerging from behind a cloud, revealed his face. "Wait! Do I know you? You remind me of someone I met in the marketplace."

"Oh, no," said Aladdin. "I'm a prince. My servants go to the marketplace for me."

"Well," said Jasmine. "I'm not interested in marrying you. Now, please go."

Aladdin's shoulders slumped. "Before I leave," he added, "I want to tell you something." He stepped onto the Magic Carpet and floated up to the balcony. "I don't think you're a prize to be won. You should be free to make your own choice."

Jasmine blinked. "Your carpet . . . floats?"

"Want a ride?" asked Aladdin, holding out his hand.

Jasmine carefully stepped onto the Magic Carpet and knelt beside him. Together, they floated out across the sleeping city of Agrabah.

"This is really fun!" said Jasmine, looking over the edge of the carpet. "Too bad Abu's not here to enjoy it."

"Oh, he doesn't like flying much—" Aladdin began. He realized too late that he'd been tricked.

"I thought so!" exclaimed Jasmine. "You *are* the boy from the marketplace. Why did you lie to me?" And why, she wondered, had Jafar told her he was dead?

Aladdin gulped. "Well, it may sound strange, but I sometimes dress as a commoner to escape the pressures of palace life. I really *am* a prince."

Remembering her own little escapade in the marketplace, Jasmine smiled and took his hand. Aladdin smiled back. For the first time in my life, he thought, things are starting to go right.

When they returned to the palace, they hovered for a moment outside Jasmine's balcony and kissed in the moonlight.

Aladdin's good fortune would not last for long. As he was returning to his guest chamber, the royal guards grabbed him from behind and dragged him away. The last thing he heard was Jafar's voice: "Make sure he's never found."

The following morning Jasmine rushed into her father's throne room.

"Oh, Father, I had the most wonderful time last night," she said. "I'm so happy—"

The Sultan stared at her with glassy eyes. "I have chosen a husband for you," he mumbled. "You . . . will . . . wed . . . Jafar."

The Royal Advisor stepped out from behind a pillar and grinned.

"You? Never!" protested Jasmine. "I choose Prince Ali."

"Prince Ali has left, like all the rest," Jafar informed her.

A voice interrupted him. "Better check your crystal ball again, Jafar."

When he saw Aladdin appear in the doorway, Jafar staggered backward. "Prince Ali!"

"Tell them the truth, Jafar," said Aladdin, holding the lamp. "Last night, you tried to have me killed. If I hadn't wished for my Genie to save me—"

"You're lying!" Jafar hissed.

"Yes . . . you're . . . lying," echoed the Sultan.

"Father, what's wrong?" Jasmine cried. "You're acting so strange!"

Aladdin wrested the snake-head staff from Jafar's grip and smashed it on the marble floor. The Sultan rubbed his eyes, coming to his senses.

"You traitor, Jafar!" He called for the guards. Jafar made a lunge for the lamp, but Aladdin was too fast for him. As the guards rushed into the room, Jafar threw down an exploding smoke pellet and, in the confusion, escaped.

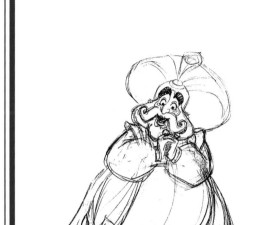

"Find him!" the Sultan ordered. He turned to Aladdin and beamed. "So, Prince Ali, my daughter has finally chosen! You will be wed at once. You will be happy and prosperous, and one day, my boy, you will become Sultan!"

Aladdin was stunned. Later, as he returned to his palace suite, the Genie floated up to him with open arms. "Congratulations, you've won Jasmine's heart. But don't forget your third wish—free the Genie!"

Aladdin looked a little guilty. "The only reason anyone thinks I'm worth anything is because of you. What if they find out I'm not a prince? Sorry, Genie, but I can't free you."

"I understand," replied the Genie. "You lied to everybody else—why not me?" Downcast, he disappeared back into the lamp.

"Go ahead and be like that," Aladdin grumbled, tossing the lamp on a cushion. He stopped himself. "What am I doing? Genie's right. I've got to tell Jasmine the truth."

At that moment, Aladdin heard Jasmine call from the garden. "Prince Ali, come quickly!" Aladdin hurried outside—but she wasn't there.

In the evening, a huge throng gathered in the palace courtyard to celebrate Jasmine's birthday and await the announcement of her engagement. The Sultan, with Jasmine at his side, stood proudly before them.

"People of Agrabah," he announced, "the day has come at last. Princess Jasmine will be wed—to Prince Ali Ababwa." With a flourish, he pulled back a curtain and gestured to Aladdin to step forward.

"Jasmine, listen," Aladdin whispered, smiling weakly. "There's something I've got to tell you about myself—"

Before he could finish, a fierce wind sprang up. Billowing clouds formed and swirled down from the sky. Before everyone's astonished eyes, the Genie appeared, grown to an immense size. He ripped the palace from its foundation and set it down hard on a nearby mountaintop.

"What's going on?" sputtered the Sultan, trying to regain his balance. "And Jafar, what are you doing here? And how dare you wear my turban!"

"I'm Sultan now," Jafar proclaimed, holding up the lamp. "You see, Aladdin, you were careless to leave this lying about. Like all parrots, my clever Iago imitates voices. It was he, not Jasmine, who called you to the royal garden. While you were looking for her, Iago stole the lamp for me!"

Jafar briskly rubbed it with his sleeve. The Genie appeared instantly and smiled sadly at Aladdin. "Sorry, kid. I have a new master now."

"Genie," Jafar ordered, "for my second wish, I wish to be the most powerful sorcerer in the world! And with my new power, I'll reveal Prince Ali for what he really is."

The Genie sighed and snapped his fingers. Jafar laughed wickedly and waved his staff at Aladdin. In a flash, he was once more a peasant in rags. He looked imploringly at Jasmine. "I tried to tell you. . . ."

"And now," Jafar roared at Aladdin, "I banish you to the ends of the earth!"

Knocked off his feet, Aladdin was whirled up into a high palace tower. With an enormous blast, the tower rocketed into the sky and disappeared.

As the days passed, Jasmine and her father, both bound in chains, watched in disgust as Jafar whiled away his time polishing the crown jewels.

"What do you say, my dear Jasmine," Jafar would ask her, "with you as my queen, we could—"

"Never!" Jasmine replied each time.

Then, late one afternoon, an unexpected visitor slipped through an open window. Quietly, he crept up behind Jafar, but Jafar heard him and spun around. Aladdin stood smiling at him.

"You!" Jafar roared. "How many times do I have to kill you!"

Aladdin raised his dagger. "Come and fight me yourself, you cowardly snake." He winked at Jasmine.

"Cowardly snake, am I?" hissed Jafar. Furious, he conjured up his newly granted powers and changed himself into an enormous snake. As he squeezed his coils tight around Aladdin, the Genie looked on, helpless.

"The Genie has more power than you'll ever have," Aladdin grunted.

"What are you saying?" asked the Genie. "Why are you bringing me into this?"

Aladdin continued. "The Genie gave you your power—he could take it away. Face it, Jafar, you're still second best!"

"Yes . . . you're right. His power does exceed my own. . . ." Jafar stopped to think. "But not for long!"

He uncoiled himself from Aladdin and transformed back into a man. Rubbing the lamp, he made his third and final wish: "I wish to be an all-powerful Genie!"

Jafar cried out in triumph as he rose from his lamp. "I'm a Genie! I have absolute power! I can control the universe!"

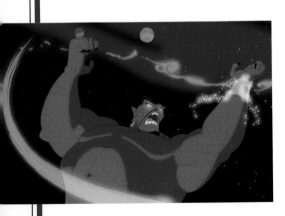

Aladdin grabbed Jafar's lamp. "You wanted to be a Genie," he told him. "Now you must put up with everything that goes with it! Unless someone summons you, you must stay inside your lamp."

Jafar, realizing his fate, let out a terrible scream. "NOOO!" In a swirl of black smoke, he was sucked down into the darkness of the lamp.

"You've still got one wish left, Master," the Genie said, patting Aladdin on the back. "Just say the word and you're a prince again."

Aladdin put his arm around Jasmine. "I love you," he said, "but I have to stop pretending to be something I'm not."

"I understand," said Jasmine, trying not to cry. "I just wish we didn't have such a stupid law."

Aladdin turned to the Genie. "I wish for your freedom."

The Genie was stunned. "Really? I'm free?" He flew out from his lamp and somersaulted about the room. "I'm FREE!" He hugged and kissed Aladdin. "You'll always be a prince to me!"

The Sultan spoke up. "And to me, too! You've certainly proven your worth as far as I'm concerned. As Sultan, I will change the law—Jasmine shall marry whomever she pleases!"

Jasmine threw her arms around Aladdin and kissed him. "Tell me something," she asked, "how did you ever get back from the ends of the earth?"

Aladdin grinned. "Jafar forgot the Magic Carpet was up in the tower. Want a ride?"

Jasmine laughed and stepped onto the Magic Carpet. Holding hands, they floated through the starry sky back to the enchanting city of Agrabah.

ALADDIN
Behind the Scenes

Disney's 1992 release *Aladdin* broke away from the fairy-tale, heightened realism of the Oscar-nominated *Beauty and the Beast* to define a fresh and winning new style. The wacky improvisations of Robin Williams as both the voice of the Genie and as the narrator who opens the movie helped give the animators license to make *Aladdin* an all-out comedic turn, pushing the boundaries of visual and verbal humor as far as possible. For the narrator's scene at the beginning of the movie, the filmmakers put together a box full of odds and ends, covered it, and brought Robin Williams and the box into a recording studio. The resulting hilarious stream of ideas was translated into visual madness by the animators. "I've always loved animation that has a sense of enjoying itself on-screen," says Eric Goldberg, supervising animator of the Genie. This character provided a perfect opportunity for "animation that looked like the characters were having a good time."

Directed by Ron Clements and John Musker, *Aladdin* not only stretched the boundaries of the Disney animated film with the humorous tone of its story-telling, it conquered new ground in terms of artistic style. One of the first artists to work on the film was production designer R. S. Vander Wende, who brought to the project very clear ideas about the look and style of the environment he wished to create. Recalls background artist Natalie Franscioni-Karp, "Our mission was to take something unreal and give it reality—to make a fantasy environment that looked believable." Goldberg, who was the first animator to work on the film, and whose background in commercials gave him a keen eye for distinct graphic styles, recalls that Vander Wende's original concepts for the environments inspired him to take an equally stylized approach to the characters. Goldberg created a Genie "simplified and curvy, with not a lot of anatomy—a character that seemed to belong to the 'Hollywood Arabian' world Vander Wende was envisioning."

Aladdin set a standard for a unified approach to the filmmaking that has been a part of the creative process on Disney animated features ever since. Explains Goldberg, "It was the first time in this generation that the Studio had got together all the lead animators, the art director, and the directors and designed the character and backgrounds to exist in the same universe." The integrated design process permitted the artists to create a world in which the backgrounds make as strong a statement about the personality of a character as the animation itself. Jasmine's room resembles a birdcage, reflecting her trapped situation. The egg motif in the columns, throne, and oil lamps in the Sultan's throne room mirror his rounded shape and soft-boiled character. When Jafar takes over as Sultan, the shapes in the throne room are reorganized to echo the far more angular silhouette of the elegant and sinister villain.

As a natural jumping-off point, the artists drew on the art and culture they were representing for visual inspiration. In early 1991, layout supervisor Rasoul Azadani returned to his hometown of Esfahān in Iran to photograph buildings and interiors from the Islamic world of the fifteenth century. The artists drew for style and color ideas on Arabian calligraphy and on Persian miniature paintings from about A.D. 1000 to 1500 Background supervisor Kathy Altieri notes, "We used the colors that appear in those miniatures—very specific shades of red, blue, green, and antiqued gold—punched up to a high degree of saturation and brightness."

A color key for the magic carpet ride suggests the influence of Persian miniature paintings.

THE LION KING

The starry African night had passed. As the morning mist rose
with the sun, eager birds, flying from every nest, filled the
sky with the sound of wings. Below, the ground trembled
as thousands of elephants, hippos, antelopes, and giraffes hurried
across the land. By the time creatures of every size and sort arrived
at the foot of Pride Rock, the sun shone hot on their backs.

A hornbill named Zazu flew down from his perch and circled
above the patient, waiting animals. He reported back to the king.
"All is ready, Sire," he said. King Mufasa nodded. The ceremony
would begin.

Rafiki, the wise old baboon, made his way forward through the
crowd. Leaning on his walking stick, he hobbled to the top of the
rock. There, King Mufasa and Queen Sarabi proudly presented their
newborn son to him. Rafiki smiled at little Simba. He cracked open
a ripe gourd and smeared its fragrant juices over Simba's brow.
Then he sprinkled a handful of earth over the tiny cub. Taking
Simba in his arms, he stood on the pinnacle of Pride Rock and held
him high for all to see. At once, the animals fell to their knees to
honor their new prince.

One member of the royal family wasn't there. The king's
brother, Scar, stayed away and sulked. "I was first in line for the
throne until that little hair ball was born," he muttered to himself.
"Now Simba's to be the next lion king." He smiled thinly. "But not
if I can help it!"

The months passed quickly for Simba, and just about every day he learned something new. Early one morning when the mist was still rising, Mufasa took Simba for a walk around the plain. As they strolled, the sun broke through the haze.

"Look, Simba." Mufasa said. "Everything the light touches is our kingdom—the Pride Lands." Simba looked wide-eyed across the brightening plain. "A king's time as ruler rises and falls like the sun," his father continued. "One day, Simba, the sun will set on my time and will rise with you as the new king."

Simba stood quietly and watched a line of zebras approach the water hole. Several tiny gazelles, already drinking, raised their heads as a flock of chattering birds landed and hungrily poked about the reeds for insects.

"Everything you see," said Mufasa, "lives together in a delicate balance. As king you must respect this."

"Dad," Simba interrupted, "don't we eat animals?"

"Yes, we do, Simba," Mufasa answered, "but let me explain. When we die, our bodies nourish the grass. Many other animals eat grass to stay alive. And so, in a way, we are feeding them. You see, we're all connected in the great Circle of Life."

As Simba thought about all his father had told him, he noticed a distant shadowy place, untouched by the sun's warm rays. "That land is beyond our domain," Mufasa warned him. "You must never go there."

At that moment, Zazu flew in with the morning report. "Well, the buzz from the bees," he began, "is that the leopards are in a bit of a spot, and the baboons are going ape—"

An anxious mole suddenly popped up from a hole in the ground. "Sire," the mole said in a raspy voice, "bad news from the underground. Hyenas are in the Pride Lands!"

"Zazu, take Simba home," Mufasa ordered and bounded off.

"I never get to go anywhere," Simba complained.

"Oh, young master," Zazu replied, "when you are king, you can chase those mangy scavengers from dawn till dusk."

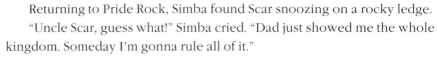

Returning to Pride Rock, Simba found Scar snoozing on a rocky ledge. "Uncle Scar, guess what!" Simba cried. "Dad just showed me the whole kingdom. Someday I'm gonna rule all of it."

"Forgive me if I don't leap for joy," Scar grumbled. After a moment, his eyes popped open. "Did he show you . . . everything?"

Simba scuffed his paw in the dust. "Well, no," he answered. "Not that place to the north. Dad says I can't go there. What's out there, anyway?"

Scar shook his head. "Sorry, Simba, I just can't tell you. Besides, an elephant graveyard is—"

Simba brightened up. "An elephant what?"

"Whoops! I've said too much. Just do me one favor." Scar grinned at his nephew. "Promise me you'll never visit that dreadful place. Only the bravest lions go there."

"Sure, Uncle Scar," Simba replied. "See ya—gotta go now."

"Remember," Scar whispered, "it's our little secret."

Simba dashed off to find his best friend, Nala. "Wait'll she hears about this!" he said to himself.

He found Nala with the rest of the pride behind the Rock. "Hi, Nala," he said. "Want to come out and play?"

"Not until my daughter is finished with her bath," Sarafina told him.

"What do you want to do?" Nala asked. "Wrestle, climb trees?"

Simba paused a second. "Uh . . . just go to the water hole."

Sarafina looked at Simba's mother. "What do you think, Sarabi?"

"It's all right with me," Sarabi answered, "as long as Zazu goes with them."

Simba frowned. "Oh, all right," he agreed. "Come on, Nala, let's go."

Simba and Nala raced across the plain with Zazu flapping madly to keep up. They headed toward a patch of tall grasses. "Run in there," Simba said, panting. "We have to ditch the dodo." They plunged into the thicket and hid. Giggling, they peeked up at Zazu as he circled in confusion. Finally, he flew off to look elsewhere.

Nala grinned at Simba. "Where're we really going?"

"Follow me!" he yelled. Nala charged after him, leaped on his back, and flipped him over.

"Pinned ya!" she said. "Now—where're we *going*?"

Simba laughed and scrambled to his feet. "To an elephant graveyard! And we'd better hurry before Zazu shows up!"

Simba led Nala toward the far border. "It's getting foggy," said Nala, peering through the gloom. "I can hardly see."

WHOOOOSH! A geyser of steam erupted inches away, spinning them both off their feet. "Nala! This is it!" hooted Simba. "The elephant graveyard!"

A field of huge gray bones lay strewn before them. "This is really creepy," Nala breathed. "Look at that giant skull! I wonder if its brains are still in there."

"There's only one way to find out," Simba answered. He started to climb into the eye socket.

"There you are!" squawked Zazu, fluttering down through the mist and shaking off his damp feathers. "We're way beyond the Pride Lands. And right now we're all in very real danger. We must leave before it's too late."

"It's already too late," chuckled a voice, followed by whoops of laughter. Shenzi, a foul-smelling creature, stepped from the shadows accompanied by her two comrades, Banzai and Ed.

Zazu fluttered backward. "Hyenas!" he gasped to the cubs. "Run!"

Shenzi cut them off. "Well, well, well. What have we got here? A trio of trespassers?" The hyenas all giggled.

"Quite b-b-by accident," stuttered Zazu. "A simple navigational error, I assure you."

Shenzi sniffed around Zazu. "I know this one," she said. "You're Mufasa's little stooge."

Banzai circled Simba. "And that would make you . . ."

"The future king!" Simba announced, standing as tall as he could. "So, you'd better watch out!"

The hyenas fell to the ground, laughing hysterically and kicking their feet in the air. Simba and Nala made a break for it.

"Not so fast!" Shenzi snickered, grabbing Simba. "Didn't you know it's dinnertime?" She gave him a good pinch. "And you'd make the perfect cub sandwich."

"*r-r-r . . .*" Simba tried to roar.

"Was that a roar?" Banzai inquired. "Or a squeak?"

"*ROARRRRR!!*"

The hyenas whipped around to find Mufasa glaring down at them. "Your Majesty," Shenzi sputtered. "We were just—"

With a sweep of his paw, Mufasa swatted Shenzi and sent her flying. "Silence!" he commanded. "If you ever come near my son again . . ."

Giggling, the trio slunk off into the fog.

Zazu took Nala home, leaving Mufasa alone with Simba. "You could have been killed," he said to his son. "You deliberately disobeyed me. And what's worse, you put Nala in danger."

"I'm sorry, Dad," Simba sobbed.

Mufasa's voice shook. "I was afraid I'd lost you."

Simba looked up in surprise. "Dad, I didn't think kings were ever afraid."

"Even kings get scared," Mufasa replied. "Like everybody else." He gave his son a playful cuff.

"Say, Dad? We'll always be pals, right?"

Mufasa paused and looked up at the twinkling stars. "Simba, let me tell you something my father told me. The great kings of the past look down on us from those stars."

"Really?" Simba asked, staring up at the boundless night sky.

Mufasa nodded. "Remember, whenever you feel alone, those kings will always be there to guide you. And so will I."

Simba rubbed his head against his father's side. "I'll remember," he promised.

Meanwhile, in a musty cave not far away, Shenzi, Ed, and Banzai stood cowering before Scar. "I'm disgusted with you three," Scar snarled. "I practically gift wrapped those cubs for you—and you let them get away!"

"Well, ya know, boss," Shenzi told him, "it wasn't like they were exactly alone."

"Yeah," Banzai agreed. "What were we supposed to do? Kill Mufasa?"

Scar grinned. "Precisely."

"Hey, great idea—no king!" the hyenas yipped.

"*I* will be king, you giggling fools!" Scar snapped. "Stick with me and you'll never go hungry again."

The next day, Scar led Simba down to the bottom of a deep gorge. "Wait here on this rock," he said. "Your father has a marvelous surprise for you."

Simba hopped onto the rock and eagerly looked around.

"Now, don't run off," instructed Scar. "You don't want to end up in a mess like you did with the hyenas, do you?"

Simba gulped. "You know about that?"

"Simba, my boy," he replied, "everybody knows about that." He loped away and left his nephew all alone.

Standing at the top of the gorge, Scar narrowed his eyes and observed the massive herd of wildebeests browsing along the rim. In the distance, he spied Mufasa with Zazu, making their usual morning rounds. "Excellent," he murmured to himself. "Everything is working out perfectly." Anxiously, Scar scanned the bluff for the hyenas. They were ready and waiting.

"There's the signal!" yelled Shenzi. "Let's go!" Whooping crazily, the hyenas dashed among the peaceful wildebeests. Confused and frightened, the herd stampeded down into the gorge.

Simba jumped from the rock and ran for his life. He was about to be trampled when he scrambled up a dead tree. He clung to a limb as the wildebeests thundered past.

Scar dashed up to Mufasa. "Brother!" he shouted. "There's a stampede! Simba's down there!"

Mufasa lunged down into the gorge. Zazu flew ahead, frantically searching for Simba. "He's over there, Your Majesty!" he cried. Mufasa hurled himself into the frantic herd and snatched Simba from the limb. Thrashing his way to the side of the gorge, he spotted an overhanging ledge and tossed his son to safety. A charging beast knocked Mufasa back down, and he was swept away in the flow. Gravely wounded, Mufasa made a valiant leap and clung to a steep incline. He clawed his way up toward a ledge, where he found Scar peering down at him.

"Brother," gasped Mufasa, hanging onto the jagged rock. "Please . . . help me."

Scar looked deep into Mufasa's eyes. "Long live the King," he hissed and pushed Mufasa backward into the gorge.

Simba clambered up onto a ledge, just in time to see his father vanish into the stampede. Choking back tears, Simba searched the dust-filled gorge. Then he felt his heart drop. Mufasa's broken body was lying on the ground.

"NOOO!" Simba screamed. When he rushed to his father's side, he realized he was dead. Sobbing, he buried his face in Mufasa's tangled mane.

Scar ambled over to him. "Now see what you've done," he said.

Tears streamed down Simba's face. "It was an accident," he wailed. "There were wildebeests . . . and Dad tried to save me. I didn't mean for it to happen."

"Of course you didn't mean it," replied Scar. "No one ever means for these things to happen. But the king is dead, and if it weren't for you, he'd still be alive. Oh, what will your mother think?"

"What'll I do?" asked Simba.

"Run away," Scar answered. "Run away and never return."

Simba looked out across the shimmering plain toward the desert. He nodded. With his head cast down, he turned his back on Pride Rock and trudged away.

The hyenas sidled up to Scar. "We did it, boss," Shenzi bragged.

Scar shook his head. "The job's only half done." He gestured toward the tiny cub disappearing over a rise. "Finish it!"

Yipping, the hyenas chased after Simba, and Scar returned to Pride Rock. Looking sorrowful, he delivered the sad news to the pride.

"Mufasa's death is a terrible tragedy," he lamented. "But to lose Simba as well is, for me, a deep personal loss."

The other lionesses nuzzled Sarabi in sympathy.

"So it is with a heavy heart," Scar announced, "that I assume the throne. . . ."

The hyenas squatted on the rise, watching Simba make his way into the desert.

Shenzi shook her head. "There ain't no way I'm going out there."

"Yeah, I hate it when the sun burns you to a crisp," Banzai said. "But we gotta finish the job."

"He'll never make it," Shenzi replied. "He's as good as dead."

The hot afternoon sun bore down on Simba. Buzzards circled overhead, waiting. But he didn't care. He collapsed on the sandy ground and passed out cold. The buzzards flocked to the ground and prodded him.

"YEEEEE-HAAAAAAAA!" Out of nowhere, a meerkat astride a warthog came galloping in and scattered the buzzards in all directions.

"Aw, Timon," said the warthog. "Look, it's just a little lion. He's so cute and all alone. Let's keep him."

"Pumbaa, old buddy, are you nuts?" cried the meerkat. "Lions eat guys like us!"

Pumbaa thought it over. "But maybe he'll be on our side."

"That's the stupidest thing I ever heard," Timon said. "But, hey! I've got it! Maybe he'll be on our side."

"So, we're keeping him?"

"Of course! Who's the brains in this outfit anyway?"

Pumbaa gently picked up Simba with his tusks and carried him to their shady forest home. Soon, Simba opened his eyes.

"You okay, kid?" Timon asked. "You were that close to being dessert for some buzzards."

"Who cares?" Simba responded.

Pumbaa was curious. "So, where're ya from?"

"It doesn't matter. I can't go back—I did something terrible."

"Look," Timon told him, "when the world turns its back on you, you turn your back on the world, right?"

Simba shook his head. "That's not what I was taught."

"Then maybe you need a new lesson," said Timon. "Repeat after me: *Hakuna matata*. It's the rule we follow. It means no worries, no responsibilities."

"Hakuna matata," repeated Simba, liking the sound of it. Simba decided to stay with his new friends. "Maybe they're right," he said to himself. "I gotta put my past behind me. No more worries!"

Days became weeks and weeks became months. Years slipped by and Simba grew from a cub into a lion. The brown spots on his coat faded and a bushy golden mane covered his head and shoulders.

One night Simba, Timon, and Pumbaa were lying on the grass, gazing up at the twinkling sky.

"Ever wonder," said Pumbaa to his friends, "what those sparkly dots are?"

"Someone once told me the great kings of the past are up there—watching over us," replied Simba.

"Ya mean a bunch of royal dead guys are watching us?" Timon scoffed. "Who told you that?"

Simba wandered away to be alone. He wondered what would his father think of him now. He flopped down on the ground and sighed. His breath carried a wispy puff of milkweed into the treetops. A fresh breeze picked it up and blew the milkweed all the way across the desert to the Pride Lands, and into the waiting, outstretched hand of Rafiki.

Pulling the milkweed apart, the old baboon examined the seeds. His eyes filled with tears of joy. "Simba," he murmured, "you're alive!" He nodded slowly to himself and began to prepare for his journey.

The next day, Simba was strolling about looking for something to eat when he heard Timon cry out: "Help! She's going to eat us!"

Simba tore through the underbrush and saw Pumbaa hiding in an old log. Nearby, a lioness, crouching in the grass, was about to spring at Timon. Simba leaped out and tackled her. As they wrestled, the lioness flipped him on his back and pinned him with her paw. Simba looked up at her in surprise. "Nala?"

The lioness peered down at him. "Simba?"

Timon watched in shock as the two lions roared in delight and hugged each other. "Hey, what's goin' on here?" he yelled. Simba introduced Nala to his friends.

But Nala couldn't keep her eyes off Simba. "I can't believe you're alive. Why did Scar tell us you were dead?"

Simba shrugged. "It doesn't matter," he answered.

"Of course, it matters," she insisted. "You're alive! And that means you're the king!"

Pumbaa dropped to his knees and stretched out flat. "Your Majesty," he said. "I gravel at your feet."

Timon yanked him up. "It's not *gravel*," he corrected him. "It's *grovel*—and don't! He's not the king."

Simba made a face. "Well, actually, she's right."

Timon's mouth dropped open.

Nala smiled at him. "Could you and Pumbaa excuse us for a little while?" she asked. "I'd like to talk to Simba."

"Sure," Timon responded in a huff. "Come on, Pumbaa. Let's give them a little privacy." He muttered as they walked away. "This is one big surprise— you think you know a guy . . ."

Nala's eyes welled up with tears. "I really missed you, Simba. It's like you're back from the dead. You don't know how much this will mean to everyone."

Simba nuzzled her. "I missed you, too."

"Then you'll come home?" she asked, smiling.

Simba looked away. "I can't. I live by new rules now. Hakuna matata— no worries, no cares."

"Listen to me," pleaded Nala. "You have to come back to the Pride Lands. Scar's in power now. He's let the hyenas take over and everything's destroyed. There's no food, no water—Simba, it's your responsibility. Your father would want you to come home."

Simba blinked back his tears. "My father's dead," he told her. To himself he added, "and it's all my fault."

That night Simba couldn't sleep. He wandered down and stretched out beside a weedy stream. "Nala's wrong," he thought. "I can't go back. It wouldn't change anything." He looked up at the stars. "You said you'd always be there for me—but you're not." Gradually, he became aware of a faint sound—the sound of someone singing a little tune:

"*Asante sana, squash banana, we we nugu, mi mi apana.*"

PLOP! A stone dropped into the water, almost hitting him on the head. Startled and annoyed, Simba looked up to find an old baboon squatting by the side of the stream.

"Who are you?" asked Simba.

Rafiki looked him in the eye. "The question is," he asked in return, "who are *you*?"

Simba blew out his breath. "I thought I knew, but now I'm not so sure."

"Well, I know who you are," Rafiki said, hopping to his feet. "You're Mufasa's boy." He scampered into the underbrush.

"Wait!" Simba called out, charging after him. "You knew my father?"

Rafiki paused. "I *know* your father," he said.

Simba felt sorry he had to tell the old baboon the sad truth. "I hate to tell you this," he said, "but my father died a long time ago."

"Wrong!" Rafiki corrected him. "Your father's alive. Follow me."

Simba thought his heart would burst with joy. He dashed after Rafiki, following him through the underbrush toward a deep pool.

Rafiki pushed some tall reeds aside. "Look down there," he whispered.

Simba gazed into the starlit water. But all he saw was his own reflection staring back at him. "It's not my father," he said, disappointed. "It's just me."

"Look harder," Rafiki urged him and touched the surface with his finger.

Simba peered into the water again. His reflection began to shimmer. Suddenly, he was staring into his father's eyes.

"You see?" said Rafiki. "He lives in you."

"*Simba.*"

Simba leaped to his feet. It was his father's voice coming from somewhere above. "Father, where are you?" he called, looking up at the night sky. The shadowy clouds parted, and Mufasa's image emerged among the stars.

"*You have forgotten who you are,*" said Mufasa. "*And so, you have forgotten me.*"

"Oh, no, Father," Simba cried out. He felt a sob rising in his throat. "I'd never forget you."

Mufasa continued in a softer voice. "*Look inside yourself, my son. You are more than what you have become. You must take your place in the Circle of Life.*" His voice faded away. "*Remember who you are. You are my son and the one true king. Remember who you are.*"

"Please don't leave me, Father," Simba pleaded. But Mufasa had vanished.

"Most peculiar weather, eh?" remarked Rafiki.

"I know what I should do," replied Simba, "but going back means facing my past. And I've been running away from it so long."

Without any warning, Rafiki whacked him hard on the back with his walking stick.

"Ow!" exclaimed Simba. "What's that for?"

"It doesn't matter now," Rafiki replied with a twinkle in his eye. "It's in the past."

Simba stretched his stinging back. "Even so," he said, "it still hurts."

Rafiki scratched his head, pretending to think. "Yes," he agreed, "the past can hurt. But the way I see it, you can run from it or you can learn from it." He waved his walking stick over Simba's head. Simba ducked. "You see? So what are you going to do?"

"First, I'm going to take your stick!" Simba kidded. "And then I'm going back home!"

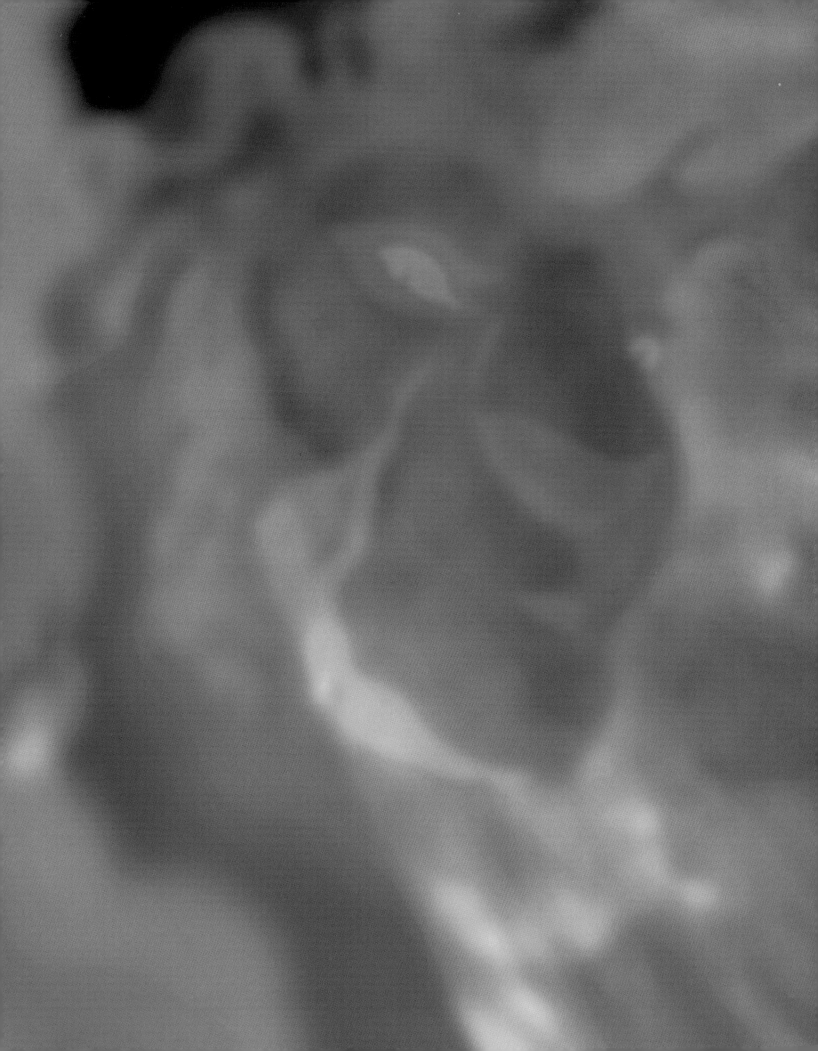

In the forest, Pumbaa and Timon were snoring loudly when Nala shook them awake. "Where's Simba?" she asked. "I've looked everywhere."

Timon rubbed his eyes. "We thought he was with you."

Just then Rafiki swung down from a tree limb. "You won't find him here," he chuckled. "The king has returned."

Simba didn't stop running until he saw Pride Rock against the pale morning sky. But it was nothing like the home he remembered. No animals were left, the earth lay parched, and the only signs of past life were wildebeest bones, lying near the dry water hole.

For a long time he gazed at the ruined kingdom. Nala appeared and quietly stood at his side. "It's awful, isn't it," she said. "What made you come?"

Simba choked back his tears. "I finally got some sense knocked into me. And I've got the lump on my back to prove it."

"We're gonna fight your uncle for this?" asked a familiar voice.

"Timon?" asked Simba, turning around. Pumbaa trotted up with Timon on his back. "What are you guys doing here?"

Timon squared his shoulders. "Well, Simba," he said, "if this is important to you, we're with you to the end."

Simba smiled at his friends. "Thanks, fellas, I can use all the help I can get!"

In the distance they could hear the hyenas whooping with laughter.

"Pumbaa, Timon," Simba ordered calmly, "you'll have to divert the hyenas. Nala, you find my mother and rally the lionesses. I'll look for Scar."

Scar waited impatiently for Sarabi outside his cave on Pride Rock. A storm was brewing, and as he paced back and forth, his mane blew in the hot wind.

"You called?" Sarabi asked.

"Where's your hunting party?" he demanded. "The hyenas need food."

"It's over, Scar," she told him. "There is no food. The herds have moved on. Our only choice is to leave the Pride Lands."

"We're not going anywhere," Scar snarled.

Sarabi was stunned. "Then you are sentencing us to death," she said. Scar looked away but Sarabi stood firm. "If you were half the king Mufasa was, you would never—"

Scar whirled around and swatted her hard. "I AM TEN TIMES THE KING MUFASA WAS!" he roared. Out on the plain, lightning flashed and thunder shook the air. Quietly, the figure of a lion stepped out of the shadows.

"M-M-Mufasa?" stammered Scar. "It can't be. You're dead!"

Sarabi raised her head. "Mufasa?" she asked groggily.

Simba went to her side and nuzzled her. "No, Mother, it's me."

"Simba?" Scar said, nervously. "I'm a little surprised to see you . . . alive."

"Give me one good reason why I shouldn't rip you apart," Simba demanded.

"Y-You know," began Scar, "the pressures of ruling a kingdom—"

Simba cut him short. "—are no longer yours," he finished. "I'm back to take my place as king. Step down or fight!"

Scar was growing panicky. Out of the corner of his eye, he saw Nala and the lionesses assembling, ready to defend Simba. Lurking behind them, the hyenas silently gathered.

"I'd hate to be responsible for the death of a family member, wouldn't you agree?" Scar asked, raising his voice for all to hear. "Go on, Simba. Tell everyone who's responsible for your father's death!"

Simba bowed his head, ashamed. "I am," he answered. Sarabi gasped. Simba sadly turned to her. "It's true, Mother," he said, "but it was an accident."

"Murderer!" roared Scar.

"No!" protested Simba, backing out of the cave. He stumbled over the ledge. Barely able to hang on to the jagged rock, he desperately looked up at Scar.

"This looks familiar," Scar said in Simba's ear. "You look just the way your father did—*before I killed him*."

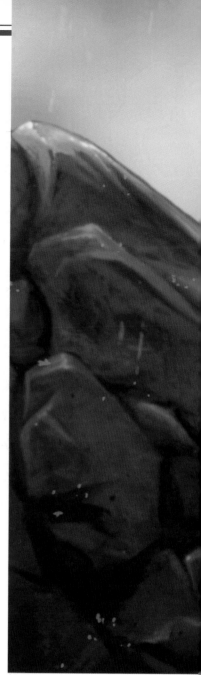

The words filled Simba with rage, and a new strength surged through his body. Letting out a deafening roar, he sprang at Scar and gripped him by the throat. "Tell them what you just said!" he commanded. "Tell them!"

Scar could hardly breathe. "I did it," he wheezed.

"Louder!" ordered Simba. "So everyone can hear you."

"I KILLED MUFASA!" Scar yelled.

Furiously, the lionesses attacked him. Nala sprang to Simba's side, and a fearsome fight followed as the howling hyenas descended from all sides to defend their leader.

Like a huge wailing animal, the wind moaned around Pride Rock. A lightning bolt flashed, setting the dead grasses ablaze. In seconds, the air was blanketed in thick black smoke. Fleeing the flames, Scar dashed on to a ledge. Simba was right at his heels.

"Nephew, I am family!" Scar begged. He didn't notice Shenzi, Banzai, and Ed creeping up behind Simba. "It was the hyenas' fault. They're the real enemy. Please, I'll do anything." When they heard this, the hyenas slunk back off the ledge.

Simba thought for a moment. "Run away, Scar," he said. "Run away and never return."

"Yes, of course, Your Majesty," replied Scar. He started to turn away, but all of a sudden, he spun around and kicked red-hot embers into Simba's face. Simba staggered, and Scar flung himself upon him. They fought on the charred ground. In the struggle, Scar fell backward off the ledge, hitting the ground below. The betrayed hyenas closed in on him.

Simba stood in the refreshing rain. Its cool water would soon bring life back to the land. Sarabi and Nala rushed forward to greet him. Then they

stepped back and let him pass. Slowly, Simba climbed to the top of Pride
Rock. He gazed up at the sky and heard his father's voice. *"Remember. . . ."*

Simba threw back his head and let out a triumphant roar.

Years later, all the animals gathered, once again, at Pride
Rock. As they waited on the soft grassy plain, Zazu flew
down and circled the crowd.

"Sire," he reported back to the king, "everyone is here."

While Timon and Pumbaa watched proudly, King
Simba and Queen Nala presented their new son to Rafiki.
Gently, the old baboon took the cub in his arms and held
him high. All across the Pride Lands, the animals bowed
low to welcome their future Lion King.

THE LION KING
Behind the Scenes

In the beginning of *The Lion King*'s journey from idea to finished film, back when it was known as *King of the Jungle*, the only certainties were that it would be a story about growing from childhood to adulthood; that it would feature animals, probably lions; and that it would be set in Africa. The making of *The Lion King* was a journey of discovery; it was a film that revealed itself to its creators as their ideas unfolded. "We weren't basing the movie on a fairy tale or an existing story," explains director Roger Allers, who, along with director Rob Minkoff and producer Don Hahn, led the creative team on Disney's 1994 summer blockbuster. "We developed the story visually and verbally at the same time. Ideas flowed back and forth among the writers and the story people in a great creative swirl."

The development of the opening song, "The Circle of Life," was, for many members of *The Lion King*'s creative team, one of the things that helped define what the movie would ultimately become. "Music is a great way to tell a story when words don't quite reach you," says Hans Zimmer, composer of the award-winning score. Elton John and Tim Rice developed the memorable tune and simple lyrics for "The Circle of Life." The piece then passed to Zimmer who, with African-born musician Lebo M, reinterpreted the original song, adding African rhythms and Zulu chants. As producer Hahn recalls: "We went over to Hans's studio to listen to his arrangement for 'The Circle of Life.' It was just thrilling. We said we needed some sort of cry in the wilderness at the beginning because the sun is rising and all the animals are going to see the newborn king. We needed some sort of call to worship. And Lebo M said, 'Oh, I think I can do something.' The first thing that came out of his mouth is the piece that ended up in the film. It was just so great, we never changed it."

Art director Andy Gaskill calls Africa "the unspoken character in this film," and the artists worked to evoke the same depth in visual storytelling as the song-writing team had revealed through music. The artists created subtle atmospheric conditions—leaves rustling in the trees, lions' manes blowing, and moving clouds that cast shadows on the ground. The background artists painted loosely, drawing on their knowledge of African terrain. The result was an organic environment, with no architectural details to speak of, and a majority of scenes with a realistic color scheme. Dramatic weather conditions such as wind and lightning helped the film come alive, and the drama unfolded against a symbolic cycle of seasons and weather, as drought and fires gave way to rain and rejuvenation.

The Lion King was for many of the animators the first opportunity to draw four-legged creatures realistically since *Oliver & Company* in 1988. Wildlife expert Jim Fowler from *Wild Kingdom* visited the Studio on several occasions with lions and other creatures native to Africa to discuss behavior and give the animators some firsthand knowledge of their subjects. Anatomy consultant Stuart Sumida gave lectures on comparative anatomy, skeletal structure, and action analysis. Artist Jean Gillmore made dozens of sketches of animals for the animators to draw from. Ruben Aquino, who animated the adult Simba, was the first artist assigned to *The Lion King*, and his earliest assignment was to research forms of animal locomotion. "Animating four-legged creatures from certain angles can be very difficult," says Aquino. "The more we understood the anatomy of these creatures, the easier it was to animate them."

The challenge to the animators was not merely to animate realistically but to create personalities within the confines of believable animal behavior. "With *The Lion King*, we had less to work with than on other films. There are no props, no hands—it's a pretty sparse environment," says producer Don Hahn. "The artists had to be inventive at every turn." The animators learned to concentrate on overall body attitude, using angles of the head and subtle facial expressions. For example, the raising of an eyebrow might be their sole means to express a particular emotion.

The animators worked with the voice actors to create a cast of distinct and winning personalities. The range of acting styles runs the gamut from the subtle Shakespearean shadings of Jeremy Irons as Scar to the sonorous tones of James Earl Jones as Mufasa. And from the wildly comedic talents of Whoopi Goldberg and Cheech Marin as two malevolent hyenas and Ernie Sabella and Nathan Lane as Pumbaa and Timon to the sincerity of Matthew Broderick as the adult Simba. That same range is reflected in the style of different parts of the film. "We were going from crazy, comic shtick to big, stirring drama. We took a lot of care with transitions to help the audience move in and out of these sequences," says Roger Allers. With the emotional content of the film ranging from the death of a parent to a flatulent warthog, the filmmakers took their cue from the message of their opening number: there's a place in the world for all these different expressions of life.

POCAHONTAS

One foggy morn in 1607 the harbor dock in old London town was
crowded with families and friends bidding farewell to the good
ship *Susan Constant* and its crew of adventurers—all set to sail far
across the ocean to the New World.

One young fortune-seeker, named Thomas, kissed his worried-looking
mother. "I'll be fine, Mum," he assured her. He stepped back to let a tall, fair-
haired man, armed with a musket and shiny sword, pass by.

"That's Captain John Smith," pointed out Thomas. "I'll be safe with him
along. They say you can't fight Indians without John Smith!"

A carriage, drawn by four prancing horses, pulled up and Governor
Ratcliffe, the leader of the expedition, climbed out. He wore a thin black
mustache, a plumed hat, and two pigtails, neatly tied with little scarlet ribbons.

Ratcliffe climbed out of the coach, followed by his servant, who was
carrying his pug dog Percy on a tassled satin pillow. He strode haughtily
onto the boat.

The ship's bell clanged. "Cast off!" shouted a sailor. The Union Jack
snapped in the freshening wind and the ship was underway.

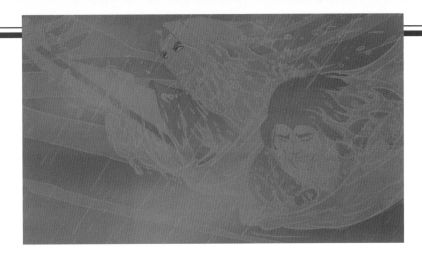

Two days out a fearsome storm tossed the sleeping men from their berths. Up on deck, sailors scrambled up and down the rigging furling the sails. The wind, roaring like a wild animal, ripped the Union Jack to shreds. As the swamped ship listed far to one side, a wave exploded over the rail.

"Man overboard!" shouted a sailor. "It's young Thomas!"

Without hesitating, John Smith tied a rope around his waist and dove off the stern. The salt water stinging his eyes, he battled the waves, searching for Thomas. Finally, he found him, and three brawny sailors hoisted the exhausted men aboard. As Thomas lay gasping for breath on the deck, Governor Ratcliffe strutted out from his dry cabin.

"Don't lose heart, men," said Ratcliffe. Smiling, he reassured the crew. "This little storm will be a mere memory in no time. Remember what awaits us in the New World—freedom, prosperity, the adventure of our lives!" As he returned to his cabin, he mumbled under his breath, "And the mountains of gold you witless peasants will dig up for me!"

Late that afternoon, Smith and Thomas leaned on the rail and watched the setting sun.

"Yes, sir," Thomas exclaimed. "I'm gonna get me a pile of gold, build a big house, and if any Indian tries to stop me . . . I'll blast him. So," he said turning to John, "what do you think the New World will be like?"

"Like all the others, I suppose," answered John. "I've seen hundreds of New Worlds. What could possibly be different about this one?"

Over the horizon, far to the west, a river wound its way through the forest and met the sea. Long ago, people built a village along its shore and were provided with all the riches they needed from the abundant waters and fertile land.

Early one morning, a young woman named Pocahontas paddled her canoe along a forest stream. As always, a raccoon named Meeko was with her. Hovering close to her shoulder was another friend, a rosy-throated hummingbird called Flit.

"I need some advice from Grandmother Willow," Pocahontas told them. She floated into a sunny glade and quietly sat before an ancient willow tree. The bark on the tree gradually changed into the face of a kindly old woman.

"Good morning, child," Grandmother Willow greeted her. "I was hoping you'd be coming to see me."

"Good morning, Grandmother Willow," Pocahontas said. "I need to talk to you. Father wishes me to marry the young warrior Kocoum."

Grandmother Willow wrinkled her nose. "Kocoum? He's so serious!"

"I know," agreed Pocahontas. "But Father thinks I'm not serious enough! He says a chief's daughter should accept more responsibility and that marrying Kocoum is the right path for me." She fingered a smooth white shell hanging from a necklace around her neck. "Father even gave me Mother's necklace—the one she wore on the day of her marriage."

Grandmother Willow thought for a moment. "You do have a bit of a problem," she admitted.

"But there's something else," Pocahontas went on. "I keep having a strange dream: I'm running through the woods and I see a spinning arrow. It spins faster and faster until it suddenly stops. Then I wake up."

"Hmmm . . . I think this spinning arrow," observed Grandmother Willow, "is pointing you to the right path."

"But, Grandmother Willow," asked Pocahontas, "what *is* my path? How am I ever going to find it?"

Grandmother Willow smiled. "As I told your mother when she was young, listen to the spirits. They are all around you—in the Earth, the Water, and Sky. If you listen with your heart, they will guide you."

A sudden breeze rustled Grandmother Willow's branches. "Listen to it, Pocahontas," she said. "Listen to the wind."

Pocahontas closed her eyes as the wind blew though her hair. "It's speaking to me," she murmured. "It's saying something's coming. Strange clouds?"

She climbed to the top of Grandmother Willow. There, above the tree-tops, she saw the towering sails of the *Susan Constant* billowing in the wind.

"What do you see?" asked Grandmother Willow.

"Clouds," answered Pocahontas. "Strange clouds."

"Better go see," Grandmother Willow advised.

By the time Pocahontas reached a ledge overlooking the river, the ship had anchored and the crew was rowing ashore. Pocahontas had never seen such strange-looking men! They had pale skin and odd clothes and some had bushy hair growing from their cheeks and chins—like animals! When the last boat reached the shore, the men stood in a circle, and their leader, a fat man in brightly colored clothes, jammed a flagpole in the ground.

"I hereby claim this land and all its riches in the name of His Majesty, King James the First of England," he boomed. "And I name this settlement: Jamestown."

One man wandered away from the group and climbed a tall tree that rose next to the ledge where Pocahontas was hiding. She backed away and, crouching behind a shrub, stared at him in wonder. His yellow hair glinted like sunlight and his eyes were as blue as a robin's egg! To Pocahontas's horror, Meeko squealed and scrambled over to him.

"Well, you're a strange-looking fellow," the man remarked and gave Meeko a biscuit from his pocket. Before gobbling it up, Meeko proudly held it up to show Pocahontas.

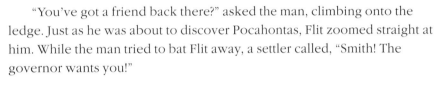

"You've got a friend back there?" asked the man, climbing onto the ledge. Just as he was about to discover Pocahontas, Flit zoomed straight at him. While the man tried to bat Flit away, a settler called, "Smith! The governor wants you!"

When Pocahontas went home, she found the whole village astir. By now, everyone had heard about the ship carrying people from a strange land. In the evening, her father, Chief Powhatan, called a meeting in the longhouse.

"I saw the strangers chopping down many trees," a brave reported. "They seem to be building a village of their own."

Another raised his voice. "They are digging holes in the earth . . . but what do they expect to find?"

Powhatan spoke to the wise medicine man at his side. "We must know more about these visitors. What do you see, Kekata?"

Kekata poured a handful of powder on the blazing fire. The coals hissed and a plume of smoke twisted upward in ghostly shapes. In silence, the elderly man observed them. "The white men are not like us," he said, at last. "They prowl like wolves, consuming all they find. Their weapons spout fire and thunder!"

Kocoum jumped to his feet. "I will lead our warriors to the river and attack. We will destroy these invaders the way we have destroyed foes in the past!"

Powhatan motioned for him to be still. "In past battles we knew how to fight an enemy," he cautioned Kocoum, "but these pale visitors are strange to us. Take some men to the river and observe them. Let us hope they do not intend to stay."

The next afternoon, John Smith knelt beside an icy stream. As he cupped his hands to drink, he saw, in the reflection, some movement behind him. In a flash, he picked up his rifle and spun around. A young woman with dark eyes and long black hair stood watching him. For a long moment, they gazed into each other's eyes. But as soon as John took a step forward, she fled.

John raced after her. "No, wait! Please, don't run away." Finally, she stopped and turned. "What's your name?" asked John.

"*Mat-ta-que-nat-u-roth*, I do not understand," she answered. But then a sudden breeze, like a loud whisper, stirred throughout the forest. It was carrying Grandmother Willow's words.

Listen with your heart, then you will understand.

"My name . . . is Pocahontas," she said, pointing to herself.

John tapped his chest. "Mine is John Smith."

She introduced him to Flit and Meeko. When John shook Meeko's paw, Pocahontas looked confused. "Shaking hands is how we say hello," explained John.

Pocahontas held up her hand and, with her palm facing him, moved it in a circle. "*Wing-gap-o*—it's how we say hello."

Just then Meeko plucked a shiny object from John's pouch and scampered off with it.

"Meeko, stop!" cried Pocahontas, embarrassed.

"He can have it," said John. "It's just a compass. It tells which direction you're going. I can get another one when I'm back in London."

"London?" asked Pocahontas. "Is that your village?"

John nodded. "It's a very big village—with streets filled with carriages, bridges over the rivers, buildings as tall as trees. . . ."

"I'd like to see these things," said Pocahontas.

"Oh, you will," John told her. "We're going to build them right here. We'll show your people how to use the land properly, and make roads and decent houses.

"Our houses are fine!" Pocahontas said, annoyed.

"But there's so much we can teach you," he continued. "We've already improved the lives of savages all over the world."

"Savages?!" Pocahontas cried out. Furious, she glared at him.

"It's just a word," John explained. "You know, a term for people who are uncivilized."

"You mean people who are *not like you*." Pocahontas led John to a rise overlooking the river and trees. "Your people do not understand the world as we do. The creatures of the forest, each rock and every bird, the fish in the rivers—they are our brothers and sisters. We are all one—with the sun, the moon, and the stars."

Flit hovered, protectively, above her shoulder. "You, me, Meeko, the raindrops and mountaintops," Pocahontas continued, "we are all a part of our Mother, the Earth." She formed a circle with her arms. "My people say life is like a giant hoop—with no beginning and no end."

As they wandered through the forest and Pocahontas spoke about the land and her people, John began to understand.

"You know, Pocahontas, what you're saying is beginning to—"

They were interrupted by the sudden beating of signal drums.

"Something's happened," said Pocahontas. "I have to go."

John called after her. "Will I see you again?" But she'd gone.

Pocahontas found a hushed crowd gathered outside the village longhouse.

"What is it?" she asked her friend, Nakoma, whose eyes were big with fright.

"Kocoum and Namontack went to spy on the white men," Nakoma informed her. "One of them shot Namontack."

Pocahontas hurried inside and found her father and Kekata beside the wounded brave. "These beasts invade our shores," Powhatan muttered to her, "and now *this*!"

"Chief Powhatan," Kekata observed, "this wound is beyond my power to heal. The white men have used one of their terrible weapons."

Powhatan's eyes narrowed with rage. He turned to Kocoum. "We'll fight this enemy," he vowed. "But we cannot do it alone. Send messengers to every village in our nation. We will call on our brothers to help." Powhatan strode from the longhouse and shouted to his people. "The white men are dangerous! No one is to go near them!"

The next afternoon, Pocahontas and Nakoma were gathering corn in a sunny field outside the village.

"We'd better pick a lot," said Nakoma, tossing ripened ears into her basket. "The warriors will probably be starving when they arrive." Looking up, she drew in her breath. "A white man is coming from the forest!"

Pocahontas whipped around. It was John! Before Nakoma could call for help, Pocahontas covered her friend's mouth. "Quiet!" she whispered. "What are you doing here?" she asked John.

He took Pocahontas by the hand. "I didn't have a chance to say good-bye."

"Pocahontas?" shouted a voice from across the field.

"It's Kocoum!" Pocahontas gasped. "Nakoma, please don't say anything." Taking John's hand, she ran with him into the forest.

"Where is Pocahontas?" Kocoum asked, approaching. Nakoma lied for her friend, but she wondered. Should she have told him the truth?

Pocahontas led John into the heart of the forest. "You took a great risk," she said, "but now that you've come, I'd like you to meet someone." Puzzled, John followed her up to a huge weeping willow.

"This place is pretty," said John, glancing around. "And to think we came all this way just to dig it up for gold."

"Gold?" Pocahontas asked, raising her eyebrows.

"Gold! It's yellow and shiny and comes from the ground," John tried to explain. "It's very valuable."

Smiling, Pocahontas pulled an ear of yellow corn from a woven basket slung over her shoulder. "Oh, here's gold," she said, handing it to him. "There's lots of it."

"No," John said, laughing. He took a coin from the deerskin pouch tied to his belt. "*This* is gold."

Pocahontas examined it and shrugged. "There's nothing like that here."

John was surprised. "Are you sure?" he asked. Pocahontas nodded. "The men aren't going to like this," he murmured. "They may just pick up and leave."

Pocahontas brightened up but then asked shyly, "What about you? Will you go home, too?"

John looked at the ground. "Well, it's not like I have much of a home to go to," he answered. "I've never really belonged anywhere."

"You could belong here," suggested Pocahontas. As she spoke, Grandmother Willow's face appeared on the side of the tree.

"Did you see that??" John cried, stumbling backward.

"Hello, John Smith," said Grandmother Willow. "Come closer." She squinted at him for a minute. "He has a good soul, Pocahontas," she decided. "And he's handsome, too."

John chuckled to Pocahontas. "Oh, I like her!"

From across the glade, they heard men's voices approaching. "Smith, where are ya, mate? Ratcliffe's lookin' for ya!"

"I'd better go before they find us," said John. He took Pocahontas's hand. "Will you meet me here tonight?"

Pocahontas nodded. "When the moon rises," she answered.

She watched him disappear and slowly shook her head. "Grandmother Willow," she said. "I know I shouldn't be seeing him again. But something's telling me inside that it's the right thing."

"Perhaps it's your dream," mused Grandmother Willow.

"My dream!" Pocahontas cried. "Do you think he's the one my spinning arrow's pointing to?"

Grandmother Willow smiled.

Pocahontas found the villagers crowded along the riverbank. They cheered as painted warriors paddled long war canoes ashore.

Kocoum's eyes shone bright. "Everything will be fine," he told her, "now that our brothers are here. Chief Powhatan will hold a war council, and then together we shall destroy the white savages!"

As Powhatan and Kekata approached the longhouse, Pocahontas reached out and held her father's arm. "Father," she pleaded, "there must be a better path to follow. Why don't you talk to the white men?"

Powhatan scowled. "They do not wish to talk."

"But if one of them wanted to talk," Pocahontas persisted, "you would listen, wouldn't you?"

Powhatan sighed wearily. "Of course," he responded. "But it is not that simple. Nothing is simple anymore."

When John emerged from the woods in Jamestown, Thomas aimed his musket at him. "Easy, Thomas! It's me!" shouted John.

Thomas looked stricken. "I-I could have killed you!" he stammered.

"Not aiming like that," John instructed him. "Don't close one eye when you aim. Keep both eyes open."

Governor Ratcliffe stormed from his tent, gnawing on a chicken wing. "Smith, where have you been?" he roared. "I figured out why we're not finding any gold—even with all our digging. The Indians have already dug it up and will do anything to keep it. They're hiding—"

John interrupted him. "They have no gold."

Ratcliffe wiped his greasy mouth with his hand. "Who told you that?"

"I met one of them," replied John.

Thomas's jaw dropped. "You met a savage?"

"They're not savages," John said angrily. "And we don't have to fight them. They can help us. They know the land and how to navigate the rivers." He pulled the ear of corn from his pouch. "Best of all, they can show us how to grow food!"

"They don't want to feed us!" Ratcliffe shouted, shaking his fist. "They want to kill us! And I say that anyone who so much as looks at an Indian will be tried for treason!"

At moonrise, Pocahontas left the village and headed toward the cornfield.

"Pocahontas, don't go," Nakoma pleaded, catching up to her. "You're turning your back on our people."

"I'm trying to help our people," she replied. "I know what I'm doing."

Nakoma watched her friend disappear into the night. In a panic, she decided she had to tell Kocoum. She found him outside his hut, sharpening his stone knife. He looked up at her as she approached.

"It's Pocahontas," Nakoma said. "I think she's in trouble."

While Pocahontas was hurrying through the cornfield, John slipped past the guards and through the fort gate. Young Thomas, who saw him go, was worried. He felt a rough hand on his shoulder.

"Follow him!" Ratcliffe hissed in Thomas's ear. "I want to know where he's sneaking off to. And remember, if you happen to see any Indians— shoot them!"

"Pocahontas," said Grandmother Willow, as they waited for John to come. "The Earth is trembling with fear. . . ."

"The warriors are here," began Pocahontas.

John came charging up to her. "My men are planning to attack your people. You've got to warn them!"

"Maybe it's not too late to stop this," insisted Pocahontas. "You have to come and talk to my father."

"I don't think talking will do much good," said John.

Grandmother Willow dipped one of her long trailing branches into the water. "Watch the ripples," she said in her gentle voice. "So small at first. Then look how they grow." She nudged John with the branch. "But someone has to start them."

John studied the widening rings of water. "All right," he said at last. "Pocahontas, let's go talk to your father." Pocahontas threw her arms around John and kissed him.

Without any warning, Kocoum sprang out from behind a bush. With a ferocious cry, he slammed John down and held a knife to his throat.

"Kocoum! Stop!" pleaded Pocahontas.

Thomas stepped out from the bushes, raised his musket, and carefully aimed. "Both eyes open," he reminded himself. Then he fired. Kocoum cried out in surprise and pain. He was dead before he hit the ground.

"You killed him!" Pocahontas screamed at Thomas.

The glade was suddenly filled with war cries, drawing closer and closer. Thomas stood dazed.

"Run!" John ordered. "RUN!"

No sooner had Thomas vanished into the forest than a group of warriors swarmed into the glade and surrounded John. Heartbroken, Pocahontas watched as John was taken away and the grieving men carried Kocoum home.

Powhatan trembled with rage and sorrow as they laid Kocoum's body before him. "Who did this?" he demanded.

"Pocahontas ran into the woods and Kocoum went out to find her," a brave explained. He gestured to John. "And then this white man attacked him."

"Your weapons are strong, but now our anger is stronger," Powhatan said to John through clenched teeth. "At sunrise, you will be the first to die." He raised his hand. "Take the white man away!"

"But, Father—," began Pocahontas. Powhatan spun around.

"I told you to stay in the village and you disobeyed me. You have shamed your father."

"I was just trying to help," Pocahontas tried to explain.

"Because of your foolishness, Kocoum is dead," said Powhatan. He turned from her while Pocahontas buried her face in her hands.

Nakoma stepped from the shadows. "Pocahontas, I sent Kocoum after you. I was so worried about you. I thought I was doing the right thing."

"All this happened because of me," Pocahontas said with tears streaming down her face. "And now I'll never see John Smith again."

"Come with me," said Nakoma. She led Pocahontas to a tiny hut guarded by two stern-looking warriors.

"Pocahontas wants to look into the eyes of the man who killed Kocoum," Nakoma told them.

"Be quick," they said, stepping aside.

Pocahontas found John kneeling with his hands tied to a post.

"I'm so sorry," she whispered. "It would have been better if we'd never met. None of this would have happened."

"Pocahontas, you must listen," John told her. "I'd rather die tomorrow than live one hundred years without knowing you."

Nakoma poked her head inside. "We'd better go."

"I can't leave you," sobbed Pocahontas.

"You never will," John said softly. "No matter what happens to me, I'll always be with you. Forever."

When Thomas ran yelling into Jamestown, the men grabbed their muskets and hurried toward him. "The savages have got John!" he cried. "What'll we do?"

Ratcliffe whipped out his sword and waved it about his head. "It's time to rescue our courageous comrade," he yelled. "Gather your weapons. At daybreak we attack!"

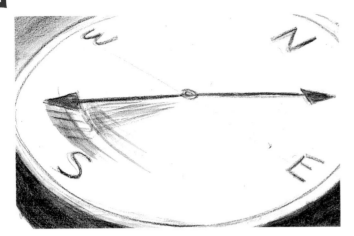

The stars were shining when Pocahontas told the terrible news to Grandmother Willow. "They're going to kill him at sunrise!" she sobbed.

"You've got to stop them," urged Grandmother Willow. "I can't," said Pocahontas. "I followed the wrong path—I feel so lost." Meeko tugged her skirt and handed her something shiny.

"It's John's compass!" Pocahontas murmured in surprise. The arrow began to spin. "It's the spinning arrow from my dream!" Suddenly, it stopped and pointed toward the horizon where the sun was beginning to rise.

"You see?" Grandmother Willow said. "Your dream *was* pointing you to John Smith. But, child, you must hurry!"

Pocahontas raced through the brightening woods. In the distance, she could see Ratcliffe's men marching from the fort and her people gathered at the top of the ridge. A sudden wind pushed her faster and faster until she felt she was almost flying.

Powhatan stood over his prisoner and raised his war club.

"No!" screamed Pocahontas, throwing herself over John.

"Stand back, Daughter!" demanded Powhatan.

Defiant, Pocahontas looked up at him. "Father, I love him," she answered. "If you kill him, you'll have to kill me, too. Look around you. This is where the path of hatred has brought us. This is the path I choose, Father. What will yours be?"

A sudden breeze sprang up and leaves swirled around the waiting warriors. Standing silent, Powhatan closed his eyes and listened to the wind. Slowly, he lowered his club and faced his waiting men.

"My daughter speaks with a wisdom beyond her years," he told them. "We all come here with anger in our hearts. But she comes with courage and understanding. From this day, if there's to be killing—it will not start with me."

He stepped back. "Release the prisoner."

The braves, stirred by Powhatan's words, lowered their weapons.

"This is our chance! Fire!" Ratcliffe yelled to his men.

No one moved. Thomas quietly laid his musket on the grass, and the rest of the men followed.

"Fine!" stated Ratcliffe. "I'll settle this myself." He raised his musket and fired at Powhatan. John lunged at the chief, knocking him out of the way. Clutching his side, John fell.

"He's shot John!" cried out Thomas. At once, Ratcliffe was surrounded by his furious men and carried off, shouting and kicking.

Pocahontas cradled John in her arms.

Three days later, the settlers were on the shore, readying the *Susan Constant* to take John home. Pocahontas and Powhatan appeared from the forest, and behind them, their people carried armloads of blankets and corn.

Pocahontas hurried to John, who was lying on a blanket in the shade, and knelt beside him. She tucked a small leather pouch in his shirt. "It's bark from Grandmother Willow," she explained. "It will help with the pain."

"Will you come with me?" asked John.

Pocahontas looked toward her people, standing quietly alongside the settlers. Her eyes brimmed with tears.

"I can't," she answered. "There is peace between our people now. I don't know what might happen if I leave."

John tried to raise himself. "Then . . . I'll stay."

Pocahontas gently settled him back down. "If you stay, you will die. You must go." She pressed his hand to her cheek while he rested.

Later, Pocahontas watched alone from a cliff as the *Susan Constant* sailed from sight.

"Good-bye, John," she said softly. "You will never leave me. No matter what happens, I will always be with you. Forever."

POCAHONTAS
Behind the Scenes

When the animators and artists who worked on *Pocahontas* (1995) talk about their experiences making this film, they use words such as *passion, sensitivity, sincerity*. They talk with hope about the messages of the film: that our existence together is fragile, that we need to see and try to understand one another, that one person *can* make a difference. They express their heartfelt wishes that in some small way the movie might block the road to prejudice. At the same time, they speak artistically of nuance, stillness, and economy of movement. They talk about simplicity of line and subtlety of expression. They speak of growing, through the making of this film, into better artists. "The filmmakers stretched themselves in many ways to make *Pocahontas*—first in its content, second in its design, and third in the level of execution that we were asking of our crew," says Eric Goldberg.

Directed by Goldberg and Mike Gabriel, and produced by James Pentecost, *Pocahontas* is the first Disney animated feature inspired by an actual historic figure. "We felt a lot of responsibility in bringing a story like this to the screen," says director Gabriel, who came up with the idea for the project during a Thanksgiving dinner with his family. The filmmakers drew on some of the finest talent from within the Native American community to voice the native characters, among them Russell Means as Chief Powhatan and Irene Bedard as the speaking voice of Pocahontas. (Judy Kuhn provided Pocahontas's singing voice.) Whenever possible, the filmmakers sought out advice, comments, and participation from prominent Native American educators, leaders, and groups, having several meetings with surviving members of the Algonquin nation in Virginia. They worked to represent the customs, living conditions, dress, relationships, and values of the historical Powhatan nation as accurately as possible.

The filmmakers also consulted historical documents of the period, including John Smith's writings. Ultimately, the moviemakers chose to focus on the love story inspired by the legendary encounter between Pocahontas and John Smith in order to underscore the important themes of tolerance and understanding.

Art director Michael Giaimo, layout supervisor Rasoul Azadani, and backgrounds supervisor Christy Maltese worked as a unified team to create an environment of awe-inspiring beauty. Giaimo wanted the Virginia setting transformed into a mystical paradise. Inspired by the tall pine forests of that state, Giaimo placed an emphasis on strong verticals and simple, clean lines, which extended both to the pristine wilderness and to the design of the characters. Giaimo and his team worked with the natural color palette they encountered on trips to Virginia but heightened and stylized those colors for cinematic and dramatic purposes. Waterfalls and swirling leaves that incorporate native motifs, misty environments, lush pine forests—all contribute an almost spiritual quality to the forest. Says Eric Goldberg, "We wanted to show that this place is so beautiful, wouldn't it be a shame if something happened to it?"

A tonal layout study concept by Rasoul Azadani with cleanup by Daniel Hu.

The principles of simplicity and subtlety that Giaimo and his team were using in the layouts and character designs were matched by the quality of the performances. "One of the things I learned on this picture in terms of design as well as acting is that less is more. Tiny expressions and subtle movements can have great impact," Pocahontas's supervising animator, Glen Keane, observes. *Pocahontas* further opened up the vocabulary of the animated film, requiring achingly fine draftsmanship on the part of all the artists, from supervising animator to cleanup artist. "A pencil-width line could make all the difference in an expression," explains Goldberg. The exquisite work of the artists in refining every detail speaks of their passion and belief in this sweet and winning story of how the love between two people can transcend hatred and intolerance.

Concept art by art director Michael Giaimo.

Wanted
$50 Bzillion
REWARD

TOY STORY

In Andy's world, Woody the cowboy was top toy. Woody wasn't just any old doll. He had a shiny sheriff's badge and a genuine cowhide vest. If you pulled the string on his back, he said all kinds of neat stuff like "Somebody's poisoned the water hole," or "There's a snake in my boot."

Woody was the only toy Andy kept on his bed all day and slept with under his cowboy bedspread at night. To show that Woody was his very own, Andy wrote ANDY in crayon on the bottom of Woody's boot.

But the most amazing thing about Woody was something Andy didn't even know. When he and the rest of the toys were left alone, they came to life. And Woody was their leader.

One afternoon, Woody called the toys together for an important meeting. Andy and his mom and baby sister, Molly, were getting ready to move on Sunday, and Woody wanted to make sure that none of the toys got left behind. Being forgotten, or lost, or—worst of all—replaced, were every toy's biggest fears.

"So, that's all settled," Woody announced. "Everybody, get a moving buddy by the end of the day."

"Do we have to hold hands?" Mr. Potato Head snickered.

"On a minor note," Woody continued, "Andy's birthday party has been moved up to today—"

The toys all gasped. "TODAY?"

Woody held up his hand. "Calm down, guys. Obviously, Andy's mom wanted to have the party before the move. Don't be worried. Listen, it doesn't matter how much we're played with. What matters is that we're here for Andy when he needs us."

Mr. Potato Head sniffed. "That's easy for you to say. You're Andy's favorite. After this party, the rest of us could land in a box marked Garage Sale."

Rex, the sixteen-inch monstrosize dinosaur, nibbled nervously on his claws. "New toys," he mumbled. "I get a nervous stomach just thinking about them."

"Pardon me," Hamm, the stout, pink piggy bank, butted in, "I hate to break up the staff meeting, but . . . THEY'RE HERE!"

The toys all scrambled up to the windowsill and watched the party guests arrive.

"The presents look bigger than last year," Slinky Dog groaned. "Gee, I think we're doomed."

"Any dinosaur-shaped ones?" asked Rex.

"For crying out loud," said Hamm, "they're all in boxes!"

"Woody," said the Bo Peep doll, "they do seem—"

Woody put his hands over his ears. "All right, all right! If I send out the troops, will you all calm down?"

"YES!" everybody shouted.

Woody turned to a plastic soldier, standing at attention on the night table. "Sergeant," he ordered, "establish a recon post downstairs. Operation Peek-a-boo. You know the drill."

The sergeant saluted. Seconds later, a platoon of plastic soldiers leaped from their storage barrel. They hoisted one of Molly's baby monitors onto their shoulders and advanced downstairs. Hiding in a potted begonia, they spied on the birthday party. As soon as Andy started opening presents, the

sergeant switched on the monitor. The toys gathered impatiently around the other monitor on Andy's night table.

"Mother Bird, this is Alpha Bravo. Nothing threatening so far," the sergeant reported. "A lunch box . . . a few board games . . . bedsheets—that's it." The toys sighed in relief. "Wait a sec—Andy's mom is going to the closet. She's pulling out another present. It's a big one. Andy's yanking off the paper . . . it's a . . . it's a . . ."

Rex shook the night table. "It's a WHAT?" he screamed. The baby monitor tumbled from the table and crashed to the floor.

"Oh, you big lizard!" said Mr. Potato Head. "Now we'll have to wait and see what the last present is."

They didn't have to wait long. The toys all scattered when they heard Andy and his friends bounding up the stairs. Woody scrambled onto the bed and flopped over, just the way Andy had left him. Andy rushed into the room with a big box in his hands. He tossed Woody off the bed and opened his new toy.

"Wow! Cool!" exclaimed Andy. "Look at those wings! Karate-chop action—awesome! And look at . . ."

Andy's mother interrupted him. "C'mon back downstairs! she called. "It's time for games and prizes."

When the kids had gone, Mr. Potato Head nudged Rex. "Did you see where Andy put that toy? On the bed! That's Woody's place."

"Woody," Rex gasped, "have you been replaced?"

Peering over the top of the bed, Woody sucked in his breath.

A shining figure in a fully equipped space suit stood in the center of the bedspread. The new toy flipped open a plastic device on its wrist and started speaking. "Buzz Lightyear to star command. Come in, star command. . . . Hmm, why don't they answer?"

Buzz gazed through his plastic helmet at the surrounding terrain. He staggered back when he discovered his cardboard box. Andy had ripped it to shreds opening his present.

"My SHIP!" he cried out. "Blast it! This'll take weeks to repair!" He switched on his recorder. "Buzz Lightyear Mission Log, Stardate 4072. I've crash-landed on a strange planet. No sign of intelligent life anywhere—"

Woody popped up in front of him. "HOWDY!" he said. Startled, Buzz sprang into a fighting stance and flashed his laser at Woody.

"Whoa," said Woody, "didn't mean to frighten you. My name's Woody and this is Andy's room. Uh, now, there's been a small mix-up. This is my spot, see, the bed here—"

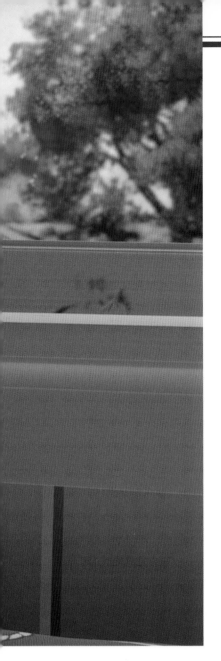

Buzz noticed Woody's badge. "Ah, local law enforcement. I'm Buzz Lightyear, space ranger. I need to repair my turbo boosters. Do you people still use fossil fuels, or have you discovered crystallic fusion?"

"Well, let's see," replied Woody, "we've got a few double-A batteries."

Buzz suddenly dove on the bed, pulling Woody down. "Unknown life-forms!" he warned. He aimed his laser at several toys peeking over the foot of the bed.

Rex raised his tiny claws above his head. "Don't shoot! It's okay! Friends!"

"They're Andy's toys," Woody explained, a little annoyed.

"All right," Buzz informed them. "You're clear to come up." He smiled at Bo Peep. "I am Buzz Lightyear. I come in peace."

Slinky Dog pressed a button on Buzz's wrist. It lit up and began to beep. "Be careful!" Buzz cautioned. "You don't want to be in the way when my laser goes off."

"That's not a laser," Woody sneered, rolling his eyes. "It's a tiny light bulb that blinks."

Mr. Potato Head scoffed. "I think you're a little envious. All you've got is a pull string—"

"All right, that's enough," said Woody. "We're all very impressed with Andy's new toy."

"Toy?" asked Buzz. "Excuse me, I think the word you're searching for is *space ranger*."

"No," responded Woody, "the word I'm searching for is *toy*. T-O-Y. Toy."

Buzz casually hit a button on his shoulder and two wings popped out. "Pure terrillium-carbonic alloy," Buzz boasted.

Woody held his sides, laughing. "The wings are plastic," he said. "Look, you're not really Buzz Lightyear and you can't fly."

"Excuse me," declared Buzz, "I *can* fly." He climbed up onto the bedpost, stood poised for a moment, shouted, "To infinity and beyond!" and took off. He headed straight to the floor, bounced off a beach ball and shot back up. Spinning upside down, he landed on a toy car, completed three vertical track loops, flipped toward the ceiling, whirled around a mobile, and made a perfect landing right in front of Woody. The toys jumped up and down and cheered.

Woody snickered. "That's wasn't flying. It was falling with style."

KAPOW! A loud explosion rattled the window. The toys all hurried to look. In the yard next door, a boy was kneeling over a tiny toy.

"How nice," observed Buzz. "A happy child at play."

Hamm grunted. "That's Sid. And he doesn't play with toys—he tortures them. Or gives them to his dog Scud to chew up!"

Woody peered through Andy's toy binoculars. "It's a Combat Carl," he reported, sadly. "Sid's tying a firecracker on his back."

Rex covered his eyes. "I can't bear to watch!"

KAPOW!

By the end of the week, Woody was getting pretty upset. Now, Andy kept Buzz on his bed every night while *he* ended up in the toy box. Andy even got himself a Buzz Lightyear bedspread. Worst of all, Buzz was sporting ANDY written in permanent marker on the bottom of his space boot.

Friday night, Andy's mother suggested they go to Andy's favorite restaurant, Pizza Planet, for dinner. "You can bring one toy, Andy," she said. "Just one." When Woody overheard that, he slumped on the desk in disgust. He knew which toy Andy would choose. But when he saw Buzz rummaging around the desk, looking for a tool to fix his ship, Woody got a bright idea.

"I'll just nudge ol' Buzz behind the desk," he thought, "and when I get back from Pizza Planet, I'll apologize and say it was a mistake." He picked up the remote control for Andy's race car and aimed the car straight at Buzz.

"Oh, Buzz! Buzz Lightyear!" Woody called out. "There's a helpless toy trapped behind the desk. You gotta save him!"

"Roger!" Buzz responded, peering down the crack. "Where? I don't see anything."

Woody hit the button, and RC Car zoomed forward. Buzz quickly stepped out of the way, but then the desk lamp swung around and knocked him out the open window. "HELP!" he cried. Before he could engage his wings, Buzz landed in the bushes next to the driveway.

The toys all rushed up to the desk.

"It was an accident!" Woody tried to explain. "You guys don't think I meant to knock him out the window, do you?"

"I do," said Mr. Potato Head. "You didn't want to face the fact that Buzz just might be Andy's new favorite toy, so you got rid of him."

The toys were about to grab Woody when they were interrupted by Andy. "Be right down, Mom," he called, rushing into the room. "I've got to get Buzz!" Andy couldn't find him, so he snatched up Woody instead.

As soon as Buzz saw Andy get into the car with Woody, he bounded out of the bushes. He grabbed on to the rear bumper and held on tight until the car pulled into a gas station a few blocks away.

"I'll help you pump," said Andy, hopping out after his mom.

Buzz clambered up the back and glared down at Woody through the open sunroof.

"You're alive!" exclaimed Woody. "This is great! We'll go back to Andy's room and you can tell everyone that it was all a big mistake!"

Buzz dove in and grabbed Woody by his neckerchief. "You tried to terminate me!" he yelled. They began to wrestle and tumbled out the open door.

"Okay, Mr. Lightweight," Woody shouted. "Take your best shot." Suddenly, the car door slammed. Before they could climb back in, Andy's mother drove away. "Oh, no," gasped Woody, watching the car turn the corner. "I don't believe it! I'm a *lost* toy!"

Buzz began speaking into his wrist communicator. "Mission log. The local sheriff and I seem to be at a huge refueling station of some sort—"

Woody smacked Buzz hard on the helmet. "It's all your fault! First you show up in your stupid little cardboard spaceship—and now you've taken away everything that's important to me."

Buzz frowned at him. "Don't talk to me about importance. Because of you, the security of the entire universe is in jeopardy. I alone have vital information that will save it. And you, my friend, are responsible for delaying my rendezvous with star command."

Woody couldn't believe his ears. "YOU ARE A TOY!" he shouted. "You aren't the real Buzz Lightyear. You're an action figure—a child's plaything!"

"You are a strange little man and you have my pity," replied Buzz. He strode off.

Woody stepped back as a delivery truck pulled up to the pump. When he saw the Pizza Planet rocket painted on the side, he hooted with joy. He'd just hop aboard and be back with Andy in no time. But wait a minute! He could never show his face in Andy's room without Buzz.

"Buzz! Buzz! I've found a spaceship!" he yelled, pointing to the picture on the truck. "If we stow away, we'll get you on the next ship and you can make your rendezvous with star command."

Minutes later, Woody and Buzz were wandering around inside Pizza Planet. Buzz was ecstatic. The intergalactic video games with their zapping laser rays made him feel right at home. "Now all I need is a ship that's headed to Sector Twelve," he thought.

Woody spotted Andy coming out of the refueling section chomping on a pizza. "Perfect," he whispered to Buzz. "We'll just hop Molly's stroller and we'll be home free. . . . Buzz?"

He turned just in time to see Buzz climbing through the hatch of a huge game shaped like a spaceship. He leaped in after him and found Buzz standing before a throng of green rubber aliens. "This is an intergalactic emergency and I need to commandeer your ship. Who's in charge here?"

The aliens raised their arms in unison and pointed skyward. A mechanized pick-up device loomed above them. "The CLAW," they all intoned. "The claw chooses who will stay and who will go."

Woody was frantic. "Buzz, we have to get out of here before somebody—"

Suddenly, a coin dropped into the slot and the claw began to move.

"WOW! A Buzz Lightyear and a cowboy!" whooped a familiar voice. Woody froze in terror. It was Sid.

"Excellent!" Sid exclaimed. Working the controls, he plucked up Woody and Buzz.

"You have been chosen," the aliens cried. "Farewell."

The next day, Sid yanked Woody and Buzz from his knapsack and slammed them on the desk.

"All right, cowboy, what do you have to say for yourself?" He pulled Woody's string.

"I'd like to join your posse, boys, but first I'm going to sing a little a song," recited Woody.

Sid snorted and picked up an electric drill. "Not gonna tell us where you stashed the gold, huh?"

Hannah, Sid's little sister, poked her head in the door. "Mom says your fish sticks are ready. Hurry up!"

"Woody, look!" shouted Buzz, after Sid had gone. "Sid's left the door open!"

They tiptoed toward the stairs, turned the corner, and bumped right into Scud. "Split up!" yelled Buzz.

With Scud snapping at his heels, Woody fled into a closet piled high with junk. Down the hall, Buzz dove through an open door into a dark room.

"Calling Buzz Lightyear!" summoned a voice from inside the room. "Come in Buzz Lightyear! This is star command. Do you read me?"

At once, Buzz flicked open his wrist communicator. "Star command," he responded, excitedly, "I read you loud and clear—"

Buzz stopped dead when he looked up and saw a flickering television set. "Yes, kids," the voice from the TV continued, "the world's greatest superhero is now the world's greatest toy. Every Buzz Lightyear comes with a locking wrist communicator, real-life karate-chop action, pulsating laser light, and, best of all, high-pressure space wings." The words NOT A FLYING TOY flashed across the screen.

Stunned, Buzz stumbled back into the hall. He couldn't believe it. There were a million Buzz Lightyears. All exactly like him. Woody's words echoed in his head: "You can't fly. You're a TOY!"

When Buzz saw an open window above the stairwell, he decided to prove to himself, once and for all, that he could fly. He shinnied up the banister and popped open his wings. "To infinity and beyond!" he shouted, leaping out. He landed so hard at the bottom of the stairwell, he snapped off one of his arms. He stared dull-eyed up at the ceiling. Woody was right—he was nothing more than a child's plaything.

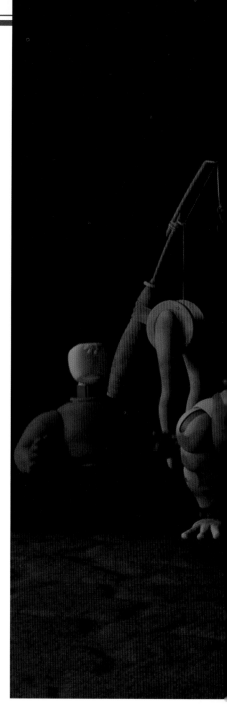

When Woody finally located Buzz, he was shocked to see Buzz's arm lying next to him.

"Buzz!" Woody gasped. "Are you okay?"

"It's just an arm," Buzz moped. "A stupid, little, insignificant *toy* arm. Look at me! I can't even fly out a window—"

"That's it!" Woody cried. "We'll escape out Sid's window!" He snatched up the broken arm and dragged Buzz back to Sid's room. Then he lugged a string of Christmas lights from the closet and tied one end to Sid's bedpost. Standing on the windowsill, he shouted across to Andy's bedroom window.

"Help, help, you guys! Buzz and I are being held in Sid's room!"

"Woody!" said Rex, surprised. "What're you doing over *there*?"

"It's a long story," Woody yelled. "I'll tell you when we get there." He pitched the lights over to Slinky Dog. "Grab hold! Buzz and I are coming over!"

Suspicious, Mr. Potato Head called back, "I don't think so! Where's Buzz?"

"He's right here," Woody shouted. But Buzz, still moping, wouldn't come to the window. "Get up here, Buzz, and give me a hand."

Buzz tossed his arm up to Woody. "Here, catch."

Woody glared at him. "You're a big help." In desperation, he used the arm to pretend that Buzz was waving hello. But the toys could see that it was snapped off. Horrified, they slammed the window shut.

"Thanks, Buzz," said Woody, hurling the arm across the room. "Now there's no way out!"

They heard a rasping sound coming from under the bed. One by one, Sid's toys began to emerge. Woody felt sick to his stomach when he saw them. The toys had all been mangled by Sid and reassembled into monsters. Their leader, Babyface Spider, lurched forward and picked up Buzz's arm. Slowly, they all crawled toward Buzz.

"Buzz!" cried Woody, racing over to him. "They're coming for you!" Buzz just sat there. The toys pushed Woody aside and surrounded the defenseless space ranger.

"You're not going to get him!" Woody shouted, shoving his way in. Then he stared in surprise. "Hey, Buzz. They fixed your arm! Well, what do you know—these guys are on our side."

Downstairs, the back door slammed. "It finally came!" Sid yelled, thumping up the stairs. He burst into the room with a big box in his hands. He ripped it open and lifted out a twelve-inch rocket with THE BIG ONE stamped on its side.

"Now," he said, looking around the room, "what'll I blow up? Hey, where'd that wimpy cowboy doll go?" Then he saw Buzz lying on the floor. "To infinity and beyond!" he shouted.

Sid pulled out his toolbox and set it on top of a milk crate. He strapped Buzz to the rocket with a big wad of tape. He was about to rush downstairs when he heard a clap of thunder. It started to rain.

"Oh, no," Sid groaned, "now I'll have to wait till morning."

Late that night, when he was sure Sid was sound asleep, Woody peeked out from the milk crate where he was hiding and whispered to Buzz. "Hey! Hey, Buzz! I'm trapped in here. See if you can get this toolbox off the crate, will ya? Then I'll get that rocket thing off you."

"Who cares if I get blown up?" Buzz mumbled. "I'm just a toy."

"Whoa, hey!" said Woody. "Being a toy's a lot better than being a space ranger. There's a kid over in that house who thinks you're the greatest. And it's not because you're a space ranger, it's because you're a toy. *His* toy."

Buzz looked up gloomily. "But why would Andy want me?"

"Why *wouldn't* Andy want you?" said Woody. "Look at you! You've got wings, you light up, you talk, your helmet flips up and down. You're a really *cool* toy." Woody stared at the floor. "I'm the one who should be strapped to that rocket. What chance does a toy like me have against a Buzz Lightyear action figure?"

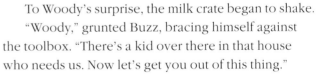

To Woody's surprise, the milk crate began to shake.

"Woody," grunted Buzz, bracing himself against the toolbox. "There's a kid over there in that house who needs us. Now let's get you out of this thing."

While Buzz pushed with all his might, the sun slowly began to rise. He just managed to topple the toolbox off the crate when Sid's alarm sounded. Sid rubbed his eyes and jumped out of bed. Snatching up Buzz, he bolted from the room.

Teary-eyed, Woody turned to Sid's toys. "Please, you've got to help me save Buzz," he pleaded. "He's my friend." Babyhead creaked up to Woody and nodded.

"Okay," Woody said. "I think I know how we can do it. But it'll mean breaking a very big rule. . . ."

In the backyard, Sid was preparing to light the rocket. He positioned Buzz in the center of the sandbox and took out a match.

"Mission Control to Houston," he began, "request permission to launch—" He scowled when he saw Woody lying on the ground nearby. "Hey! How'd you get out here?" He stuck the match in Woody's vest pocket and carried him over to the barbecue grill. "Oh, well. We'll just have ourselves a little cookout later."

"Reach for the sky," said Woody.

"H-Huh?" stammered Sid.

"That's right, I'm talking to you, Sid," Woody continued. "We don't like being blown up or smashed or ripped to shreds. So, from now on—play nice!"

Sid backed up. "W-W-W-We?"

"WE," said Woody. "Your *toys*."

From all over the yard, Sid's toys appeared, limping, scraping, and squirming toward him.

"MOM!" Sid screamed. "They're alive!" Flailing his arms, he dropped Woody and fled into the house.

"Nice work, fellas," Woody said to the toys. Buzz, still attached to the rocket, offered Woody his hand.

From the driveway next door, they heard a car starting up. "Good-bye, house!" Andy sang out.

Woody and Buzz stared at each other. "IT'S MOVING DAY!" they screamed and charged across the yard. They were just in time to see the car drive away. Then the moving van pulled away from the curb.

"Let's go!" shouted Buzz. Running up behind the van, he grabbed a rope trailing off the back and hoisted himself onto the bumper.

"C'mon, you can do it, Woody," Buzz yelled.

Woody lunged for the rope. Hanging on, he looked at Buzz and sighed in relief. "We made it!"

All of a sudden, Scud shot out of nowhere and clamped down on Woody's boot. "Buzz," he gasped, "I can't hold on. Take care of Andy for me—"

Woody was about to let go when Buzz leaped onto Scud and shook him loose. Woody scrambled up and tugged open the van door. He searched desperately for the box marked ANDY'S TOYS.

When Woody grabbed RC Car and tossed him into the street, the other toys in the box all went berserk. "AAAGH," Rex screamed. "He's at it again!"

"Get him," yelled Mr. Potato Head, "before he gets another one of us." The toys all piled on top of Woody. Then, holding him by the arms and legs, they heaved him out the back. Woody sailed through the air and landed right in RC Car. Buzz was next to him, driving.

"Nice of you to drop in," said Buzz. "Now, let's catch up to that truck!"

They were closing fast when RC Car started to cough and his wheels slowed down. His batteries were dead.

"Great," Woody groaned. "Could anything else possibly go wrong?"

"Woody!" Buzz cried. "The rocket!"

Smiling, Woody took Sid's match from his vest pocket. He struck it on the pavement and lit the fuse.

Buzz wrapped his arms tightly around Woody. "This is Mission Control. Prepare for liftoff!" he announced.

"Roger!" replied Woody, gripping RC's steering wheel. With a loud *PHITTT!* the rocket shot forward toward the open van, but at the last second, it veered straight up. Woody dropped RC into the truck as he and Buzz sailed skyward.

"Wait a minute!" said Woody. "Is this the part where we blow up?"

"Not today!" shouted Buzz. He snapped open his wings, the tape ripped off, and the rocket fell away.

"We're flying!" cheered Woody.

Buzz grinned. "We're not flying. We're falling with style!"

"But we missed the van!" Woody said.

"I'm not aiming for the van," Buzz replied.

Woody looked down as they approached Andy's car and saw Andy through the open sunroof. They landed with a soft thud into a box next to the boy.

"Mom!" he shouted. "I found Woody and Buzz!"

His mother smiled at him in the rearview mirror. "I told you they weren't lost."

Andy hugged his two favorite toys. "Yup," he said. "They must have been here the whole time!"

TOY STORY
Behind the Scenes

F or director and former Disney animator John Lasseter, *Toy Story* (1995) was the realization of a long-held dream. Ever since he first encountered computer animation, Lasseter had wanted to make a feature-length animated film with only computer tools and technology. After years of developing that technology and producing computer-animated shorts, his dream became a reality when Pixar Animation Studios joined together with Disney Feature Animation to create the first feature-length computer-animated film.

What the director loves most about computer animation is its ability to give life to inanimate objects. "To me there's no object that can't become a personality," says Lasseter. Through computer animation the creative and technical teams at Pixar were able to show their audience a familiar world from an entirely new perspective. That perspective—imagining what toys might do, think, and feel if they were alive—reflects the passions of the filmmakers. "If there's one thing animators know and love, it's toys," says story cocreator Andrew Stanton. The filmmakers wanted to show toys behaving in ways we've all always imagined or wished they could. "The motivating emotion for the film was that desire to believe in our toys," adds Stanton.

John Lasseter (kneeling) and crew at work at a design station at Pixar.

Even though the artists were working in a brand-new medium, their first priority was to develop the characters and story. No matter how dazzling the technology, Lasseter contends, people will walk away from a good movie remembering the characters and their relationships. "We're storytellers who happen to use computers," comments Lasseter. The key to defining clear characters in this film was to determine the various toys' personalities using traits that would result from the appearance and identity of the toys themselves. What was the toy built to do? How was it made? What materials were used? So Mr. Potato Head keeps going all to pieces and blowing his top, while Rex the dinosaur's rigid plastic construction and wimpy little arms prevent him from being a truly ferocious beast.

The daunting task of creating a completely imaginary universe filled with talking, thinking toys required the talents and creative efforts of dozens of animators and technicians joined in an extraordinary creative partnership. The animators

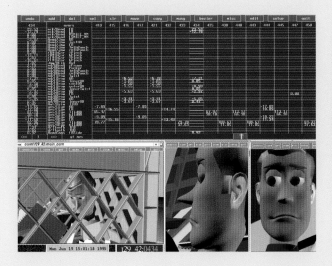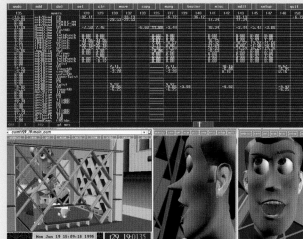

An animator's workstation display at two points in the sequence in which Woody is trapped in a milk crate.

came from the entire spectrum of animation media, including traditional hand-drawn, stop-action, and clay animation. For many, this was the first time they were animating using the computer. The only requirement for the animators was that they be able to express ideas and emotions through the characters.

Supervising Technical Director Dr. William Reeves led the technical team in solving the unique set of challenges the story posed. Working closely with the directors, animators, and art director, the technical group created and tested the models for every character, prop, and set, from Buzz Lightyear to a bowl of Froot Loops cereal. They created "shader" programs, which describe or define the surface appearance of every exposed area or object in terms of color, reflectivity, texture, and bumpiness; and "texture maps," components of a shader that may be painted or scanned, and that describe a surface as a picture or an image. Texture maps were used to create the reflection in Buzz's helmet, Sid's Megadork poster, and the wallpaper in Andy's home.

The artists designed virtual sets as complex as the miles of suburban streets for the final chase, articulating every leaf and replicating real outdoor lighting conditions. Because the computer easily creates a too-perfect world, the technical artists concentrated on populating *Toy Story*'s world with a host of dents, scuffs, dirt, and dust—all imperfections that would help this created universe feel more "real." They even devised ways to re-create the worn and comfortable texture of faded denims. From the architecture of Pizza Planet and the eerie designs of the Mutant Toys to the light cast through rain falling outside Sid's bedroom window the night before Woody and Buzz make their escape, the technical group worked to provide the tools that would allow the directors, writers, artists, and animators to realize their ideas on film.

In March 1996, Lasseter received a Special Achievement Award from the Academy of Motion Picture Arts and Sciences for his work on *Toy Story*. "This medium broadens the horizon for what can be done in animation," says Ralph Guggenheim, who coproduced the film with Bonnie Arnold. "It adds another possibility to the animated forms that already exist, such as hand-drawn, clay, sand, stop-motion, and puppet animation, but computer animation is so new it has yet to be defined." The possibilities, as Buzz Lightyear might suggest, are infinite.

THE HUNCHBACK OF NOTRE DAME

On long-ago sunny days in the city of Paris, children gathered in the cobblestone square before the great Cathedral of Notre Dame. They sat on the steps and listened to the tales of Clopin, the gypsy storyteller.

"Today," Clopin once began, "I will tell you the story of the bell ringer of Notre Dame—the one who calls the faithful to prayer. What I say is true, for I saw it with my own eyes. It is a story of terror and love, great sadness and joy. It is the tale of a monster and a man. At the end, you decide, who is the monster and who is the man?"

It began one freezing night on the river.

A group of gypsies sat huddled in a small boat as it floated past Notre Dame. They were not welcome in Paris and hoped to arrive unnoticed. But the cruel judge, Claude Frollo, had been alerted by his spies. Hidden in the shadows near a snow-covered bridge, he waited on horseback, surrounded by his soldiers.

As the boat drifted up to the pier, Frollo charged forward, his black cape billowing behind him. "Arrest those gypsies," he ordered his men. A woman, clutching a tiny bundle, leaped from the boat.

"You there!" a soldier shouted. "What are you hiding?"

Frollo glared down at the woman. "Stolen goods, no doubt. Take them from her."

Terrified, she fled. Frollo, astride his steed, thundered after her. She hurried through the icy streets to the steps of Notre Dame. "Please, protect my child and me—grant us sanctuary!" she cried out, pounding on the door.

Frollo galloped up and snatched the bundle. The gypsy woman fell, striking her head on the stone steps. She was killed instantly.

Frollo unwrapped the bundle. "An infant!" he exclaimed in surprise. His surprise turned to disgust when he found that the child was ugly and misshapen. Seeing a well in the courtyard, he decided to drop the baby into it. "This is an unholy demon!" he muttered, holding the child above the dark opening. "I am sending it back to Hell, where it belongs."

"Stop!" cried the Archdeacon, rushing toward Frollo. "You have already spilled innocent blood. Now you would add this child to your guilt?"

"I am guiltless," protested Frollo. "She ran—I merely pursued her."

The Archdeacon pointed to the statue of Notre Dame, holding her infant son in her arms. "You can lie to yourself," he told Frollo. "But you can never hide what you've done from the eyes of Our Lady, Notre Dame."

Panic gripping him, Frollo feared for his immortal soul. "What must I do?" he asked.

"Care for this child," replied the Archdeacon, "and treat it as your own."

"What?" cried Frollo. "You wish me to be saddled with this deformed—" He paused. "Very well, as you wish. But let him live here with you in your church—in the bell tower, perhaps."

The Archdeacon consented.

"Who knows?" Frollo thought to himself. "Our Lord works in mysterious ways. Even this fool creature may be of use to me . . . someday."

The child was given a cruel name. Frollo called him Quasimodo, which meant "the half-formed one." Every day the minister visited the church to give the boy his lessons. The rest of the time, Quasimodo's only companions were the gargoyles. To everyone else, they were grotesque stone figures, but to him, they were his friends—Hugo, Laverne, and Victor. And when he was alone he talked to them.

Twenty years passed. Quasimodo grew strong pulling the thick ropes and ringing the heavy bells. Townspeople caught glimpses of him, silhouetted in the tower, and referred to him as the Hunchback of Notre Dame.

Early one morning, Hugo excitedly leaned over the bell tower railing. Below, the town square stirred with activity. Everybody was getting ready for their favorite holiday—the Festival of Fools.

"Quasi," Hugo called out. "Get over here! Nothin' like balcony seats for the ol' F.O.F."

"It's a treat to watch the colorful pageantry of the simple peasant folk," Victor observed, yawning and stretching his wings. "But you must admit, it's a rather peculiar holiday. Imagine, they dress as fools and then crown the most foolish-looking one King of the Festival!"

"Aw, don't be so stuffy, Victor," said Hugo. He glanced around. "What's keeping Quasi? Watching the festival is always the highlight of his year."

"What good is watching a party," said Laverne, shuffling across the balcony, "if you never get to go?"

They found Quasimodo inside the bell tower, staring at a miniature town that he'd carved over the years. It was of the city he knew only from above.

"I . . . I just don't feel like watching the festival," he told them.

Laverne touched his shoulder. "Did you ever think of going down there?"

Quasimodo looked up, surprised. "You know I can't do that! Frollo says the world's a cruel place and that nobody would like me. He says I should stay here and be grateful that he took me in, you know, after my heartless mother abandoned me."

"Quasimodo," said Victor. "Frollo might not be right. You may find the world isn't such a bad place after all. Why don't you give it a try?"

"Yeah!" added Hugo. "Don't you want to play Bobbin' for Snails?"

"Take it from an old spectator," Laverne advised. "Life's not a spectator sport. If watching is all you're going to do, you're going to watch your life go by without you."

Quasimodo went out to the balcony and gazed at the bustling square. "All my life," he murmured, "I've wanted to go down there. To be free." He closed his eyes. "If I could be free, for just one day, my heart would sing with joy."

Then, at last, he made a decision. He hurried to his room and yanked his cloak from the hook. "You're right!" Quasimodo said to his friends. "I'll go to the festival, but I sure hope I don't run into Frollo."

Victor patted him on the shoulder. "Better to beg forgiveness than to ask permission."

On a street below, Phoebus, the dashing Captain of the Guard, led his horse, Achilles, through the jostling crowd. After years away, he had been called back to serve under Frollo.

Phoebus stopped to watch a gypsy woman dancing in the street. Her white goat, Djali, gaily pranced alongside. As she whirled about, beating a tambourine, people tossed coins into a hat on the ground. Phoebus tossed in a coin of his own. She smiled at him. He was surprised to feel his heart thump—he'd never seen such a beautiful woman!

"Esmeralda!" a gypsy boy shouted to her. "The soldiers are coming!"

As Esmeralda bent down to scoop up the hat, one of the soldiers grabbed it.

"All right, gypsy," he demanded. "Where'd you get this money?"

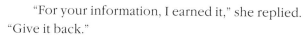

"For your information, I earned it," she replied. "Give it back."

He raised the hat higher. "Gypsies don't earn money," he jeered. "They steal it."

Suddenly, Djali butted him from behind. The surprised soldier yowled and dropped the hat. In a flash, Esmeralda snatched it up, dashed past Phoebus, and vanished into the crowd.

The soldiers started after her. As they ran toward Phoebus, he yanked hard on the reins and pulled Achilles directly into their path. One soldier bumped into the horse and fell.

"Achilles, sit!" Phoebus commanded. Obediently, the animal settled himself down on top of the soldier.

"Hey!" yelped the furious man. "Get this horse off me!"

Phoebus appeared shocked. "Oh, dear, I'm terribly sorry. What a naughty horse!"

The second soldier drew his sword. "I'll teach you a lesson, peasant!" he threatened.

Phoebus threw back his cloak, exposing his armor and rank, and whipped out his sword.

"C-C-Captain!" stammered the soldier, snapping to attention. "At your service, sir."

"And now, you two," Phoebus told them, "I wish to be escorted to the Palace of Justice."

Phoebus found Frollo out on the palace balcony observing the festivities.

"You must be the gallant Captain Phoebus," said the minister, turning to greet him. "You have come to Paris in her darkest hour. It will take a firm hand to save the weak-minded from being misled."

"Misled?" inquired Phoebus.

"By the gypsies," Frollo explained. "They live outside the normal order. Their heathen ways inflame the people's lowest instincts. They must be stopped." Frollo paused to watch three ants scurrying along the stone railing. "For twenty years," he went on, "I've been . . . *taking care* . . . of the gypsies." Smiling, he crushed the tiny insects under his fingertip, one by one. He pulled up a loose stone and revealed a nest of swarming ants.

"But their hideaway, called the Court of Miracles, has never been uncovered," he informed Phoebus. "I demand that you find this gypsy nest and destroy it!" Trumpets suddenly blared, heralding the climax of the festival. "Ah, duty calls. We must watch the fools crown their king."

Quasimodo wandered about in the square below the palace balcony. Thrilled, and a bit bewildered, he was carried along by crowds of merrymakers wearing masks and topsy-turvy costumes.

"Excuse us!" two people cried out, bumping into him. Dressed as a horse with a tail at both ends, they galloped, laughing, up to the festival grandstand. Knocked off balance, Quasimodo stumbled into a tent and tipped over a table. A woman, fastening a headdress, hurried over to him. It was Esmeralda.

Quasimodo tried to duck away. "I didn't mean to—"

"You're not hurt, are you?" Esmeralda asked, helping him to his feet. Seeing that he was all right, she showed him outside. "By the way," she grinned, "great mask!"

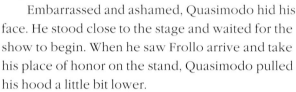

Embarrassed and ashamed, Quasimodo hid his face. He stood close to the stage and waited for the show to begin. When he saw Frollo arrive and take his place of honor on the stand, Quasimodo pulled his hood a little bit lower.

A man with a plumed hat appeared before the crowd. "Come one, come all," he shouted. "I, Clopin, present the lovely Esmeralda!"

Esmeralda danced onto the stage in a swirl of bright, silky scarves. She sashayed over to Frollo and wrapped a scarf around his stiff neck. He felt his face grow hot.

"What a disgusting display," Frollo muttered to Phoebus, but the captain was enthralled. Quasimodo, too, felt his heart throb with joy. Up in the tower, he'd never imagined anything could be so beautiful. When she finished, he clapped wildly with the rest of the crowd.

"Now," announced Clopin, "the moment you've all been waiting for! It's time to crown the King of Fools. So don't be shy. Come on up. The audience will vote for the most foolish mask." His eyes got big when he spotted Quasimodo. Esmeralda saw him, too, and pulled him up onstage with the others. Quasimodo's hood fell back from his head.

"No, no," he groaned. The audience cheered and stamped their feet.

"He's the winner!" they yelled. Clopin motioned to Esmeralda. "Remove the gentleman's mask, so we can see who he is."

Esmeralda gently tugged at Quasimodo's face. Then she realized it wasn't a mask at all! "Oh," she stammered, "I'm so . . . sorry."

Someone from the crowd called out. "It's the Hunchback of Notre Dame!"

"Quasimodo!" they all roared. "The King of Fools!" As they rushed forward to crown him with a jester's cap, Quasimodo felt a surge of happiness. Frollo was wrong about people not liking him. They wanted him to be King!

All of a sudden, someone threw a rotten egg and hit Quasimodo—*SMACK!*—in the face. "Now he's even uglier than before!" a woman jeered. Everybody laughed. Soon they were all pelting Quasimodo with spoiled fruit and vegetables. When he tried to escape, several men threw a rope around him and tied him to a pillory.

Frantic, Quasimodo looked beseechingly at Frollo.

"Master, please help me!" he cried out.

Phoebus turned to the minister. "Sir, request permission to stop this cruelty."

"Not yet, Captain," Frollo instructed him. "A lesson needs to be learned here."

Esmeralda hurried through the crowd to Quasimodo's side. The crowd hushed as she wiped his face with her scarf. She took a knife from her pocket and began to cut the ropes.

Frollo stormed over to her. "You! Gypsy girl! Get away from him!" he ordered.

"Yes, Your Honor," answered Esmeralda, "just as soon as I free this poor creature."

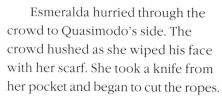

"I forbid it!" Frollo thundered.

Esmeralda finished cutting the ropes. "You mistreat this poor boy the same way you mistreat my people," she told him. "You speak of justice, yet you are cruelest to those who need you the most."

"How dare you defy me! You will pay for this insolence." He signaled to Phoebus. "Arrest her!"

Esmeralda laughed. "Just try to catch me!" She tossed some powder in the air and disappeared in a cloud of colored smoke.

"Witchcraft!" Frollo muttered to himself.

"What a woman!" breathed Phoebus.

"Find her, Captain," commanded Frollo. "I want her alive!"

After Phoebus and his men rode off, Frollo glared at Quasimodo.

"I'm sorry, Master," Quasimodo said, weeping. "I will never disobey you again."

Hanging his head in shame, he slowly walked back to Notre Dame and shut the door behind him.

Moments later, Esmeralda, disguised in a monk's robe, quietly slipped into Notre Dame. Holding Djali, she stood entranced as glowing light filtered through the stained glass windows. She removed her robe and then, sensing she was not alone, she whirled around. Phoebus stepped from the shadows.

"You gave us quite a chase," he said. "I'm very impressed." He smiled at her. "My name is Phoebus. I was coming to apologize to you."

Esmeralda was surprised. "You're not arresting me?"

"Not as long as you're in here," replied Phoebus. "I can't."

"So, if you're not going to arrest me," Esmeralda asked, "what do you want?"

"I'd settle for your name," answered Phoebus.

After pausing a moment, Esmeralda told him.

The cathedral door flew open. "Good work, Captain!" said Frollo, striding forward.

Phoebus stepped closer to Esmeralda and drew his sword.

"You tricked me," she muttered.

"Claim sanctuary," Phoebus whispered to her, "and you'll be safe. The church will protect you." Esmeralda kept silent. "Say it!" Phoebus repeated through his teeth.

Phoebus turned and addressed Frollo. "I'm sorry, sir. She claimed sanctuary. There's nothing I can do."

"Then drag her outside," said Frollo.

From the rear of the cathedral, an angry voice broke in. "Frollo! You will not touch her!" The Archdeacon came forward. "Don't worry, my child," he said aloud so Frollo would hear. "Judge Frollo learned years ago to respect the sanctity of the church."

Frollo whispered to Esmeralda. "You think you've outwitted me, but I am a patient man." He leaned close and stroked her hair. "Such a clever witch."

After the soldiers left, Esmeralda hurried to the door and peeked outside. There were men posted at every door. Quietly, the Archdeacon came up behind her. "Don't act rashly," he counseled. "It would be unwise to arouse Frollo's anger further. I heard you tried to help Quasimodo, but you can't right all the wrongs of this world by yourself."

"Well," retorted Esmeralda, "no one out there is going to help, that's for sure!"

"Well, perhaps, there is someone in here who can," the Archdeacon responded. He withdrew, leaving Esmeralda alone with her thoughts.

For a few moments, Esmeralda gazed at the wondrous ceiling, arching toward heaven. Mindful of the Archdeacon's words, she prayed for help. When she opened her eyes, she glimpsed Quasimodo watching her from behind a pillar. Realizing he'd been seen, he fled.

"Wait," Esmeralda called. "I'd like to talk to you." With Djali clattering at her heels, she ran up the stone steps to the bell tower.

"Here you are!" she exclaimed, out of breath, when she finally found him. "I'm really sorry about this afternoon."

"It's okay," Quasimodo mumbled.

Esmeralda glanced around the tower. "What is this place?"

"This is where I live," he replied.

Esmeralda noticed the little city set up on the table. "Did you make this all by yourself?" she asked, studying the carved houses and tiny wooden townspeople. "This is really beautiful."

"Thank you," said Quasimodo. Shyly, he looked down at the floor.

Esmeralda smiled at him. "You're a surprising person, Quasimodo."

She moseyed around the room and admired the tall pillars and arched windows. "Imagine having all this to yourself!"

"Well, it's not just me," he explained. "There's the gargoyles and, of course, the bells." He held out his hand. "Would you like to see more?" He led her up a little stairway to the roof.

Esmeralda and Quasimodo stood side by side and gazed out over the darkening city. Before them, the sun dipped from sight. The orange sky turned deep blue and the moon slowly rose among the twinkling stars. "I could stay up here forever," she murmured.

"You could, you know," Quasimodo said. "You have sanctuary."

Esmeralda smiled sadly. "But not freedom. Gypsies don't do well inside stone walls."

"But you aren't like other gypsies," said Quasimodo. "Frollo says they're all evil. He teaches me everything about the world. He raised me, you know."

Esmeralda was stunned. "How could such a cruel man raise someone like you?"

"Cruel?" asked Quasimodo. "Oh, no, he saved my life. He took me in when no one else would. You see, I'm a monster."

Esmeralda gently took Quasimodo's hand and studied the lines on his palm. "Gypsies believe people's hands tell a lot about them. And I don't see a single monster line."

She looked into his eyes. "I'm a gypsy and you just said you don't think I'm evil. So, maybe Frollo is wrong about both of us."

Quasimodo studied the soldiers down in the square.

"You helped me," he said, at last. "Now I'd like to help you. The guards are watching the doors, but we'll climb down."

Esmeralda gulped. "Climb down?"

"You carry your goat," Quasimodo explained, "and I'll carry you. The trick is not to look down."

He picked them up and vaulted over the side. Holding tight to Esmeralda, he glided along a flying buttress and, skipping from ledge to ledge, landed on a steep roof. A loose tile shot out from under him.

"WHOOAH!" he shouted, balancing on one foot. They sailed off the roof into the air. At the last second, he reached out and caught himself on the wing of a gargoyle. He dropped the last few feet to the square.

"I hope I didn't scare you," he whispered.

"Not for an instant!" joked Esmeralda. Growing serious, she held his hand. "Leave this place. Come with me to the Court of Miracles."

"Oh, no," responded Quasimodo. "I'm never going out there again. This is where I belong."

"Then I'll come back," she said. "After sunset." Esmeralda took a talisman from around her neck. "If you ever need a safe place, this will show you the way. Just remember: when you wear this woven band, you hold the city in your hand."

She kissed him on the cheek. With Djali in her arms, she hurried into the darkness.

As Quasimodo climbed back to his tower, wondrous thoughts filled his head. All his life, he'd watched lovers walking, hand in hand, along the river far below. What was it like to be happy and love someone, he'd wondered. Now he knew. But he dared not think it—was it possible Esmeralda might really care for him?

Several streets away in the Palace of Justice, Frollo knelt in tortured prayer. "Help me," he begged. "You know my thoughts are pure, but the gypsy woman continues to tempt me. You must not let me fall under this witch's spell."

A guard knocked on the door. "Minister Frollo! The gypsy woman has escaped!"

Frollo uttered a strangled cry. "I'll find her . . . if I have to burn down all of Paris!"

At dawn, Frollo's troops stormed the sleeping city—ransacking houses, setting shops afire, and arresting gypsies. On the outskirts of Paris, Frollo led his soldiers in a desperate search. They stopped in front of a mill.

"This is a gypsy refuge," Frollo said to Phoebus. "Burn it."

"With all due respect, sir," Phoebus replied, "I was not trained to murder the innocent."

"Insolent coward!" yelled Frollo. He leaned down from his horse, grabbed a torch from one of his men, and tossed it onto the thatched roof. Hiding among the gathering crowd, Esmeralda watched in horror as the mill exploded in flames.

"Frollo, you are a madman!" cried Phoebus, racing into the thick smoke. A few moments later, just before the mill collapsed, Phoebus burst outside with two children in his arms. Behind him, the miller and his wife staggered out, gasping for breath.

"Captain," Frollo snapped. "You are to be punished for your disobedience." He gestured to his men. "Shoot him!"

Hastily, Esmeralda found a stone and threw it hard at Frollo's horse. The

startled animal reared, throwing Frollo to the ground. Phoebus hurled himself onto the riderless horse and galloped toward a bridge. But when Phoebus was halfway across, a soldier's arrow hit its mark. Phoebus toppled from the horse and fell into the river. The soldiers rushed to the bridge.

"Don't waste your arrows," Frollo called out. "Leave the traitor to rot in his watery grave."

Esmeralda watched the soldiers disappear down the road. Then she dove down to the bottom of the river and, using all her strength, pulled Phoebus to shore.

Quasimodo and the gargoyles stood on the balcony of Notre Dame and looked out over the burning city.

"Don't worry, Quasi," said Hugo. "If I know Esmeralda, she's three steps ahead of Frollo, and when things cool off, she'll be back."

"Do you really think so?" Quasimodo asked.

"Quasimodo?" a voice whispered from behind him.

"Esmeralda?" he cried, spinning around and rushing inside. "I knew you'd come back!"

"You've done so much for me already, but I must ask your help one more time. It's Phoebus. He's wounded and a fugitive now, like me."

"Bring him in, quickly," said Quasimodo. She motioned to two men waiting in the stairwell. They stepped forward, carrying Phoebus, and placed him on Quasimodo's bed.

Esmeralda attended to his wound. "Fortune must have been with you, Phoebus. The arrow almost pierced your heart."

"I'm not so sure it didn't," Phoebus whispered. He squeezed her hand and pulled her toward him.

As they kissed, Quasimodo looked away and choked back a sob. He thought his heart would break. Before Esmeralda left, she turned to Quasimodo. "Promise me you won't let anything happen to him."

"I promise," Quasimodo answered.

Suddenly, he heard the familiar clatter of Frollo's carriage in the square.

"My master's coming!" he cried to Esmeralda. "You must go. Take the south tower steps. I'll hide Phoebus."

Frollo stared up at Notre Dame. "I put guards at every door," he muttered to himself. "How did she manage to escape? She must have had help. . . ." A broad smile crossed his face. Of course—Quasimodo!

Moments later, Frollo entered the bell tower. "Quasimodo, I just thought I'd pay you a little visit," he said, poking about the room. He stopped before the miniature town and picked up a newly carved figure. "I haven't seen this one," he remarked. "It looks just like . . . that gypsy witch!"

Quasimodo backed away, petrified. Frollo's eyes grew dark with rage. "I know you helped her escape," he hissed. "And now all of Paris is burning because of you."

"But sh-sh-she was kind to me," stuttered Quasimodo.

"That wasn't kindness—it was cunning!" stormed Frollo. "She's a gypsy. Gypsies are not capable of real love. Think, boy. Think of your mother!"

Picking up Quasimodo's carving knife, he plunged it into the wooden figure and set it afire. "She's a witch!" he roared as he watched it burn. "But she'll be out of our lives soon enough."

"What do you mean?" asked Quasimodo.

"I know where her hideout is," Frollo answered, letting his words sink in. "And tomorrow at dawn, I will attack with a thousand men."

As soon as Frollo left, Phoebus struggled out from under the bed. "We've got to warn Esmeralda!" he told Quasimodo. Holding his side, he limped to the door. "Aren't you coming?"

Quasimodo shook his head. "I can't disobey Frollo," he replied.

"Well," said Phoebus before leaving, "I'm not going to stand by and watch Frollo murder innocent people."

Quasimodo took Esmeralda's necklace from inside his shirt. Why should he help her, he thought. Frollo was right—she'd only pretended to like him. Yet, she did rescue him at the festival. And risked her life doing it. Frollo hadn't helped him at all. Still, Frollo was his master. But . . . Esmeralda was his friend.

He hurried after Phoebus. Together, they examined the amulet Esmeralda had given to Quasimodo.

"Must be some sort of code," Phoebus said.

Quasimodo murmured to himself. "When you wear this woven band, you hold the city in your hand. You know what—I think it's supposed to be a map! See? The cross in the middle represents the cathedral. These lines are the city streets. The bead is placed where the city graveyard would be. I'll bet that's where we'll find the Court of Miracles!"

Quasimodo put his arm around Phoebus and helped him across the square. Smiling, Frollo watched from the shadows. Keeping a safe distance behind, he followed them with his troops.

At the edge of the city, Quasimodo and Phoebus passed through a creaky iron gate and wandered among rows of tombstones. In the center of the graveyard, an obelisk stood silhouetted in the bright moonlight.

"Look! It's shaped like the bead on the map," whispered Quasimodo. He leaned against it and tried to read the inscription. Suddenly, the marble cover creaked open, revealing a staircase lit by flickering torches. Phoebus and Quasimodo crept down the worn steps and found themselves in a large chamber connected to a series of tunnels. Gypsies instantly sprang out from all directions and surrounded them.

Clopin was among them. "Tie and gag these spies!" he ordered.

"No," pleaded Quasimodo. "You've got to listen. . . ."

"Wait!" cried Esmeralda, hurrying from a tunnel. "These men aren't spies. This is the soldier who saved the miller's family, and Quasimodo helped me escape from the cathedral."

Phoebus addressed the crowd. "We're here to warn you," he said. "Frollo's attacking at dawn!"

Esmeralda put her arm around him. "You took a terrible risk coming here, but we're very grateful."

"Don't thank me," Phoebus said. "Thank Quasimodo. Without his help, I never would have found this place."

"*Nor would I!*" boomed Frollo.

He stepped from a passageway flanked by armed soldiers. "After twenty years of searching—the Court of Miracles is mine! And, dear Quasimodo, you led me right here. I always knew you'd be of use to me one day."

He glared at Phoebus. "Back from the dead . . . a *miracle*, no doubt. But we shall remedy that." He smiled widely at all the gypsies. "There will be a little bonfire in the square tomorrow night and you're all invited to attend."

Quasimodo collapsed at Frollo's feet. "No, please, Master," he whimpered.

Frollo pushed him away. "Take this one back to the bell tower," he said to his men. "And make sure he stays there."

All the next day, Quasimodo knelt chained between two pillars in the tower. Too depressed to struggle, he stared at the floor.

"C'mon, Quasi, snap out of it!" pleaded Hugo. "You gotta save your friends."

"It's all my fault," he mumbled.

Victor and Laverne tried to make him listen. "You can't let Frollo win," they insisted.

Quasimodo roared, "Leave me alone!"

"Okay," Victor said, sadly. "I guess there's nothing we can do."

"We're only made out of stone," added Laverne. "We just thought you were made of something stronger."

At sunset, Quasimodo heard the prisoner carts rolling into the square. An angry mob pressed against the line of soldiers circling the platform. In one of the carts, Phoebus watched helplessly as Frollo's men dragged Esmeralda up the steps and tied her to a stake atop a pile of wood and straw.

"The time has come, gypsy," Frollo said to her under his breath. "You stand upon the brink of the abyss. But even now it's not too late. I can save you from the flames of this world and the next. Choose me or the fire!"

Esmeralda stared coldly at him. Frollo trembled with rage.

The judge's voice boomed above the commotion. His voice carried all the way up to the bell tower. "The prisoner Esmeralda refuses to recant. She has been found guilty of the crime of witchcraft. The sentence is DEATH!"

The crowd roared. "She's innocent! Release her!"

"It is my sacred duty," Frollo proclaimed, "to send this unholy demon back where she belongs." He stepped forward and lit the pyre.

In a surge of anger, Quasimodo threw back his head and shouted, "NOOOO!" With all his might he strained against his chains. The pillars trembled and began to crack and then came crashing down. As they fell, the tremor caused the bells of Notre Dame to sway.

The clanging of the great bells stirred the crowd below. Looking up, they saw Quasimodo leap out from the bell tower and swing down toward them. He landed on the platform, shoved Frollo back, and untied Esmeralda. She slumped in his arms, unconscious from the heat and choking smoke.

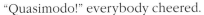

"Quasimodo!" everybody cheered.

Battling his way through the soldiers, Quasimodo disappeared with Esmeralda into Notre Dame and bolted the doors. Moments later, he appeared high on a balcony before the rose window. He lifted Esmeralda in his arms and cried out, "Sanctuary!"

The crowd echoed, "Sanctuary! Sanctuary! Sanctuary!"

Frollo was desperate. "Seize the cathedral!" he ordered his men. They lifted a heavy beam on their shoulders and rammed it against the solid doors. "Again!" yelled Frollo.

In the confusion, Phoebus freed himself and the gypsy prisoners.

"Citizens of Paris!" he shouted, leaping atop a cart and waving his sword. "Frollo has persecuted our people, ransacked our city . . . and now he has declared war on Notre Dame herself. Will we allow it?"

"NEVER!" the people responded, surging forward. A terrible battle ensued.

The doors of Notre Dame shuddered, ready to break apart. From above, Quasimodo and the gargoyles watched in panic. "C'mon!" he cried. "I just thought of something."

They followed Quasimodo up to the workshop, where a cracked bell was being repaired. A huge vat of molten lead stood steaming in the center of the room.

"You've got to tip this thing!" Quasimodo shouted.

Hugo, Victor, and Laverne threw themselves against the red-hot cauldron. "This is one time," said Hugo, "when it's good to have hands of stone."

With Quasimodo giving it a final shove with his foot, the vat toppled over. The fiery liquid streamed across the stone floor, over the balcony, and onto the square. Dropping the battering ram, the soldiers fled. But Frollo, in a fury, jammed his sword into a break between the doors and squeezed through. He bounded up the tower steps and found Quasimodo kneeling by Esmeralda's still body.

Out of the corner of his eye, Quasimodo saw Frollo pull a dagger from beneath his cloak. Crying out in rage and surprise, he wrenched it away and knocked Frollo to the floor.

"You killed her," sobbed Quasimodo. "You say the world's a dark cruel place, but now I see that the only thing dark and cruel about it is people like you."

Esmeralda's eyes fluttered open. "Quasi. . . ?" she murmured.

"Esmeralda!" he cried. "You're alive!"

"She lives!" gasped Frollo. "I should have known you'd risk your life to save this gypsy witch, just as your own mother died trying to save you!"

Quasimodo reeled from shock. "What did you say?"

Frollo drew his sword and advanced toward Esmeralda. Quasimodo swept her up in his arms and scrambled out a window onto a gargoyle. He hoisted Esmeralda safely to the balcony above.

"And now, Quasimodo," Frollo growled, climbing out after him, "I'm going to do what I should've done twenty years ago." He swung his sword at Quasimodo, knocking him off balance. Flailing his arms, Quasimodo grabbed onto a ledge and hung by his fingertips. Esmeralda frantically reached down and clutched his wrists.

Frollo pulled himself onto the gargoyle. Straightening up, he held his sword high over Esmeralda and smiled.

"And He shall smite the wicked," he recited, "and plunge him into the fiery pit."

Before he could strike, the gargoyle cracked beneath him and broke off. Screaming, Frollo plummeted to his death.

"Quasimodo!" Esmeralda sobbed. "I can't hold on any longer!" Just as she lost her grip, two arms reached from a window below and pulled Quasimodo in. Phoebus leaned out and grinned up at Esmeralda.

Back inside the bell tower, Quasimodo hugged his friends. He took each by the wrist and joined their hands together. As they kissed, he smiled.

When Phoebus and Esmeralda appeared on the steps of the cathedral, the elated crowd called out to them. Esmeralda turned and beckoned to Quasimodo. He took a few steps forward and looked around shyly. Everyone fell silent.

A little girl let go of her mother's hand and walked up to Quasimodo. She reached up and gently touched his face. Then, she led him into the square. As Quasimodo stood blinking in the early morning sun, the townspeople welcomed him—the hero of Notre Dame—with cheers.

THE HUNCHBACK OF NOTRE DAME
Behind the Scenes

Written in Paris more than a century ago, Victor Hugo's novel *Notre-Dame de Paris* provided a dramatic and exciting template for an animated feature film and a brand-new challenge to the artists of Disney Feature Animation: to adapt in animation a complex classic by an acknowledged literary master. Hugo's sprawling story, with its grand spectacle, melodramatic structure, and cast of archetypal characters, contained within it a simple message: It's what's inside a person that counts. The Disney animators focused on that idea and envisioned in *The Hunchback of Notre Dame* (1996) a story full of hope and optimism, concentrating on the figure of the bell ringer Quasimodo and his fervent wish to join the world he sees from the isolation of his bell tower.

The filmmakers streamlined the basic structure of Hugo's novel while adapting his memorable and well-drawn characters to the spirit of the film. In their hands, Quasimodo was transformed from a vicious, antisocial, half-human creature into an emotionally deprived, appealing young man. The gypsy Esmeralda evolved

Layout art of the bell tower by Tom Shannon.

from an impressionable, exotic, but ultimately helpless victim of Frollo's obsession into a capable, self-possessed heroine. Phoebus metamorphosed from Hugo's self-centered, vainglorious, untrustworthy, and shallow cad into a witty, brave individual full of good humor and self-deprecating charm. The Disney artists invented the gargoyles Hugo, Victor, and Laverne partly to leaven the seriousness of the film with broad topical humor and partly as a device to draw out elements of Quasimodo, allowing the audience to see the bell ringer's endearing humor and humanity.

The different environments in the film were designed to reflect the characters most closely associated with them. The objects and structure of the bell tower communicate aspects of Quasimodo's life to the audience—his preoccupations, loneliness, and imagination. Frollo's Palace of Justice is spindly, elongated, and severely angular, his own room devoid of furnishing. Its bareness and austerity match Frollo's rigidity and self-denial. Unlike Frollo's unyielding, cold environment, the gypsies' home,

Esmeralda's eyes fluttered open. "Quasi. . .?" she murmured.

"Esmeralda!" he cried. "You're alive!"

"She lives!" gasped Frollo. "I should have known you'd risk your life to save this gypsy witch, just as your own mother died trying to save you!"

Quasimodo reeled from shock. "What did you say?"

Frollo drew his sword and advanced toward Esmeralda. Quasimodo swept her up in his arms and scrambled out a window onto a gargoyle. He hoisted Esmeralda safely to the balcony above.

"And now, Quasimodo," Frollo growled, climbing out after him, "I'm going to do what I should've done twenty years ago." He swung his sword at Quasimodo, knocking him off balance. Flailing his arms, Quasimodo grabbed onto a ledge and hung by his fingertips. Esmeralda frantically reached down and clutched his wrists.

Frollo pulled himself onto the gargoyle. Straightening up, he held his sword high over Esmeralda and smiled.

"And He shall smite the wicked," he recited, "and plunge him into the fiery pit."

Before he could strike, the gargoyle cracked beneath him and broke off. Screaming, Frollo plummeted to his death.

"Quasimodo!" Esmeralda sobbed. "I can't hold on any longer!" Just as she lost her grip, two arms reached from a window below and pulled Quasimodo in. Phoebus leaned out and grinned up at Esmeralda.

Back inside the bell tower, Quasimodo hugged his friends. He took each by the wrist and joined their hands together. As they kissed, he smiled.

When Phoebus and Esmeralda appeared on the steps of the cathedral, the elated crowd called out to them. Esmeralda turned and beckoned to Quasimodo. He took a few steps forward and looked around shyly. Everyone fell silent.

A little girl let go of her mother's hand and walked up to Quasimodo. She reached up and gently touched his face. Then, she led him into the square. As Quasimodo stood blinking in the early morning sun, the townspeople welcomed him—the hero of Notre Dame—with cheers.

THE HUNCHBACK OF NOTRE DAME
Behind the Scenes

Written in Paris more than a century ago, Victor Hugo's novel *Notre-Dame de Paris* provided a dramatic and exciting template for an animated feature film and a brand-new challenge to the artists of Disney Feature Animation: to adapt in animation a complex classic by an acknowledged literary master. Hugo's sprawling story, with its grand spectacle, melodramatic structure, and cast of archetypal characters, contained within it a simple message: It's what's inside a person that counts. The Disney animators focused on that idea and envisioned in *The Hunchback of Notre Dame* (1996) a story full of hope and optimism, concentrating on the figure of the bell ringer Quasimodo and his fervent wish to join the world he sees from the isolation of his bell tower.

The filmmakers streamlined the basic structure of Hugo's novel while adapting his memorable and well-drawn characters to the spirit of the film. In their hands, Quasimodo was transformed from a vicious, antisocial, half-human creature into an emotionally deprived, appealing young man. The gypsy Esmeralda evolved from an impressionable, exotic, but ultimately helpless victim of Frollo's obsession into a capable, self-possessed heroine. Phoebus metamorphosed from Hugo's self-centered, vainglorious, untrustworthy, and shallow cad into a witty, brave individual full of good humor and self-deprecating charm. The Disney artists invented the gargoyles Hugo, Victor, and Laverne partly to leaven the seriousness of the film with broad topical humor and partly as a device to draw out elements of Quasimodo, allowing the audience to see the bell ringer's endearing humor and humanity.

Layout art of the bell tower by Tom Shannon.

The different environments in the film were designed to reflect the characters most closely associated with them. The objects and structure of the bell tower communicate aspects of Quasimodo's life to the audience—his preoccupations, loneliness, and imagination. Frollo's Palace of Justice is spindly, elongated, and severely angular, his own room devoid of furnishing. Its bareness and austerity match Frollo's rigidity and self-denial. Unlike Frollo's unyielding, cold environment, the gypsies' home,

the Court of Miracles, is organic, chaotic, and loose. "Though forced to live in the ruins underneath Paris, the gypsies have made their space a reflection of their own creative energies," says producer Don Hahn.

A storyboard sketch by Paul and Gaëtan Brizzi.

Fittingly enough, several sequences of *The Hunchback of Notre Dame* were developed at Disney's Paris Studio. Coproducer Roy Conli and sequence directors Gaëtan Brizzi and Paul Brizzi led the studio in storyboarding and producing several sequences of the film, including the dramatic musical opener "The Bells of Notre Dame." Several members of the creative team in California took trips to Paris to learn about the cathedral and the medieval town surrounding it, taking photographs and drawing sketches of Notre Dame. They sought to create "a grimy, lived-in Paris," according to directors Gary Trousdale and Kirk Wise. The layout department developed a roughened-up Paris, exaggerating the vertical scale of the buildings to intensify the impression of a claustrophobic medieval town. Living in the shadows of the town is a cast of computer-generated medieval Parisians, whose presence adds to the scope, spectacle, and sense of chaos during the Festival of Fools and the final battle sequence.

An imposing presence in the novel, the cathedral also presides over the events and characters in the film. Towering above the cramped, congested town, Notre Dame makes its moods known through ever-changing shifts in shadows, lighting, and color. Snow blows around a cold cathedral in Frollo's presence, while a warmly welcoming Notre Dame embraces the solitary Esmeralda during her ballad "God Help the Outcasts." In the finale of the film, the cathedral becomes the literal battleground against which Quasimodo and Frollo play out their confrontation, and Quasimodo finally gains the freedom he seeks.

ACKNOWLEDGMENTS

The producers of *Disney's Treasury of Children's Classics: From "The Fox and the Hound" to "The Hunchback of Notre Dame"* would like to thank the following people for their contributions to the creation of this book: Katie Alexander, Roger Allers, Lizza Andres, Andreas Deja, Doug Engalla, Natalie Franscioni-Karp, Mike Gabriel, Vance Gerry, Michael Giaimo, Eric Goldberg, Ed Gombert, Howard Green, Ralph Guggenheim, Don Hahn, Ann Hansen, Mark Henn, Laurence Ishino, Stacie Iverson, Robin Jacobson, Eva Larson, Zoë Leader, Bobby Lee, Tim Lewis, Burny Mattinson, Barbara Gerald Owens, Steve Rogers, Russell Schroeder, Peter Schneider, Thomas Schumacher, Lella F. Smith, Jeanette Steiner, Michael Stern, Zelda Wong.

Produced by Welcome Enterprises, Inc.
575 Broadway, New York, NY 10012

Editors: Hiro Clark, Wendy Wax
Art Director: Gregory Wakabayashi
Designer: Jon Glick
Behind the Scenes Author: Ellen Mendlow

Library of Congress Cataloging-in-Publication Data

Ingoglia, Gina.
Disney's treasury of children's classics : from The fox and the hound to The hunchback of Notre Dame / adaptations by Gina Ingoglia.
-- 1st ed.
p. cm.
Summary: A collection of well-known fairy tales, folk tales, and stories, illustrated with scenes from Walt Disney films.
ISBN 0-7868-3113-8 (trade). -- ISBN 0-7868-5042-6 (lib.)
1. Children's stories, American. 2. Children's stories, English.
3. Fairy tales. 4. Tales. [1. Short stories. 2. Fairy tales.
3. Folklore.] I. Title.
PZ5.I485D1   1996

[Fic]--dc20   96-22820
                                                                 CIP
                                                                 AC

FIRST EDITION
1 3 5 7 9 10 8 6 4 2
Printed in Hong Kong.